Praise

"With Marina, I think I finally understand the term "book boyfriend"—she is definitely a "book girlfriend.""—*Vivielle Montes*

Whisk Me Away

Whisk Me Away "was exactly what I hoped for…and then some. From the first bite (er, chapter), I was hooked by the irresistible setup: two rival pastry chefs with sizzling tension, creative drive, and just enough baggage to make the stakes feel real. Regan's passion and persistence clashed so beautifully with Ava's cool confidence, and watching them go from frosty to fiery was a total delight. This isn't just your average 'rivals forced to work together' trope. There's heart here, real emotional growth wrapped in buttery layers of tension, vulnerability, and personal redemption (and growth)…If you're into slow-burn sapphic romances with snark, sweetness, and soul, this one's worth devouring."—*Brian's Book Blog*

"Beers excels at creating settings that readers can simply lose themselves in, and the retreat, with its cozy kitchen drama and low-key reality TV vibes, feels both aspirational and intimate. The ensemble cast of diverse pastry chefs brings texture to the story, offering moments of humor, camaraderie, and friendship. And, as always, Beers' accessible prose and natural dialogue keep the story flowing smoothly."—*Women Using Words*

Can't Buy Me Love

"Everything about the story and the characters was exciting and I adored every minute. It had everything from the magical moments of instant attraction to the misunderstandings that cause all the drama that every great romance needs…A great story, lots of humorous moments, some heartfelt ones, and lots of cute getting to know one another ones as well. I really, really enjoyed the story and will definitely be reading it again."—*LesbiReviewed*

Aubrey McFadden Is Never Getting Married

"Georgia Beers has become a household name in the world of LGBTQ+ romance novels, and her latest work, *Aubrey McFadden Is*

Never Getting Married, proves she is worthy of the attention. With its captivating characters, engaging plot, and impactful themes, this book is a pure delight to read. Its enemies-to-lovers narrative tugs at the heart, making one hope for resolution and forgiveness between its leading ladies. Aubrey and Monica's push-and-pull dynamic is complicated and knotty, but Beers keeps it fun with her quick wit and sense of humor. The crafty banter ensures that readers have a good time."—*Women Using Words*

Playing with Matches

"*Playing with Matches* is a delightful exploration of small town life, family drama, and true love…Liz and Cori are charming characters with undeniable chemistry, and their sweet and tender small town, 'fake-dating' love story is sure to capture the attention of readers. Their journey reminds readers of the importance of love, forgiveness, family, and community, making this feel-good romance a true triumph."
—*Women Using Words*

Peaches and Cream

"*Peaches and Cream* is a fresh, new spin on the classic rom-com *You've Got Mail*—except it's even better because it's all about ice cream!… [A] delicious, melt-in-your-mouth scoop of goodness. Bursting with tasty characters in a scrumptious story world, *Peaches and Cream* is simply irresistible."—*Women Using Words*

Lambda Literary Award Winner *Dance with Me*

"I admit I inherited my two left feet from my father's side of the family. Dancing is not something I enjoy, so why choose a book with dancing as the central focus and romance as the payoff? Easy. Because it's Georgia Beers, and she will let me enjoy being awkward alongside her main character. I think this is what makes her special to me as an author. While her characters might be beautiful in their own ways, I can relate to their challenges, fears and dreams. Comfort reads every time."
—*Late Night Lesbian Reads*

Camp Lost and Found

"I really like when Beers writes about winter and snow and hot chocolate. She makes heartache feel cosy and surmountable. *Camp*

Lost and Found made me smile a lot, laugh at times, tear up more often than I care to share. If you're looking for a heartwarming story to keep the cold weather at bay, I'd recommend you give it a chance."—*Jude in the Stars*

Cherry on Top

"*Cherry on Top* is another wonderful story from one of the greatest writers in sapphic fiction…This is more than a romance with two incredibly charming and wonderful characters. It is a reminder that you shouldn't have to compromise who you are to fit into a box that society wants to put you into. Georgia Beers once again creates a couple with wonderful chemistry who will warm your heart."—*Sapphic Book Review*

The Secret Poet

"[O]ne of the author's best works and one of the best romances I've read recently…I was so invested in [Morgan and Zoe] I read the book in one sitting."—*Melina Bickard, Librarian, Waterloo Library (UK)*

On the Rocks

"This book made me so happy! And kept me awake way too late."—*Jude in the Stars*

Hopeless Romantic

"Thank you, Georgia Beers, for this unabashed paean to the pleasure of escaping into romantic comedies…If you want to have a big smile plastered on your face as you read a romance novel, do not hesitate to pick up this one!"—*The Rainbow Bookworm*

Flavor of the Month

"Beers whips up a sweet lesbian romance…brimming with mouth-watering descriptions of foodie indulgences…Both women are well-intentioned and endearing, and it's easy to root for their inevitable reconciliation. But once the couple rediscover their natural ease with one another, Beers throws a challenging emotional hurdle in their path, forcing them to fight through tragedy to earn their happy ending."—*Publishers Weekly*

Fear of Falling

"Enough tension and drama for us to wonder if this can work out—and enough heat to keep the pages turning. I will definitely recommend this to others—Georgia Beers continues to go from strength to strength."
—*Evan Blood, Bookseller (Angus & Robertson, Australia)*

One Walk in Winter

"A sweet story to pair with the holidays. There are plenty of 'moment's in this book that make the heart soar. Just what I like in a romance. Situations where sparks fly, hearts fill, and tears fall. This book shined with cute fairy trails and swoon-worthy Christmas gifts…REALLY nice and cozy if read in between Thanksgiving and Christmas. Covered in blankets. By a fire."—*Bookvark*

The Do-Over

"*The Do-Over* is a shining example of the brilliance of Georgia Beers as a contemporary romance author."—*Rainbow Reflections*

The Shape of You

The Shape of You "catches you right in the feels and does not let go. It is a must for every person out there who has struggled with self-esteem, questioned their judgment, and settled for a less than perfect but safe lover. If you've ever been convinced you have to trade passion for emotional safety, this book is for you."—*Writing While Distracted*

Calendar Girl

"A sweet, sweet romcom of a story…*Calendar Girl* is a nice read, which you may find yourself returning to when you want a hot-chocolate-and-warm-comfort-hug in your life."—*Best Lesbian Erotica*

Blend

"You know a book is good, first, when you don't want to put it down. Second, you know it's damn good when you're reading it and thinking, I'm totally going to read this one again. Great read and absolutely a 5-star romance."—*The Romantic Reader Blog*

Right Here, Right Now

"[A] successful and entertaining queer romance novel. The main characters are appealing, and the situations they deal with are realistic and well-managed. I would recommend this book to anyone who enjoys a good queer romance novel, and particularly one grounded in real world situations."—*Books at the End of the Alphabet*

"[A]n engaging odd-couple romance. Beers creates a romance of gentle humor that allows no-nonsense Lacey to relax and easygoing Alicia to find a trusting heart."—*RT Book Reviews*

Lambda Literary Award Winner *Fresh Tracks*

"[T]he focus switches each chapter to a different character, allowing for a measured pace and deep, sincere exploration of each protagonist's thoughts. Beers gives a welcome expansion to the romance genre with her clear, sympathetic writing."—*Curve magazine*

Lambda Literary Award Finalist *Finding Home*

"Georgia Beers has proven in her popular novels such as *Too Close to Touch* and *Fresh Tracks* that she has a special way of building romance with suspense that puts the reader on the edge of their seat. *Finding Home*, though more character driven than suspense, will equally keep the reader engaged at each page turn with its sweet romance."—*Lambda Literary Review*

Mine

"Beers does a fine job of capturing the essence of grief in an authentic way. *Mine* is touching, life-affirming, and sweet."—*Lesbian News Book Review*

Too Close to Touch

"In her third novel, Georgia Beers delivers an immensely satisfying story. Beers knows how to generate sexual tension so taut it could be cut with a knife...Beers weaves a tale of yearning, love, lust, and conflict resolution. She has constructed a believable plot, with strong characters in a charming setting."—*Just About Write*

By the Author

Romances

Turning the Page

Thy Neighbor's Wife

Too Close to Touch

Fresh Tracks

Mine

Finding Home

Starting from Scratch

96 Hours

Slices of Life

Snow Globe

Olive Oil & White Bread

Zero Visibility

A Little Bit of Spice

What Matters Most

Right Here, Right Now

Blend

The Shape of You

Calendar Girl

The Do-Over

Fear of Falling

One Walk in Winter

Flavor of the Month

Hopeless Romantic

16 Steps to Forever

The Secret Poet

Cherry on Top

Camp Lost and Found

Dance with Me

Peaches and Cream

Playing with Matches

Aubrey McFadden
Is Never Getting Married

Can't Buy Me Love

This Christmas

Whisk Me Away

That's Amore

The Great Popcorn Romance

The Puppy Love Romances

Rescued Heart

Run to You

Dare to Stay

The Swizzle Stick Romances

Shaken or Stirred

On the Rocks

With a Twist

Visit us at www.boldstrokesbooks.com

THE GREAT
POPCORN
ROMANCE

by

Georgia Beers

2025

THE GREAT POPCORN ROMANCE

ISBN 13: 978-1-63679-910-0

THIS TRADE PAPERBACK ORIGINAL IS PUBLISHED BY
BOLD STROKES BOOKS, INC.
P.O. BOX 249
VALLEY FALLS, NY 12185

FIRST EDITION: DECEMBER 2025

CREDITS
EDITORS: LYNDA SANDOVAL AND STACIA SEAMAN
PRODUCTION DESIGN: STACIA SEAMAN
COVER DESIGN BY INKSPIRAL DESIGN

Acknowledgments

With this book, I finally realized something that you, my readers, probably already know: I seem to enjoy writing about women who run their own small businesses…which is interesting, as I've never run my own. However, I do understand what it means to be passionate about something, and just the idea of having that little place, that little location that houses everything you're passionate about, ignites something in me. Poptacular, the popcorn shop in this book, fit that bill perfectly, and as I was writing her, I completely, one hundred percent understood Hannah Kramer. She's a woman who doesn't need to be rich. She just wants to be able to pay her bills while doing the thing she loves most in the world. And that, I can relate to. I imagine many of you can. I hope you love her the way I do.

On to the thank yous:

I've grown a lot in the past year or two—a strange thing for a middle-aged woman to say, but I feel it's the truth. I've learned a lot about myself. I've learned a lot about those close to me and those I care about, and not everything—in any of those categories—has been positive. But what I do for a living has been a huge factor in helping me discover the best versions of myself, and I will be forever grateful to the Universe for allowing me this incredible career. Somebody asked me recently about retirement, and I just laughed. I can't imagine not writing sapphic romances. I just can't. So don't worry. I'm not going anywhere.

As always, thank you to everyone at Bold Strokes Books who keep things running smoothly behind the scenes.

Thank you to my unstoppable editors—I would not be the writer I am today without them helping me be better. Lynda Sandoval is a pro at lifting me up, even when she's teaching me (or reminding me of something she's already taught me 27 times), and that means more than she knows. Stacia Seaman never fails to see something I didn't or catch something I missed, and I'm not sure how she does it. I don't know what I'd do without either of them. Together, they make me the best writer I can be, and I don't foresee myself ever not learning from them with each and every book.

To my crazy, unconventional family of littles: Thank you for the privilege of watching you grow and become the amazing tiny humans you're becoming (way too quickly! slow down!). Every day, I wake up knowing how lucky I am to get to be a part of the process. Gigi loves you more than you know.

Every now and then, I feel a strange desire to thank my dog. It may sound silly to some, but Archie is my rock, my constant, my compass. He has been by my side for almost five years now, through some very tumultuous, emotional points in my life, and I honestly can't imagine being without him, though I know one day I'll have to. So, even though he has no idea I'm typing this, I want you to know how grateful I am to be his mommy and how lucky I feel to have him in my life.

And last, but never, ever least: the biggest thank you I can muster to you, my readers. You've supported me for longer than I'm comfortable admitting. If you keep showing up, I'll keep writing you stories. Thank you from the bottom of my very grateful heart.

THE GREAT
POPCORN
ROMANCE

CHAPTER ONE

Caramel is sexy.

Hannah Kramer had always thought so, even as a teenager making it for the first time, and she smiled now as she stirred. The secret to good caramel was timing and temperature. Too hot and it burned and became bitter. Not hot enough and it didn't flow well. Like Goldilocks's porridge, it had to be just right.

Like it was now.

She took the pot off the stove, still stirring, and carried it to the mixer, where a batch of fresh popcorn rolled and tumbled in a mesmerizingly endless circle, the large pot spinning at a medium pace. She poured the caramel in slowly, watching the rich brown stream as it began to coat each piece. She scraped the pot as clean as she could and inhaled deeply, the warm, sweet scent of fresh caramel popcorn filling the air of her small shop.

Caramel was one of her best-selling flavors, so she made it fresh every morning at Poptacular, the gourmet popcorn shop she'd been running almost single-handedly for more than three years now. Plopping the empty caramel pot into the sink full of soapy water, she wiped her hands on her apron, tucked an escaping lock of hair behind her ear under her hat, then slipped her hands into her apron pockets and wandered out into the shop toward the front door, where she stood and watched the main drag of Sunset Valley slowly wake up for the day.

Across the street was the Coffee Cup, the only business that opened before she did. As she watched, the front door swung open and Shana Franklin, the manager, came out. She glanced both ways—totally unnecessary, as there was exactly zero traffic so far that morning—and scooted across the street to Hannah, who unlocked and opened the door.

"God, I love the smell in here," Shana said, handing Hannah a large, steaming cup. "It's guinea pig time."

Hannah took the top off the cup and inhaled deeply. "OMG, speaking of loving the smell."

"I tweaked the pumpkin spice this year. Tell me what you think." Hannah blew on the coffee, then took a sip. "Oh," she said, then let the tastes sit on her tongue before sipping again. "I like it."

Shana watched her face for a moment before venturing, "Too heavy on the cinnamon?"

Hannah nodded slowly. "Maybe pull back on that and kick up the nutmeg a titch?"

"Exactly what I was thinking, too."

"I like it, though. It's very fall." Hannah gestured with her head for Shana to follow her into the back of the shop, where the popcorn and caramel had blended perfectly. She turned the mixer off, shook open a bag, and filled it for Shana. Who didn't even let her close it before she took a handful and ate it.

"Goddamn, girl, I don't know what you do to this, but it's like magic." She chewed and grabbed more. "No. It's like crack, let's be honest."

Hannah laughed. "You always say that."

"It's always true." Shana held up the bag in thanks, then headed back across the street where things were starting to pick up. The Coffee Cup was the only coffee shop in the teeny-tiny town of Sunset Valley, and Shana had a slew of regulars that came every day without fail. She also owned her own building.

Hannah envied those things.

She had regulars, yes, but not nearly as many as Shana did. Bradley McFarland owned her building; he'd inherited it last year when his dad had passed away, and so far, he hadn't jacked up her rent. But each day, she was low-key braced for a phone call or text.

With a soft sigh, she watched cars pull in and out, filling and vacating the spaces in front of the coffee shop. It would be like that for the next two hours, easily. She wished her business was that steady.

"Popcorn isn't a necessity, it's a luxury," she said aloud to the empty shop. It was what her grandmother always told her when she was explaining why great customer service was so important. "People don't *need* popcorn, but they want it. And you need to make them remember your shop, make them think of Poptacular when they're telling their friends about their amazing vacation. You have to make them *want* to come back."

She stood behind the counter and leaned on her hands as she looked around at the shop she'd worked at—and loved—since she was a kid. It wasn't big. People didn't sit at tables to eat popcorn, so there was no need for any kind of dining area. And the popping and mixing equipment took up a lot of space, so the back of the shop was larger than the front. Below the counter was a display case with her most popular flavors listed. They were in airtight containers, some empty and some full—the candied flavors had a longer shelf life than the more savory ones, so they could stay in the display case for a few days—signs in fun and fancy lettering telling customers each flavor combination. Kaitlyn, one of her employees, dabbled in calligraphy as a hobby, so Hannah had enlisted her to make the signs. She did not disappoint.

Behind her on shelves were pre-bagged flavors in small, medium, and large, as well as the tins she liked to use for gifts or when a customer ordered more than one flavor. She noted that her tin supply was running low, knew she should order more, but was pretty sure she still owed the vendor for the last order she'd placed. Yeah, they'd have to wait.

And now she was thinking about money—or more accurately, the lack of it—and that wasn't something she was ready to deal with. Nope. Time to take her mind off it the best way she knew how.

"Let's make a new flavor." Again, she said it out loud to the empty shop. She did that a lot: talked out loud when nobody was around. Her grandmother used to do the same thing, she'd said, and Hannah was never bothered by emulating her grandma. Glancing up at the wall in the front of the shop, she blew a kiss to the framed photo of her, standing in front of Poptacular the day it opened. "Miss you, Grams."

The small notebook in her apron pocket was a fixture, and her loved ones always teased her about it. Her neighbor—fifteen-year-old Parker, who lived across the hall in her apartment building—couldn't understand why she didn't jot her notes on her phone.

"You have an app exactly for note-jotting," Parker had said to her one day, tapping on her own screen with a fingertip. "It's literally called Notes." Her exasperation was clear, and Hannah found it amusing.

"I like to write it down on paper," she tried to explain. "I like the act of writing it, the feel of it, scribbling and crossing out and stuff. It relaxes me."

Parker had sighed like the most put-upon person on Earth. "You're so weird, Han."

Now she flipped through the pages—the well-worn pages, considering how many times she'd opened it, scribbled in it, and shoved it back into her pocket again—to the notes she'd jotted yesterday for a couple new flavors she wanted to experiment with.

The back door opening surprised her so much, she let out a little yelp.

"Hey, little sis," Kyle said, mischievous smile on his face.

"You scared the bejesus out of me," Hannah said, hand pressed to her chest. "My God."

He didn't apologize. He never did. Scaring her was his thing and had been since they were kids. He'd never passed up an opportunity to hide in a closet or around a corner and jump out at her when she least expected it. He grabbed a bowl off a shelf and scooped some of the fresh caramel corn into it, then popped some into his mouth, humming with approval. "I love it when it's still warm."

Hannah took the mixing pot of popcorn off the spinner and dumped the remaining caramel corn onto the cooling tray. As she pulled on her plastic gloves, she glanced at her brother. "You need a haircut," she commented, noting his sandy hair had started to flip a bit at the ends. It was the end of August, so he was clean-shaven now, but she knew come next month, he'd grow in his beard. Their mother didn't approve of it, but Hannah thought he looked handsome with it.

"Thanks, *Mom*," he said, eating another handful of the popcorn.

She began sifting the corn through her fingers, spreading it, tossing it, doing both those things gently so as not to crush the kernels. The point was to keep it from clumping. All the candied popcorn flavors needed to go through this ritual, and Hannah loved it. She found it soothing, sifting popped kernels through her fingers.

"How are the BBs?" she asked. Kyle had three-year-old twins, Brody and Brianna. Hannah lovingly referred to them as the BBs.

"Good. All good."

He munched and there was another length of silence.

"Are you just here to watch me work?" she finally asked after he stood quietly for a long moment. "Don't you have some drywall to hang?" Kyle was a contractor. His company had built many of the new houses in Sunset Valley, and he was often so busy, she didn't see him for weeks.

"I do," he said. "I just wanted to remind you that we've got the meeting with Jeff this afternoon."

"I know." Did she snap that? Maybe not, but it was a little bit snarky. She gave him an apologetic look. "I'll be there, okay? I don't need you to remind me every single day."

Her brother held his hands up like a robbery victim. "Okay, okay. Just trying to help." And he was. She knew that.

"I'm sorry," she said with a sigh. "A little stressed here lately."

He nodded as if he totally got it, then tossed another handful of caramel corn into his mouth.

He didn't stay long after that, just long enough to grab a bag of the chocolate banana split popcorn—the BBs' favorite—and he was on his way.

"Mr. Doom and Gloom," she muttered as she watched Kyle's truck pull away through the front windows. She hated when he popped in simply to remind her that business wasn't good. That's what the meeting with Jeff was about. He was their CPA. His father had handled the finances for Poptacular when their grandma had been around— another Sunset Valley native who'd taken over the family business— and he liked to give Hannah suggestions on how to make more money on her shop. Terrible suggestions, but she knew he was only trying to help.

Hannah blew out a hard breath and turned to do what she always did when she was feeling pressure: create something new. Experimenting with new flavors was her favorite thing, so she got to work. Today's new flavor? Dill pickle. There were a couple other popcorn shops in the country with dill pickle as their best-selling flavor, so she'd decided it was time to give it a shot.

Fresh popcorn was popping—would she ever not love the sound? the smell?—and she had a pot on the small stove, the burner set super low, with melting butter in it. Consulting her notebook, she threw dried dill weed, garlic powder, sea salt, and black pepper into a bowl and whisked it all together. The smell was already lovely, but she knew the popcorn was going to need that punch of dill pickle flavor. That's where the actual, literal dill pickle juice came in.

"We'll try just a bit at first." Two tablespoons of pickle juice went into the butter, and she stirred it until it was blended, a weirdly off-gold color. Into the mixer went the freshly popped corn, and once it was turning and tumbling, she slowly poured the butter over it.

Now she could smell pickles.

Once the butter had mixed in well and coated the popcorn, she sprinkled the seasoning mix over it and let it toss for a few more minutes before she stopped it, snagged out a few bites, and gave it a try.

"Holy shit, that's good," she said quietly as she munched. "Wow."

Onto the giant table went the popcorn, and then she bagged it up to sell today. She reserved some of it for samples—that went into an airtight container so it wouldn't go stale sitting out in the open. By the time she'd bagged it up, labeled and priced it, shelved the bags, and started on another batch, the back door opened, and Kaitlyn came in for her shift.

"Hey, boss. Oh, wow, it smells like pickles in here." Kaitlyn was a walking dichotomy, something Hannah loved about her. At nineteen, she'd finished up her freshman year in college only a couple months before and was home for the summer. She was the goalie for her school's ice hockey team, and she was the strongest, most muscular woman she'd ever know. At nearly six feet tall and probably a good two hundred pounds of muscle, Kaitlyn cut an imposing figure. But imposing was the last word Hannah would use to describe her. Her hobbies were calligraphy, botany, and baking. When she wasn't in the gym lifting weights, of course. She was also kind, a little sensitive, and soft-spoken.

Hannah adored her.

"What do you think?" Hannah asked, holding out a sample of the dill pickle popcorn.

Kaitlyn dutifully tasted it, and her brown eyes went wide. "Wow. That's amazing." She grabbed more, munched, and nodded. "So good."

"Can you make a New Flavor sign?"

"On it."

These were the moments that made Hannah happy. Coming up with or simply perfecting a new flavor, flipping over the Open sign in the window, propping the door open to let the wonderful aroma of fresh popcorn waft out into the street and draw people in. She stood on the sidewalk in front of Poptacular, hands on her hips, and simply inhaled the fresh August air. Fall was coming, and that meant extra tourists. The leaf peepers. Upstate New York in autumn drew all kinds of people who didn't get the color-changing leaves at home. They'd come here. They'd look at the leaves. They'd buy popcorn.

"What color?" Kaitlyn called from the back. "I'm thinking green."

Hannah smiled, nodded at a gentleman walking by, and turned to go back into her shop.

❖

Kyle was already at Jeff's office when Hannah arrived. Of course he was. He and Jeff were buddies, having played football together in high school. She pulled her ten-year-old Toyota into the parking spot next to Kyle's truck, took in a big breath, and blew it out.

This meeting likely wasn't going to go well. She knew that. Meetings with Jeff never did. Bracing for it was still hard, though.

"Inhale through the nose," she said quietly, then followed her own directions. "Exhale through the mouth." She sat for another moment before muttering, "All right. Let's get this over with."

Jeff's office was small but nice. He was one of two CPAs in Sunset Valley, and he did quite well. Of course, it didn't hurt that his father had established most of the clientele, and Jeff didn't have to do much work as far as finding new clients. He basically inherited a fully functioning, successful business, and he ran with it.

"Hi, Hannah," said Sheila, Jeff's receptionist.

"Hey, Sheila, how are you?" She handed over a bag of s'mores popcorn, Sheila's favorite. "Brought you something."

Sheila's smile grew. "You didn't have to do that." Immediately, she went to work on the twist tie and dug in. Her shoulders dropped and her eyes closed, and her approval was clear. "So. Good." She indicated the short hall to her right. "You can go right in. They're waiting for you."

Seated behind his enormous mahogany desk, tall and lean with huge hands and broad shoulders, Jeff didn't look anything like a CPA. Hannah always thought he'd look more at home on a basketball court taking free throws than behind a desk crunching numbers. His hair was cut much shorter than the last time she'd seen him, and when she commented on it, he ran a hand over his head.

"Shorter and grayer," he said with a grin, then stepped out from behind the desk to wrap her in a hug. "Good to see you." He noticed the bag of popcorn in her hand, and his dark eyes lit up with anticipation. "Chili lime?"

"What else?" She handed it over, and he set it on the desk.

"I'll dive into that when I'm alone and nobody can see me inhale the entire bag in one sitting."

She grinned at him. A nod at Kyle and she took the chair next to him, doing her best to mentally prepare.

It didn't work, though, because by the time she pushed out the doors of Jeff's office building, she was angry and close to tears.

Kyle hurried after her and caught her arm just as she reached her car. "Hey," he said, his voice soft. "Come on." His grip was gentle but firm.

She wouldn't meet his eyes.

"Han. Come on. This isn't a surprise. Business has been on a downslide for months now."

"But fall is coming," she said, immediately irritated by the pleading tone of her voice. "It always picks up then and through the winter."

"And then it slows down again." Kyle was clearly trying not to upset her further, but as the other half of Poptacular—the silent partner, as Hannah referred to him—he also had a stake in the business's success. Or failure. "Look, you heard Jeff. We're not suggesting you close the doors. But, Han, we've gotta do *something*. We're hemorrhaging money."

"I love how it's suddenly 'we,'" she sniped, yanking her car door open. "It's never 'we' unless there's bad news." She dropped into the driver's seat and waited, as Kyle had his hand on the door.

"Han. Come on. I'm trying to help."

She sighed because she knew he was right. Still, she was too raw. "I know," she said softly, then gave the door a little tug so he'd move his hand. He did, and she closed the door and started the engine. She didn't look at him again as she drove away.

Once back at Poptacular, she went into the tiny, closet-sized office (closet-sized because that's exactly what it had once been), closed the door, and let the tears flow. Quietly, because she didn't want to worry Kaitlyn, whose concerned face had followed her all the way to the back, even as she waited on a customer.

Why was she so upset? This wasn't even the first time she'd had a meeting like this. It was, like, the third or fourth. Kyle telling her she should start thinking about selling the business wasn't new. It happened once or twice a year.

But this time was different, because he wasn't wrong. Poptacular wasn't clearing enough of a profit to justify keeping its door open for much longer. And rent could and probably would go up at any time. Bradley would be stupid not to raise it at some point.

She had no idea how she'd afford it.

Moving to another location was suggested last year by Kyle, but everything seemed so much more expensive, and this place was perfect. Plus, it had been here for decades. The customers knew it, especially the locals. They expected its presence.

She grabbed her hoodie off the back of her chair, wadded it up into a ball, held it to her face, and screamed into it. Hopefully, Kaitlyn didn't hear, but she was so frustrated, she needed to let loose. And just like always, her frustration and worry slowly turned into anger.

Anger was better.

Anger made her creative.

Hands on her desk, she pushed to her feet. "Okay. Enough wallowing, Kramer," she said out loud to the empty office. "Put this negative energy to good use." She tied her apron back on and pulled out her little notebook. Might be time to give the spiced curry idea a try.

❖

"I know it's asking a lot."

Well, wasn't that a damn understatement? But there was real concern in Kyle's voice. Even over the phone, Riley Shaw could hear it. Not that he hadn't called before and been concerned, but this was different. There was almost a…desperation to his tone.

Riley stood in her bedroom and looked down at her open suitcase, packed for her first vacation in more than three years. No big deal, just a lake house she'd found on Airbnb, someplace quiet with solitude where maybe she could drink wine by the water, read some of the huge stack of books she continued to buy but had no time to read, and not answer her constantly ringing phone. But this was Kyle. They'd been best friends in high school and beyond. And while they'd drifted a bit over the past few years, he was still Kyle, and she still loved him like a brother. If ever she needed something, she knew he'd drop whatever he was busy with to help her. It wasn't even a question that she'd do the same.

"I didn't know who else to call," he went on. "And this is kinda your wheelhouse, isn't it? Helping struggling businesses?"

He wasn't wrong, and of course she'd help. Of course she would. "Okay," she said. "I'll see what I can do."

"Oh my God, Ri, that's amazing. Thank you so much." The utter relief in his voice was as clear to her as the desperate worry had been just a moment ago.

"Anything for you, man. Truly." She sat on her bed and blew out a breath. "I can be there the day after tomorrow, all right? I'll just drive." Sunset Valley was about a four-hour drive from Boston, and she could use the time to think about ways to help…at least until she was able to see things for herself.

"Perfect. That's perfect."

"You'd better prepare your sister. She's not going to be happy about my presence."

"I know. I'll pave the way. Don't worry." Kyle thanked her profusely several more times and they finally hung up.

Riley flopped backward onto her bed and stared at the ceiling. There was a lot to get done. She'd have to cancel her reservation at the Airbnb—she'd end up eating her deposit, but she could afford it. She needed to redirect her assistant, fill him in on her change of plans. And she'd have to alter some of the clothes in her suitcase. No use for a bathing suit or beach towel in Sunset Valley. Nope. She should get up and do that stuff now.

She didn't.

Instead, she lay there while visions of Hannah Kramer filled her head against her will. Petite, full of energy and sunshine. And infuriatingly stubborn. Annoying as hell. Nobody had ever made Riley want to throw herself off a cliff the way Hannah Kramer had when they were growing up. She didn't expect it to be any different this time around. In fact, it would likely be worse, because Riley was going to come in and tell her how to run her business. For her own good and the good of the bottom line, sure, but nobody liked being told they were doing things wrong. Especially by a person they butted heads with anyway.

She, Hannah, and Kyle had all worked together at Poptacular when they were teens and the Kramers' grandmother had owned it. Mrs. Kramer was awesome, funny, and kind. The customers loved her, and she really knew flavor. Riley was amazed every time she came up with some new, obscure taste combination, and the customers ate it up, literally. She remembered seeing glimpses of that in Hannah, when they weren't arguing. If she closed her eyes, she could picture Hannah's hair—not quite blond, but not exactly brown—the color of a wheat field in the sunlight. The intensity of her brown eyes always surprised Riley. High cheekbones, made so prominent whenever she smiled. And every time she bent to scoop popcorn out of a bin, her ass— *Aaaand that's enough of that.* She needed to pull her head out of Fantasy Land and put it back into Reality, the place where Hannah was going to hate her.

She blew out a breath. "Yeah, this is gonna be fun." She pushed to her feet, determined to scrub any inappropriate—and irritating— memories of her teen years out of her brain, and began unpacking her beachwear. "Apologies, sexy new bathing suit," she said sadly as she stroked the satiny material of the black one-piece. "We'll meet again one day."

By the time she was ready for bed the next night, she'd taken care of everything necessary for the trip. Justin, her assistant, was up to speed on her change of plans. She'd canceled her Airbnb, sadly, and reserved herself a room at the Sunset Valley Resort and Spa. If she was going to miss her vacation, she could at least get a massage and a pedicure while she was doing Kyle a favor, right? She checked her phone one last time before plugging it into its charger next to her bed.

Tomorrow at this time, she'd be in Sunset Valley, a place she had so many mixed emotions around. So many, she wasn't even exactly sure how she felt about it. Which was fine. She'd become a pro at tamping down confusing feelings and turning her focus to her work. It was no coincidence she was as successful as she was. That ability to focus solely on her work had served her well.

Slipping under the covers, she clicked the remote until she found *Law & Order* on the television. She was always able to find some iteration of it, no matter the time of day, and for whatever reason, the cops and lawyers and *chung-chung* of the soundtrack always helped lull her to sleep. As her eyelids grew heavy and her thoughts started to drift, they tugged her toward the memories she'd carefully avoided in her waking life. Wheat-colored hair in a French braid, the sway of hips in retreat, the brilliant flash of straight white teeth in a gorgeously genuine smile, a bowl of popcorn being thrown at her...

"Yeah, you'd best keep that last one in mind," she whispered to herself, tugging the covers up to her chin. "It'll probably happen again."

CHAPTER TWO

Sunset Valley had barely changed at all in the—how long was it since Riley had been there? Six years? Seven? Once she'd moved her mom to Boston with her, closer to hospitals and treatment centers, there hadn't been much reason to return.

Now, as she slowed her BMW to thirty miles per hour and glided easily into the little town, memories flooded back into her brain like somebody was pouring them in, and they floated into view, each one slowly rippling into focus as she drove. The gas station had been remodeled and updated, she noticed, new electronic signs glowing to show her the price of gas and that she could get the town's best cup of coffee inside. Bethany's Boutique looked exactly the same—Riley had a flash of Bethany, a petite redhead in her late forties, who'd helped her find a prom dress on consignment, since her mom couldn't really afford to buy her one. *She's gotta be in her sixties now. I wonder if she still works there.*

Then she was coasting into downtown, a moniker that made her shake her head with a fond smile, as Sunset Valley was hardly big enough to have an uptown, a downtown, or any kind of town, but the fountain in the middle of the street that forced the road around it was still beautiful, the August sunshine making the flowing water sparkle. She couldn't help smiling as she drove past.

And there it was. On her right. Poptacular. Riley knew if she rolled down her window, she'd be able to smell fresh popcorn. To this day, any time she smelled it, her memories of Sunset Valley would come rushing back into her mind like a tidal wave. Directly across the street was the Coffee Cup—arguably the lamest name for a coffee shop in existence, but it was cute and modern looking. She wondered how they felt about the gas station's claim to have the best coffee in town.

It was just after noon—she'd allowed herself a leisurely morning since she technically couldn't check into the hotel until three and hadn't left until after eight. The Sunset Valley Resort and Spa was on the far side of town, and she hoped maybe her room would be ready early. September was in a couple days, and that's when Sunset Valley's tourist season would begin. By mid-October, it would be in full swing, hotels full and lots more people on the sidewalks, milling in and out of shops. Fall was a big deal here.

A quick pop inside the resort told her that unfortunately, her room was not ready yet. She used their lobby restroom, and then she was back in the car. She dialed Kyle's number and got his voicemail, so she hung up and sent a text.

Just got into town. Room won't be ready for another hour. Got time to kill. Gonna head to shop, check things out.

She added an emoji of a popcorn box, then shifted into gear and headed back the way she'd come.

Sunset Valley was like a little Hallmark movie town. Everybody joked about it. One main street where most of the businesses were, the fountain in the center. In a couple months, an enormous tree would be erected near it and lit up in a public gathering. It was all so charming and clichéd and…and… "Corny," she said out loud with a shake of her head. She much preferred the bustle of the big city. Quincy Market and Chelsea Market and Pike Place. Those were the kinds of gathering places she loved, where there were so many people, you could get lost in the crowds, where nobody knew who you were, and you never stopped moving because if you did, you could be run over.

She was smiling about that as she slid her BMW into a parking spot on the street a couple doors down from Poptacular and got out. For a moment, she simply stood in the summer sunshine, let it warm her face. She inhaled deeply, because no matter how much she preferred the city, there was definitely something wonderful about the fresh air of… *not* the city. In the air here, she could smell several of the businesses. A little bit of fried chicken, probably wafting over from the diner a couple doors down. Freshly roasted coffee, the aroma drifting across the street. And, of course, popcorn. The smell of her childhood and teen years really, earthy and warm, and without her consent, her mouth watered.

"Might as well dive right in," she muttered as she grabbed her cross-body bag and slammed the car door.

Before she even moved, she took a good look at the shop. The sign for Poptacular was written in a fun, curvy font, and it was large enough to read, but over the years, the weather and the heat of the sun had faded the bright yellow. Now it was more the color of old, dried-up corn. She pulled out her phone, opened the Notes app, and began a list. Painting the sign was the first thing she typed.

As she stepped up over the curb and onto the sidewalk, she took note of the shop's appearance. Signage was decent, but the window display was nonexistent. Sure, you could look in and see the cases of popcorn behind the counter, the bags on shelves, but there was a huge space to the left of the door—probably a good six-by-four spot just itching for some kind of advertising display.

She jotted more notes.

Now that she was closer, she could see the chipping paint, the battered door handle. More notes. She pulled the door open and went inside.

It was like she'd gone back in time.

Everything was the same, from the display cases filled with popcorn to the shelves behind the counter that held bags filled with different flavors. She was sixteen again, tying an apron around her waist, tucking her hair under the baseball hat with the Poptacular logo embroidered on it—a splurge Mrs. Kramer had surprised them with. The air smelled of fresh popcorn, yes, but also so much more. Butter and salt and chocolate and cheese and—dill pickles? That was new.

The tall girl behind the counter was young—maybe twenty?— and was waiting on a customer. While said customer sampled different flavors, Riley took the opportunity to look around the small space. The photo of Mrs. Kramer on the wall made her smile and brought back a flood of memories, from her surprisingly soft voice to her full-body hugs. The woman was the epitome of what a grandma should be— warm, gentle, and loving.

The walls themselves, though…dingy and bland. She held up her phone and took a photo. A fresh coat of paint on the whole place would be step one to making things look more inviting. Also dingy was the linoleum floor, and she tried to imagine how many feet had tramped over it—especially in the clearly worn path from the door to the front of the counter—through the years. She took another photo. It was clean, she could see that. Mrs. Kramer had always been a stickler for cleanliness in her shop, and she'd pounded that into their brains when they'd worked there, how important it was for an establishment that fed people to remain as clean as possible. But it was old. Obviously. Floors were expensive, so she created a secondary list and added new flooring to that.

The customer was torn between the barbecue ranch flavor and the chili lime, and the girl behind the counter was surprisingly knowledgeable, explaining the ingredients of each flavor and what they combined best with. The customer finally decided to get one of each, and Riley mentally gave the salesgirl points for moving the product.

Riley was scanning the shelves and finding herself impressed by the flavor variety when a voice said, "Hi there. Can I help you?" But it wasn't the same voice as the young woman behind the counter. No. It was a voice that was much more familiar, albeit one she hadn't heard in literal years.

She turned to meet that dark-eyed gaze and was shocked at the way she felt it in her stomach. And a little lower.

Hannah Kramer had always been a pretty teenager. Despite her infuriating stubbornness, Riley had always found her pretty. She also hadn't seen her in over a decade, and the person standing in front of her now was no longer a pretty teenager. No, she was an absolutely stunning woman. Stunning. Even with her hair tucked up under the hat and sticking out the back of it in a ponytail, even in her white T-shirt with the Poptacular logo on it smeared with what looked like chocolate, even in stained black joggers and very old tennis shoes, Hannah was stunning. Riley had no more time to assess, though, before Hannah's brown eyes went wide with recognition.

"Riley? Is that you?" She tipped her head as if examining her, then reached out and enveloped her in a hug. She smelled like popcorn, chocolate, and home.

"Hi, Hannah." They let go and stood looking at each other. The shot of nerves that zapped through Riley irritated her.

"Wow. It's been a long time." Hannah was smiling the smile of a grown woman, and Riley wasn't sure why she was struggling with that.

"It has." She nodded. For too long. Conversation stumbled a bit there. Faltered. So Riley made herself shift into the place she felt most comfortable: business mode. "Why isn't there a window display?" She turned to look at the empty area, then held her phone up to get a photo. "That's a great advertising spot for anybody who walks by. I mean, the smell of popcorn is a great draw, but if you put something fun right here, it'll catch their eye as well as their nose. You know how much foot traffic there will be in a week or two." She turned to the empty white wall, waved a hand at it. "And here, maybe more shelves? Oh, what about a mural? That would be cool." A glance at their feet. "The floor's gross. That needs replacing." When she glanced up, she stopped short. Hannah's previous smile had vanished and now her brows dipped in a V above her nose, her lips pressed together in a thin line.

"Seriously? Your first visit in more than ten years and all you can do is criticize my shop?" There was a little emphasis on the word *my*, and she folded her arms across her chest. "Is that what you learned in the big city? How to be judgey?"

"What? I—" She stopped and blew out a breath, suddenly understanding. "Did Kyle not tell you I was coming?"

"Kyle? No." Hannah blinked rapidly several times, and Riley could almost hear the gears in her head as she put two and two together.

"Yeah. He called me and asked for my help." For the first time in the past few minutes, she remembered the other girl behind the counter and lowered her voice. "Said the shop was struggling."

A bright red splotch formed on each of Hannah's cheeks, and Riley felt an instant pang of regret for embarrassing her. *Seriously? What the hell, Kyle?* "I'm not struggling," Hannah said, clearly insulted by the word, even as she sneered it.

It wasn't uncommon for a business owner to resist her help in the beginning, especially a small business owner. Riley worked with mostly larger companies now, but she'd helped her share of small ones, and it was always the small business owners who had the most pride... to their own detriment, most of the time. She did her best to gentle her voice. "Well, from what I understand, Kyle is half owner, and he says you're struggling." Hannah's embarrassment was shifting to fury now, and Riley hurried on, hoping to cut it off at the pass. "What can it hurt to let me help? Hmm? This is what I do for a living, and I promise you, I am very good at my job."

Hannah didn't look convinced. Or happy. She looked pissed. "Well, this is the first I've heard about any of this, and I really don't appreciate you waltzing in here and telling me all the things that are wrong with my shop."

Again, the slight emphasis on *my*.

Oh, Riley was going to kill Kyle. Kill him. Dead.

"We are not struggling. We don't need your help. We are fine." Riley could tell Hannah didn't believe her own words, but she also realized this was not the time to argue with her. She'd made her angry, had insulted and embarrassed her. She was thinking about how maybe she should leave when Hannah added, "You can go." With that, she spun on her heel and disappeared into the back. The girl behind the counter pretended to busy herself straightening the bags on the shelves, but Riley was pretty sure she'd heard every word, as there was nobody else in the shop.

That right there should be a clue.

With a quiet sigh, she pushed out the door and back to her car. Once inside with the a/c running, she saw she had no response from Kyle, so she sent another text.

That was fun. Wish you'd have told me she didn't know I was coming. Thanks, asshole.

She always talked to Kyle like that, so it wasn't unusually harsh, but she was still thinking about killing him. Her stomach rumbled loudly.

"Fine," she muttered, shifting the car into gear. "Food before murder."

"Are you fucking kidding me, Kyle?"

Hannah was closed in her closet office in the hopes that Kaitlyn wouldn't hear her verbally rip her brother a new one over the phone. The size of the space prevented her from angrily pacing around, which was what she really wanted to do, so she stood in the middle of the tiny room and practically vibrated with rage.

"I meant to tell you," Kyle said. "And I was going to meet Riley there. Then I had to deal with an electrical issue on this new project and had to focus on that instead of the shop. I'm really sorry, Han."

Instead of the shop. Well, wasn't that just typical? But she could picture her big brother running his hand through his sandy hair. He wasn't a mean-spirited guy, so she believed him when he said he'd meant to tell her. But that wasn't the point. At all.

"You seriously called in a consultant without even asking me? A fixer? We own the shop together, you know."

"I do know that. That's exactly why I called Riley. Because we own the shop together and it's in trouble. I'm sorry if you don't want to accept that, but it's true, and you know it."

"But…Riley Shaw?"

"Han. This is what she does now. I've told you that. She helps struggling businesses, gets them back on their feet. She's very successful, and she came here as a favor to me. So could you at least be nice to her? Listen to what she has to say?"

By the time they hung up, she was pretty sure Kyle was feeling better about things. Hannah, on the other hand, was not. And it wasn't just because Kyle hadn't consulted her. No, it was more than that. It was because it was *Riley*.

She opened the door to her office and headed back out into her work area. The cotton candy flavor was running low, so she set the popper to pop a new batch and went to work on the coating.

Memories assaulted her as she put butter, corn syrup, floss sugar, and some salt into a large pot on the stove. With those memories came a barrage of mixed emotions. That was the thing that had always frustrated her about Riley Shaw—from the time she'd met her when she was eleven years old and Riley was thirteen, right up until today—that confusing amalgamation of feelings. Young Riley had frustrated her at first, giving Kyle so much attention and Hannah so little. Looking back now, it made sense. Riley had been headed into her teen years and likely didn't want to be saddled with an eleven-year-old who followed her around like a puppy. Conversely, Hannah was suffering from her first big crush, and she wanted nothing more than to be around Riley every second she could—a constant source of irritation for her big brother, who was also harboring a crush.

She stirred the mixture as it started to heat up. The popcorn was overflowing, so she tipped it into the rack and got a second batch going, then scooped a bunch into the pot for the mixer and set it there to wait. A deep inhale of the wonderful aroma reminded her how she'd never get sick of the scent of freshly popped popcorn.

Riley and Kyle had started to hide on her, and that stung. Again, she could look back with adult eyes and understand why, but she also had the memories of how much it hurt to be left out by the two people who meant the most to her in her very small world. She was so young.

She'd been quiet as a child, just as she was now, a little shy, and it was hard to make friends when you weren't gregarious and outgoing. Her grandmother took note of this, she knew now, and asked if she thought she'd like to help out in the popcorn shop. Hannah could still remember the day she asked, could still feel that whole-body rush of adrenaline, pride, and excitement. She became a sponge, soaking up anything her grandmother would teach her, from how to pop the popcorn exactly right to how to blend some of the flavors. Back then, of course, there had only been a half dozen or so flavors, but Hannah watched everything her grandmother did. And not only did she have a blast working at Poptacular, she was good at it. In fact, this cotton candy flavor she was currently making had been her idea in the beginning.

Smiling as she stirred the mixture in the pot, she remembered coming back from the local fireman's carnival that summer, pulling chunks from the cotton candy her mother had bought for her. "Hey, Grams, how can we make cotton candy popcorn? I think it would be great." The Internet wasn't as prevalent as it is now, so they combed through some of Grandma's food supply catalogs until they found the floss sugar. It took some experimenting to find the right amount of butter and corn syrup. They'd figured out together the need for baking soda, which she poured in now and watched foam up, making the syrupy concoction lighter and fluffier—easier to pour over the popcorn. She took the hot pot to the spinner and clicked it on, and once the corn was tumbling, she slowly poured the cotton candy coating in, just as she had the caramel that morning. In a matter of seconds, the sweet aroma filled the air.

She'd made it in several different colors, but classic pink seemed to sell the best, so she stuck to that most of the time, like now. Soon, the popcorn was coated in the pink candy flavoring, and then it would get the same treatment as the caramel did—dumped onto the cooling rack and hand-sifted to alleviate any clumping.

By the time she'd bagged up the fresh cotton candy popcorn, she felt better. Making popcorn was her yoga, her meditation, her zen, and she'd put Riley Shaw out of her mind, at least for a while. She took the bags out front and set them on shelves, then dumped the remainder in the airtight container behind the display case.

"Why don't you take your dinner break?" she said to Kaitlyn, who nodded and, a moment later, exited the shop with her purse. She'd be back in forty-five minutes, Hannah knew. Kaitlyn was a good employee, and she wished she could pay her more.

With a deep breath, she leaned her forearms on the front counter and watched Sunset Valley out the front windows.

Why isn't there a window display?

Riley Shaw's judgey voice came screeching back into her head, shattering the quiet and ratcheting Hannah's irritation up once more.

"Because, Ms. Know-it-all, I don't have time to come up with a window display." She muttered it out loud to the empty shop and shook her head. She also found herself gazing at the small empty space next to the door and wondering what exactly she could put there. Her thoughts were interrupted by customers walking in, the little bell on the door ringing cheerfully.

"It smells so good in here," the woman said. She had two kids with her, maybe four and seven. A man stood outside on the sidewalk, scrolling on his phone. The husband.

"Thank you. We make popcorn fresh every day." Hannah injected happiness into her voice, and the woman left with three large bags— one caramel, one dill pickle, and one cotton candy.

And then the shop was quiet again. There were things to be done— there were always things to be done—but her brain kept shooting her memories like little vignettes of her time at Poptacular as a kid and into her teen years.

When it had finally become clear to her that Kyle and Riley had a thing, her young heart cracked open in her chest. She remembered the day she caught them in the tiny closet office. Grams had run down the street to the small grocery store to grab a bag of sugar because they'd run through theirs experimenting with a new flavor, and though the delivery truck was due that day, it was late. Grams didn't want to wait to make fresh caramel corn, so she popped out, promising to be back in less than fifteen minutes. She left and Hannah had gone into the back area, but Riley and Kyle were suddenly nowhere to be found, which was weird.

Then she heard some kind of thump that seemed to come from Grams's office. The door was shut tight, which was also weird because Grams rarely closed it, so Hannah turned the knob and pulled it open.

Riley and Kyle jumped apart like they'd received a zap of electricity. Riley was sitting on Grams's desk, and Kyle had been standing between her knees. Hannah might have only been thirteen at that point, but she knew exactly what they'd been doing, and it turned her stomach. To her horror, she felt her eyes well with tears. She left the shop through the back door, ran all the way home, and threw herself onto her own bed to cry into her pillows.

Her very first broken heart.

The memory brought a sad smile to her face, and she shook herself back to the present. Riley and Kyle hadn't worked out for whatever reason, but they'd remained the best of friends, which was impressive for high schoolers, really. Even after Riley left for college, moved away, moved her mother away, she'd kept in touch with Kyle. They had something special, the two of them.

Something that never included me.

"Ah, well." Pushing off the counter, Hannah straightened herself up as she saw Kaitlyn heading in from her break. She could go home now if she wanted. Kaitlyn knew how to close, and it wasn't quite tourist season yet. Things wouldn't get busy for another week or two.

Instead, she went into the back and put on a fresh batch of popcorn to pop. She'd experiment with some new flavors like she always did when something was bothering her; it was her way of shifting gears, focusing elsewhere.

"Hey, Kaitlyn, how do you feel about cumin?" she called out, reaching for her spice shelf.

This was her shop. It was her life and her livelihood, and she would run it as she saw fit. She knew it better than anybody else.

Fuck Riley Shaw.

CHAPTER THREE

R iley was used to sleeping in hotel beds.
    She traveled so much for work that she was away almost more than she was home, and for the past year, that's the way she'd preferred it. She was an excellent traveler, skilled at packing thoroughly and efficiently, and sleeping away from home was never a problem. So why she had tossed and turned for the better part of last night, she had no idea. But when her alarm went off at six in the morning, her first reaction was to groan in annoyance.

Poptacular opened at ten, but she was meeting Kyle and Hannah there at nine. That gave her time to get in a run at the resort's fitness center, shower, and have some breakfast before she walked into what was without a doubt going to be an uncomfortable meeting.

Half an hour later, she was dressed in workout gear, hair pulled into a dark ponytail, and she began an easy jog on the treadmill in the resort's fitness center. She didn't understand people who enjoyed running. She didn't like it. At all. But she did like the way she felt afterward, so she forced herself more often than not. She worked herself up into a doable rhythm and let her mind go.

Riley did her best thinking while running, which was a big part of why she continued to do something she didn't enjoy. Ideas, presentations, debates—she worked them all out while on the treadmill. For whatever reason, she was able to focus fully while she ran, and today, she was focused on Hannah Kramer.

Man, she had certainly grown up. She'd been a cute enough kid; Riley remembered that version of Hannah well, and like she'd thought yesterday, Hannah had become pretty as she aged into her teen years.

But now? She wasn't just attractive. She wasn't just pretty. She was *beautiful*. Even in her stained work clothes with her hair shoved up under a hat, anybody could see her beauty. Riley had been shocked, and now she wondered if she'd covered it well enough. She was here to do a business favor for Kyle, and that didn't include ogling his little sister like some kind of creeper.

It had been so long since they'd known each other, since they worked in the popcorn shop together. She'd really been Kyle's friend, and much as Hannah had wanted to tag along with them—she worshipped her big brother—he didn't want her constantly following them. What big brother wants his little sister following him around? Riley's brain tossed her a memory then, an image of Hannah walking in on her and Kyle kissing. She was shattered, seeing her big brother like that. That much was clear. She'd left crying. What was she? Thirteen? Riley recalled that she and Kyle had been about…fifteen? Yes, she'd been fifteen years old, and it was the first and last time she'd ever made out with a boy.

She remembered having to explain to Kyle how much Hannah looked up to him, and that seeing him kissing a girl was probably not part of her image of him. She'd sent him off to talk to her, and he had, but things had never been the same after that, not between her and Hannah. Hannah had pretty much hated her after that.

And from the looks of things, not much had changed.

She picked up the pace, a sheen of sweat covering her body now as she chased that elusive runner's high. She had a list of ideas for Poptacular. Suggestions. She'd start small, since Hannah was so resistant to help. That was probably the way to go.

An hour later, she turned off the water in her shower and dried herself with a thick, thirsty towel, Hannah Kramer still on her mind—both the attractive figure and the scowl. It wouldn't be the first time she'd been brought into a business by one person over the resistance of another. It was actually quite common, so she wasn't nervous. This was her job, and she was damn good at it. Plus, it was a favor for Kyle.

Surprisingly, the face of Mrs. Kramer popped into her head then, Hannah and Kyle's grandma, whom everybody simply called Grams. Sweetest, kindest woman Riley had ever known, aside from her own mother. She had known Riley and her mom were on their own, that they didn't have much. She'd given Riley a job, constantly sent her home with free popcorn, and treated her like her own grandchild. Riley would never forget her kindness, and that vision of Grams helped her focus.

Yeah, if Hannah was going to be a pain, Riley would do this for Grams. It was that simple.

There was no need for a business suit. This was Sunset Valley, after all, plus Kyle already knew her. He didn't need to be impressed by her wardrobe. That being said, she wasn't going to dress down either. A quick check of the forecast told her it was going to be in the mid eighties again, so she chose a pair of black pants and a simple sleeveless, high-necked shell in baby blue. It would make her eyes pop and she knew that—she had a stylist who helped her once a year with a wardrobe that played to her strengths, and her sky blue eyes were definitely one of those. She added subtle silver hoop earrings, a few silver bangle bracelets, and modest heels. She twisted her dark hair behind her head with a clip but kept it soft rather than severe. Standing in front of the resort's full-length mirror, she scrutinized herself. She wanted to look professional but not intimidating. Intimidating wouldn't help her win over Hannah Kramer. Maybe nothing would, but Riley knew Grams wouldn't want Poptacular run into the ground.

She wasn't about to let that happen.

Her laptop and a folder went into her computer bag. She grabbed her purse and glanced at her watch. Just enough time for her to hit the diner a few doors down from Poptacular and get herself some breakfast.

"Here we go."

She closed the door behind her.

❖

Sunset Valley had changed quite a bit since Riley was there last, and it also had barely changed at all. Which made no sense, she realized, but it was true.

For example, the avocado toast with the egg on top she'd just finished was absolutely delicious—and not something she'd ever have expected the diner to serve, considering it had been dishing out the same Sunset scramble or eggs over easy for about four decades. She'd been pleasantly surprised by some of the menu offerings. In addition to her chosen breakfast, there was a yogurt cup with homemade granola, and also chia pudding with fresh fruit. Conversely, the chair she sat on was wobbly with uneven legs and was probably older than she was. The red vinyl booth to her left had a slice that was held closed with a piece of duct tape that was also probably older than she was, given the way it was frayed.

The diner seemed to do a good business, though, customers in and out in a steady stream in the hour Riley had taken to order and eat. Now she sat with her laptop open on the table and sipped the fresh warm-up of coffee the waitress had given her. She had another twenty minutes before her meeting, and she wanted to make sure she was ready.

Which was kind of silly because Riley Shaw never went into a meeting *not* ready. Even if it was a meeting that was simply a favor for a friend, she'd be fully prepared. She'd been doing this job long enough—and enjoyed it so much—that the prep work was nearly as much fun to her as the actual meetings themselves. She absolutely loved pulling businesses back from the brink. She loved showing people things they could be doing that they weren't, things that would help, small changes that always brought expressions of surprise to the faces of clients. Sometimes, the changes had to do with finances, both incoming and outgoing. Well, *often* they had to do with finances. They were the largest reason for business failure, obviously. But sometimes, it had to do with the employee roster. Other times, it was marketing. Often, it was all three. She suspected this might be the case for Poptacular—minus the employee roster, since she was pretty sure there was a grand total of three employees, Hannah included.

She glanced out the window where she saw Kyle's pickup pull into a spot in front of the popcorn shop. He hopped out and scooted across the street to the Coffee Cup. A few minutes later, he came out, carrying a tray with three cups in it. Riley set hers down, deciding not to finish it so she'd be able to at least sip from the one Kyle had clearly purchased for her.

He was still cute. Riley hadn't seen him in a couple years now, but he was definitely still cute. She watched as he crossed the street again, his mirrored sunglasses and slightly too-long sandy hair giving him a surfer dude air. No longer a gangly young man; his job had bulked him up. His shoulders were broad now, his muscular build clear under his black T-shirt. He wore jeans and Timberland boots, and despite the initial surfer dude descriptor, his entire look really did scream *contractor*.

Riley grinned. She loved Kyle with all her heart. He was a good man, and despite Hannah's anger with him, he was only doing what he thought was best by asking Riley for her help.

She'd do what she could.

Bill paid, she gathered up her stuff, shouldered her laptop bag and purse, and pushed out into the sunny late-August morning. The diner was only a few doors down from Poptacular, so she left her car where it was and walked the short distance. She'd forgotten how crisp and clean the air was in a small town like Sunset Valley. No smog, very little car exhaust. And the quiet! God, it was weird and wonderful. Riley'd become used to the sounds of the city. Car horns, sirens, screeching brakes, the constant buzz of endless conversation. Here, there was birdsong. Actual birdsong! Sure, there was traffic, but it was minimal and going under thirty miles an hour. The only conversation she could hear was people shouting good morning to each other across Main.

Taking one last big lungful of that fresh air, she knocked on the front door of Poptacular. She could see both Kyle and Hannah inside.

"Morning," Kyle said with a big smile as he let her in, then locked the door behind her. He was forcing it, the cheer, she could tell. For Hannah's sake, she guessed.

"Good morning," she said back as Kyle kissed her cheek. She gave him a tight hug, then met Hannah's eyes across the room where she stood behind the counter, already dressed in her apron and hat. She was not smiling. "Hey, Hannah."

"Hey."

For a moment, Riley was catapulted back in time, back to *then*. A.K. That's what she called it. There was Hannah before Riley's kiss with Kyle—B.K. And there was Hannah after Riley's kiss with Kyle—A.K. And Hannah was two different people in those times. She adored Riley and then she hated her. Simple as that.

Clearly, they were in A.K., if Hannah's stone-faced expression was any indication. The place she'd been for many, many years now.

She sighed internally, set her bag down, and pulled out her laptop. Kyle handed her one of the coffee cups she'd seen him carry across the street.

"One cream, two sugars?" he asked hopefully.

"I've whittled myself down to one sugar," she said, taking the cup, "but I'll consider this a treat. Thank you, that was nice of you."

Kyle nodded once and sipped from his own cup. Hannah said nothing. A cup was on the counter next to her, the string of a tea bag visibly dangling from it.

"Okay." Riley opened her laptop on the counter. "First of all, let's talk about goals." She folded her hands and looked from Kyle to Hannah. "Why am I here?"

Hannah gave an almost inaudible snort and picked up her tea to sip.

"What do you hope to gain by having me here?" Riley asked, trying a slightly different tack.

Kyle seemed to take a beat, as if waiting for Hannah to start. When she didn't, he spoke. "The shop isn't doing well. We're not turning enough of a profit. We're falling behind on bills. Some of our vendors are refusing to supply us because we owe them money."

Riley nodded and typed as he spoke, jotting notes, her fingers flying over the keyboard. "Okay. What else?"

Again, Kyle looked to Hannah, who sipped and gazed out the window. This time, he sighed loudly enough for them both to hear it. "We're struggling with each other. I fully admit that this is Hannah's baby. She runs the place. She makes the product. She's in charge. I'm simply a silent partner." Hannah's scoff was louder this time, and Kyle glared at her for a beat before he continued. His voice was laced with the tiniest bit of animosity now, and he enunciated very clearly as he spoke this time. "We're fighting a lot lately because my little sister is very resistant to any kind of change, and she doesn't seem to understand that if we don't do *something*, this shop that she loves so much, that is basically her life, is going to go down in flames."

That seemed to get Hannah's attention, or at least got her to stand up a bit straighter, and it was apparently her turn to glare at her brother.

Riley nodded, continued typing notes. Being tossed into the ring between two fighting siblings—or spouses or parent and child or business partners—was not new to her. At all. Granted, the fact that she'd known these two people since they were all young did make things slightly more complicated as far as her own feelings went, but she was pretty sure she could set that aside for the time being.

"All right," she said, looking from Kyle, his brown eyes sincere and hopeful, to Hannah, who didn't meet her gaze at all. "I'm going to need some things. First of all, access. I'll need to see all the financials.

Monthly bills. Debts. Incoming, outgoing, all of it. Profit statements. Overdue invoices, etcetera. I can't help if I don't have the whole picture."

Hannah still hadn't met her gaze, but her face had changed just a little. In her years in this business, Riley had become pretty adept at reading facial expressions, and right now, she could read Hannah's. There was always a tell on a person's face, and with Hannah, it was in her eyebrows. They'd been either straight across or dipping down slightly in a scowl since she'd arrived. Now the scowl was gone, replaced by a worry that was indicated by the way her brows were now curved up, just above her nose.

"Is that going to be a problem?" she asked, purposely keeping her voice gentle. Being firm or disappointed in Hannah was only going to make her more anxious, since she was already getting that from Kyle, and Riley needed her cooperation if there was any chance of her helping.

Hannah picked up her tea and shook her head. Her "no" was almost inaudible.

"Good." She turned to Kyle. "I know you're not super involved, so you don't have to hang around. I'll email you an updated report of my findings, my suggestions, stuff like that every couple of days. Yeah?"

Kyle gave one nod, clearly relieved to be excused. "Yeah. Awesome." He looked to his sister. "You good?"

The glare was back, and Riley found herself happy it wasn't leveled at her this time. "Fine," Hannah said, her gaze following her brother all the way out the door.

Now it was just the two of them

CHAPTER FOUR

Hannah wanted to crawl under something, anything, and hide. Her eyes roamed over the large popper, scanned the bottom, and she absently wondered if she could flatten herself enough to slide under it and stay there until Riley went away.

"It's funny," Riley was saying. "It's changed a lot here, but it also hasn't changed that much." She smiled softly at Hannah, clearly trying to pull her back from the brink of anger-slash-resentment-slash-worry she was standing at the edge of. "Like, I remember the popper. Well, I suspect this one is newer than the one that was here when we were kids, but it looks the same."

Hannah nodded once. "It's not the same one, but they haven't changed much." She needed to do something, to busy herself. Standing around made her feel itchy. She needed to make fresh caramel corn anyway and thought she might as well get started. She grabbed the bucket of kernels she'd chosen as the best mushroom kernels she could afford and scooped some into the popper.

"It still smells amazing in here," Riley was saying as she slowly wandered around, softly touching things or dragging her fingertips along them.

"Just wait," Hannah said, as she set the first batch of the day to popping. "Just you wait."

Riley turned to her with a wide grin that shot Hannah back in time for a moment, back to the first time she'd seen Riley, back to when just being in the same room with Riley would make her heart beat faster and her palms sweat and caused waves of…just *weirdness* in her lower body. Of course, she knew what all of that was *now*. But back then? It had scared the shit out of her because she'd had no idea what was going on in her own body. When she looked at Riley now, she had to swallow her dreamy sigh. She was still so beautiful. Why? Why did she have to still be so fucking beautiful? More. More so. She was even more beautiful because now she wasn't a kid or a gangly teenager still growing into her limbs. She was a woman, and she was fucking gorgeous. From her sleek, dark hair to her lean body—that she worked on, if the subtle definition in her bare arms was any indication—to those striking blue eyes. Hannah had always had a love-hate relationship with those eyes. They were stunning, almost shocking to see, given Riley's dark hair and olive-toned skin. But they were also all-knowing. That was ridiculous, Hannah knew, but that's how she'd always felt around Riley—like she knew things. Like she saw things. Like she looked right into Hannah's soul with those eyes and knew everything she was thinking. It was unnerving and comforting at the same time. She also smelled fantastic, like summer. Suntan lotion, and sand and surf, and coconuts. Hannah would be glad when the popcorn's scent overtook Riley's because she was having trouble thinking right now.

"Mushroom kernels," Riley said, and when Hannah glanced at her, she was reading the bucket the popcorn was in. "What does that mean?"

She cleared her throat and pointed to the popper. "I'll show you as soon as these start popping." She watched as Riley wandered and continued to lightly touch things, clearly taking a little trip down Memory Lane.

"I can still almost see your grandma here," Riley said quietly, then turned to Hannah with that soft smile. "Kinda still expecting her to walk in at any moment."

That brought a smile to Hannah's face, she couldn't help it. "I still feel that way sometimes, too."

The popcorn started to pop, and in another several seconds, it was all popping loudly, the scent filling the air. Riley lifted her nose like a bloodhound and inhaled deeply. "God, I love that smell."

Hannah snatched up a freshly popped kernel, then pulled over a bowl half full of popcorn that had been left there yesterday. "Kaitlyn, one of my employees, always makes herself a little bowl of simple butter-and-salt popcorn to munch on during her shift." She grabbed a piece of it and held it up for Riley to see. "This is butterfly popcorn. See all the little wings? They're best for simple flavors like salt and butter or experimental stuff that I only make a small amount of. Butterfly popcorn doesn't stay fresh as long and it also crushes more easily." She held up the freshly popped mushroom kernel. "Now, see how this is more like a ball? It doesn't have those wings? This is much better for holding thicker coatings like caramel and syrupy flavoring. The cotton candy popcorn. The s'mores popcorn. Cheese, too. It stays fresher longer, and because of its shape, it doesn't crush as easily. Anything made with butterfly popcorn has to be refreshed daily. Any flavors made with the mushroom popcorn will last a couple days before I have to toss it and make a new batch."

Riley actually looked interested, which was surprising. Hannah knew she could go on and on about popcorn, the way it pops, the science behind it, various flavors and which ones work best, taste best, sell best. Because of that, it wasn't uncommon for her to see eyes glaze over and smiles become pasted and artificial. She'd ruined plenty of dates this way. But Riley didn't look like she was faking her interest.

"So, are you gonna make caramel corn? Like, now?" Hope was written all over her face, so much so that it almost made Hannah laugh.

"I am."

"It's my favorite." Riley shrugged, and a tiny expression of embarrassment shot across her face. "Terrible for my teeth, but I don't care."

Hannah knew it was Riley's favorite. She remembered. "Let's make you some."

Ten minutes later, the ingredients for fresh caramel coating were heating up in a pot on the small stove, and Hannah set a second batch of corn to popping.

Working with Riley in her space was both weird and not weird at all, and she had no explanation for that. How could it be both?

"Should I stir this?" Riley asked, pointing to the caramel. Hannah nodded, then watched Riley's hands as she picked up the spatula and gave it a stir. They were both quiet for a moment before Riley spoke again, her voice soft. "So, I know this will be hard for you, having me all up in your business, but I'm only here to help. It may seem like I'm being critical at times, but that's the bottom line: I'm here to help."

The talk of business yanked Hannah back into reality, and for that, she was thankful. She gave a quick nod. "Sure." Then she took the spatula from Riley and continued making the caramel. This was not for fun. Riley was not here for fun or to catch up or to learn how to make caramel corn, and Hannah would do well to remember that. She could feel Riley's presence, how she stood close for a bit, but then moved away. It was like a heat source had been removed, and Hannah felt an instant chill.

As Riley strolled off to where she'd left her laptop and began doing…whatever on it, Hannah continued with her daily routine of making fresh caramel corn, because it made everything feel normal. Not like there was somebody here who was going to point out every wrong thing she'd been doing in running her business and possibly tell her there was no saving it. She steadied herself and focused, and before long, the popcorn and the caramel were tossing in the mixer, caramel sauce being evenly distributed as it all rolled over and over in a steady rhythm that often hypnotized her. But Riley was here, she reminded herself, so she left it and headed out into the shop area to clean out the caramel corn bin and get out some bags and hear what Riley needed from her.

Because Poptacular didn't have tables, Riley was leaning against the counter on her forearms, scrolling on her laptop, dark-rimmed glasses on her face now—*God help me*—her finger moving slowly from the bottom of her touchpad to the top and back. Hannah stared at her hand.

Oh, good, something else hypnotizing.

She gave herself a shake and pulled the bin out of the display.

"So, I'm gonna need a few things from you to get started," Riley said. She'd stopped working and fixed those gorgeous eyes on Hannah.

She nodded.

"Are your finances easily accessible?"

Hannah tipped her head. "What do you mean?"

Riley pushed herself off her forearms to standing and pulled the glasses off. "I mean, do you have a program or an app you use to pay your bills? Something you can just give me access to?"

Hannah's mind shot her an image of the folder on her tiny desk in the tiny closet office marked Invoices, and the old filing cabinet overflowing with papers and crap. She almost snorted out loud. "Um…" She grimaced and braced for the disapproval.

Instead, Riley laughed, a sweet, musical sound that seemed to echo through the empty shop. "No worries. I deal with this all the time." She waved a hand. "At some point today or tomorrow, I need you to show me what you've got, how you organize your invoices, things like that. Okay?"

"Okay." Hannah managed not to laugh at the word *organize*. At least this would give her a little time to get her shit together. Or somewhat together. Or maybe the tiniest bit together.

Riley must've seen something on her face because she reached across the counter, grasped Hannah's forearm with a warm hand, and leveled that smile at her again. "Hey. Don't worry. We're gonna figure this all out, all right? Remember, I'm here to help." She gave her arm a squeeze and let go.

Hannah felt that squeeze all the way down to her—

"Oh my God, that smells good." Riley's eyes had gone wide. "I didn't expect to smell the caramel so distinctly. Wow. My mouth is watering."

Riley's enthusiasm somehow managed to haul Hannah out of the land of concern, at least for the moment, and she grinned.

"Tell me something," Riley said.

"What?"

"Do we get to sample the fresh caramel corn? I mean, we have to make sure it's acceptable for selling, right?"

There was a beat when Hannah actually thought Riley was serious, and she had started toward the path of *What do you mean, acceptable for selling? All my popcorn is acceptable for selling. It is, in fact, delicious. Just ask my customers.* And then she saw the twinkle in Riley's eyes, the half-grin on her face, and realized she was teasing. "We absolutely have to make sure. I'd be a terrible business owner if I didn't, right?"

"The worst."

This time, Hannah's grin was a little fuller and the tiniest bit more genuine. "Follow me."

❖

"Hey, boss, how are things in Sunrise Village?"

It was good to hear Justin's voice, and his completely wrong name for the town made her laugh. She'd decided to give Hannah a bit of a break. She'd been doing pretty well, but the more Riley had talked about things they'd need to do or look into or fix, the wider Hannah's deep brown eyes had become. Giving her a break seemed the kind thing to do.

Now she stood next to her BMW and talked to her assistant on her cell. "Sunset Valley. And fine. How are things there?"

"Things here are fine. Know why?" Justin was endlessly competent. That's why Riley had hired him. The bonuses she'd discovered after he started working for her were that he was gay and he was unapologetically hip. She never had any worries when she traveled to a client—which she did more often than she stayed in her office—because there was nothing Justin couldn't handle. "Because you're supposed to be on vacation, that's why."

She sighed, flattered by his obvious protecting of her. "I know. I'm just helping out a friend."

"You're a better person than me. There's no way I'd have given up my beach vacay. No way."

She understood that. But Justin clearly didn't have a Kyle in his life. As they touched on a couple of quick things that he needed her okay on, she watched Main Street in Sunset Valley over the roof of her car. She had lived here from the time she was thirteen until she'd headed off to college. So, not terribly long. Five years, maybe? She'd come home for holidays while in college, but in her head, she'd already fully moved to the big city. She loved Boston, and when her mom was diagnosed, it only made sense to move her there, too.

But Sunset Valley was in her blood somehow, because she felt a level of relaxation here that she couldn't explain. Her muscle tension eased. Her breathing slowed. Even her heart rate seemed to downshift, and it was so weird that she knew that, that she could actually feel it. There was something about this place.

Her plan had been to head back to the resort, change into her bathing suit—which she'd decided to throw back into her bag at the last minute, and now was so glad she had—and sit by the pool while she worked. She figured there was no reason she couldn't still work on her tan, despite not being anywhere near a beach, and she would still do that, but not yet.

Bag tossed into her car, she slammed the door, locked it, and shouldered her small purse. Then she started walking.

Poptacular had been in the same spot on Main Street since Kyle and Hannah's grandmother had opened it in the nineties. According to Kyle, the locals knew it and loved it, but that wasn't enough. Not anymore. Tourism was big in Sunset Valley, especially in the fall with the leaf peepers and in the winter with the skiers.

She pulled out her phone and jotted some notes, things she wanted to ask Hannah, suggestions she wanted to make.

Digging back through her memories, she tried to take note of what businesses were new since she'd left—the Coffee Cup had been there for ages, but the microbrewery she could see across the street was new. There was also what looked like a wine bar a few doors down from that. The bakery had been there forever, as had the corner store. There were a couple of new restaurants, though.

The folks of Sunset Valley were proud. Many of the families there had been there from the beginning, since the town was settled in the early 1800s. She knew this from her first year there, attending school and learning the history of her new home. She stood on the sidewalk and gazed up and down the street, jotting notes on her phone.

They needed to take advantage of that loyalty.

Good. This was good. She headed back toward her car, passing Poptacular again. The sign hanging on the front door had been flipped from Closed to Open. Riley jotted a note about it and glanced through the windows, but saw no sign of Hannah.

Forty-five minutes later, she was spreading a towel over a white lounge chair out on the pool deck of the resort. It was just after eleven, and she sat down and slathered herself with sunscreen. Yes, she'd been blessed with a lovely olive tone to her skin, thanks to her Mediterranean mom, but that didn't mean she couldn't burn. Plus, after what her mother had gone through, Riley would do whatever necessary to protect herself from any kind of cancer. *No, thank you. Avoiding that in any way I can.*

The sky was clear blue, not a cloud in sight, and she lay back with a long sigh, sunglasses on her face and an umbrella angled so she wasn't in full sun. She loved the summers here because they didn't get crazy hot. They were too far north for that. The high eighties was unusual, so today was going to be hotter than normal, but she was fine with that.

The pool was attached to the back of the resort, so when she scanned beyond the black wrought iron fencing, she got a breathtaking eyeful of the mountains in the distance. It was a view she'd never tire of, one she didn't realize she missed until she laid eyes on it. Now? She simply sat, breathed, and took it all in.

Being back here was turning out to be more cerebral than she'd expected.

That thought, of course, turned her attention to the job ahead. And Hannah.

Aside from growing up and becoming a woman—a strikingly attractive one—she hadn't changed much. Riley had picked that up right away. She was still stubborn. Still fiercely proud. Still didn't like to be told what to do. Riley smiled now as she lay there, feeling the sun warm her body. She pictured Hannah this morning, pictured her face, how she'd gone from closed off and annoyed at Riley's mere presence to letting her help make caramel corn.

This was gonna be a tough job, she could feel that already.

Not that it was something she couldn't handle. Of course she could. She would. She'd handled much worse. She'd handled bankruptcies and one business partner stabbing the other in the back. She'd had to tell people there was no hope, that their business was going under no matter what they tried. And she'd had huge successes, businesses that had gone from teetering on the brink of bankruptcy to having skyrocketing profits.

She'd seen it all.

What she'd never dealt with, though, was a business owner who conjured up the confusing feelings of her teen years.

God, a therapist would have a field day with her right now.

She shook her head with a grin, jotted a few more notes on her phone—things she wanted to look into and possibly discuss with Kyle. And Hannah. Yes. She had to be careful not to cut Hannah out of any discussions. Kyle would be easier, that was a fact. He'd listen. He'd be willing to make changes. But he didn't run the place. He had very little to do with the day-to-day of Poptacular.

She was going to have to deal with Hannah. *Okay. Okay, I can do this.*

Again, difficult clients were nothing new. Hannah Kramer was no different than any other stubborn client she'd dealt with in her career. She set her phone down and closed her eyes, let her skin feel the comforting warmth of the sun. Her brain decided that while she tanned, she should be treated to a barrage of memories with Hannah in them. Old ones. New ones.

All Hannah, all the time.

"Terrific," she muttered.

Yeah, she was going to have to deal with Hannah. So she would. And then she would get the hell out of Dodge.

❖

Hannah spent the morning and early afternoon the way she always did. She made the usual popcorn flavors—the caramel, the cheddar cheese, the s'mores with the teeny marshmallows. After that, normally, Kaitlyn would arrive and Hannah would stay in the back experimenting while refreshing some of the more unusual flavors—turtle, loaded baked potato, mac and cheese—and coming up with new ones.

But not today.

Today, once she'd refreshed every flavor that needed refreshing, she left Kaitlyn on her own and closed herself in her minuscule office. Which was no easy feat, since she'd basically closed herself in a box. But she didn't want anybody to witness her panic as she dug through file drawers and stacks of papers and folders on her desk in order to gather the things Riley had asked for. Invoices, monthly orders, payroll.

Paperwork was her kryptonite.

She muttered a curse as she dropped a folder, and all its contents spilled onto the linoleum. Her frustration made her sweat, and the sweating made it hard to breathe, and suddenly, she was in a coffin. In a panic, she burst out of the room and straight into the chest of her big brother.

"Whoa, whoa, whoa," he said, grabbing her upper arms to keep her from falling to her knees. "What's going on? You okay?"

She looked up into his brown eyes, crinkled at the corners as he laughed, and she was suddenly seized with an anger she couldn't get a grasp of. She straightened up and punched him in shoulder.

It had no effect, of course, other than to make him look at her in surprise.

"Ow. What? I just got here. What did I do?" He rubbed at the spot, which made her roll her eyes. He was basically a walking boulder. Her tiny fist hadn't caused him pain. It never had. She knew this from their childhood when he'd annoy her until she cracked and swung at him, and then he'd laugh at her. Such a big brother thing to do.

"What did you do? What did you do? Seriously?" She blinked at him.

He blinked back, oblivious.

God, why were guys so stupid? "You brought *her* here!" She continued to stare at him, waiting for some kind of reaction.

He gave her a tiny eye roll, and when he spoke, it was with that condescending tone that he used on her when he understood something she didn't quite grasp. "Han." He used two fingers to point to his own eyes. "Look at me when I tell you this." He waited until she did. "Hear me. We. Need. Help. I know you hate letting somebody else into your little inner sanctum here, but you don't have a choice. I own half of this place, too, and I really don't want to see it go bankrupt. Just let her help."

Hannah sighed and dropped her shoulders, which had been up by her ears. He was right, and she knew it. "Fine."

"Listen, if nothing else, she's fun to look at, right?" He waggled his eyebrows at her, and she rolled her eyes at him. She punched him again, but this time, there was no fury behind it.

"Hey, you're married. What would Ashley say about you ogling another woman?"

"First of all, she wouldn't care 'cause she knows I'm a one-woman man. And looking is just that. Looking. And secondly, I was talking about her being fun for *you* to look at."

He wasn't wrong. Riley was fun to look at.

"It's been a while since you had a date. Maybe you should ask her out."

Hannah turned to him, shocked. "Um, what?"

"Why do you look so flabbergasted?" he asked, and then understanding seemed to settle in, and he nodded as he spoke. "Oh. Oh, right. Yeah, Riley plays on your team, little sis."

Gut punch.

Throb.

Before anything else could be said, his phone chimed. "Shit," he said as he read the screen. "Gotta run. Can I grab a bag of...?" He let the sentence dangle as he jerked a thumb over his shoulder, and she nodded and waved him away.

She watched her big brother as he snagged a large bag of the loaded baked potato popcorn and hurried out the front door. He was gone, but his words hung in the air like dialogue in a cartoon. She could almost see the letters, all puffy and cloudlike, hovering over her popper.

Riley plays on your team.

How was that possible? And more importantly, how had she never known this?

No. She gave her head a hard shake. It meant nothing. So what if Riley was gay? So what? It changed nothing. She was still infuriating. She was still here to point out all the things Hannah did poorly. She was still here to embarrass her.

Okay, that last one was unfair, even if it was how she felt. And Riley had come as a favor to Kyle, so even if she was angry about it, Hannah had to at least give credit where it was due. She glanced back at the tiny office where papers lay scattered all over the floor and groaned softly. Riley wanted to see all her paperwork, and much as Hannah would rather be experimenting with flavors, she knew she needed to get stuff together. There'd be another meeting tomorrow and she wanted to be ready for it, not caught off guard.

Business wasn't bad that day. Regulars like Kitty Baynard, a local kindergarten teacher, came in, as well as a few new faces, likely tourists. Kaitlyn called her out to the front a couple of times, either to help out or to answer questions from customers. Yes, most of the popcorn was made fresh each day. Coconut oil was used to pop it because it had a better, subtle flavor. Yes, the salt in the sea salt caramel was actually sea salt.

Kaitlyn had to leave a bit early for a family thing, so Hannah was left on her own for the last couple hours. She was wiping down the counter when the bell over the door tinkled to announce the arrival of a customer.

"Mr. Daniels," she said with a smile. "How are you this evening?"

"Can't complain, Hannah. Can't complain." He gazed at her, his blue eyes wet and slightly rheumy. He had to be eighty-five if he was a day. He looked like a lamppost to Hannah, tall and thin and slightly bent over at the top. His hair was pure white, but he had a good amount of it, and he was always friendly and smiling. "My God, you are the spitting image of your grandmother, do you know that?"

She did know that because he told her every time he came in. But he was sweet and kind and she adored him. "I take that as the highest compliment. What can I get for you today?"

He let his eyes roam over the display case where she had little signs announcing each flavor. "What's the newest flavor?"

"That'd be the dill pickle. I think it came out pretty good if I say so myself." She opened the lid of the bin and used a scoop to give him a sample.

His blue eyes lit right up. "Oh, that's delicious. It's got quite a pop. Is there pickling spice in there?"

She grinned at him. This was a game they played. He tried the newest flavor of popcorn and tried to guess how she'd made it. He had a great palate and was right much of the time. With a nod, she said, "Just a bit. I tried without it, but it didn't have that punch, that bite you get from a dill pickle."

"I can see how that wouldn't quite work." He munched another bite. "Let me have a large bag of that."

"You got it." She bagged it and rang it up, and like always, he dropped a twenty-dollar bill into the tip jar.

Like always, she scolded him. "Mr. Daniels, you do *not* have to do that."

"Young lady, I am an old man. I don't do anything I don't want to do any longer." With a wink, he thanked her and left.

He'd be back in precisely two days. Like clockwork.

The rest of the night was mostly quiet. She had a few sales, but not a ton, and by the time she turned the sign so it read Closed, she was dead on her feet. She wanted to go home and go straight to bed. She found that interesting because it wasn't like she'd worked any longer than a typical day for her. It was her brain. She was mentally exhausted, and she knew that was because of everything Riley Shaw had lobbed her way.

Which reminded her of the paperwork Riley wanted to see tomorrow.

"Ugh." She clicked off the lights and gathered up the messy stack of papers she'd managed to pull together throughout the day when she wasn't making popcorn or thinking about new flavors. She'd have to go through it all at home and figure out the least embarrassing way to present it all in the morning.

Bed would have to wait.

CHAPTER FIVE

Hannah was not a fun person when she was tired. She slept hard, and she didn't like to be woken up. Her mother called her an angry sleeper.

Accurate.

She stood on one side of the counter in Poptacular and Riley stood on the other. It was two hours before opening, and they had papers spread across the entire counter. Invoices. Orders. Check stubs. Mail. Notes Hannah had jotted about flavoring or seasonings or which vendors would extend her credit even when she owed them money.

Riley had her glasses on again and was looking at every fucking piece of paper like it was some historical document from the Smithsonian. But holy crap, did she look good doing it. Today, she wore jeans and a simple black tank top. Her hair was pulled back into a twist and held with a black hair clip. She'd carried that scent in with her—the sunscreen-coconut *I smell like sunshine* scent—and Hannah caught herself inhaling deeply more than once.

The rap on the front door startled both of them enough that they each jumped, then met one another's gaze and laughed softly.

Shana stood at the door holding two to-go cups, God bless her. Hannah hurried to let her in. "You are an angel and a lifesaver," Hannah said.

"Your brother came by earlier and said if I saw you guys working, to bring by sustenance." She held out a cup to Hannah. "The next iteration of the pumpkin spice." She handed the other cup to Riley. "Cream, one sugar?"

Hannah watched Riley smile and—what the hell—did it light the whole place up? Sure seemed like it did.

"Oh, I needed this," Riley said, on a sigh. "Thank you so much." She took the cup and held out a hand. "Riley Shaw."

Shana took her hand and shook it. "Shana Franklin. Lovely to meet you." Her eyes scanned the countertop covered with paperwork. "Oh, this looks fun." She turned to Hannah with wide eyes.

Hannah snorted. "It's the opposite of fun, actually." She sipped her coffee and glanced at Riley over the rim. Was that a shadow of hurt that zipped across her face? Nah. Couldn't be.

"What do you think?" Shana asked, indicating the coffee with her eyes.

"Better. I can taste the nutmeg now. I think"—she squinted and took another sip, let it sit on her tongue for a minute—"it might be the tiniest bit too sweet?"

"Ugh." Shana grimaced. "That says a lot coming from a sweet tooth like you. Okay, I'll tweak the sugar content. We still on for tonight?"

Hannah nodded. "Definitely. I'll need it." After the flash of hurt she'd seen on Riley's face, she didn't elaborate on the fact that she was meeting Shana for drinks, and what she'd meant was that she was going to need many of them after today.

"Perfect. See you at seven." Shana headed for the door.

"Wait," Hannah called, then tossed a bag of caramel corn across the shop to her. Shana caught it with little effort. "Thanks, Boo. Riley, very nice to meet you."

"Same," Riley called after her. When the door was closed and Hannah went to it and turned the lock, she added, "Very cool of her to bring us coffee."

"Shana's great. We are taste testers for each other. She likes to experiment with lattes, and I like to experiment with popcorn, and we both have pretty refined palates."

Riley seemed to watch as Shana crossed the street and disappeared back inside the Coffee Cup. "She didn't go to school when we did, did she?"

Hannah shook her head. "She moved here about ten years ago, I think. Started out as a barista at the coffee shop and worked her way up until she bought the place when her boss retired."

"Ah, I see. A fellow small business owner."

Hannah nodded but didn't say that the Coffee Cup was much more successful than Poptacular. That was probably obvious from the steady stream of people in and out of the coffee shop all day long.

Riley blew out a breath and pushed herself up to standing straight. "Well, you weren't kidding about not having your paperwork sorted."

Ouch. Okay, maybe she deserved that.

"And I know there's something to be said for doing things old school, but we really need to get you computerized. You're living in the nineties with all this paper floating around."

"That's how my grandma did it." Hannah cleared her throat, then sipped her coffee.

"I get that. But your grandma's not here, and you need a better handle on your accounting." She began sorting all the papers into piles. "Do you have a laptop?"

"Yeah." She let the word sort of hover in the air until Riley stopped shuffling papers and met her gaze.

"What does that mean?"

She wrinkled her nose. "It's not exactly, um, state of the art."

"No worries, we're gonna get you a new one."

Hannah cleared her throat again and said quietly, "I can't really afford that right now."

"I know. Lemme see what I can do."

What did that mean? Hannah was afraid to ask, so she simply watched Riley sort paper. She had beautiful hands—delicate wrists, long fingers, nails shining with clear polish. She watched for what felt like a long time.

"Okay." Riley put her hand flat on one pile and moved it from pile to pile as she spoke. "Invoices. Payroll. Vendors. Profits. Owner notes. Recipes-slash-ideas." She glanced up at Hannah, and those clear blue eyes stole her breath for a second. "I will input all this later, and then we'll talk about who to pay first. Well, after rent. We need to get that up to speed. Can you talk to your landlord? The last thing you need is to lose your space."

Hannah sighed. "Bradley McFarland's a nice guy, but he's kind of hard to get ahold of."

Riley furrowed her brow, which only made her look more attractively stern. "Did he teach us English?"

"His dad did. In fact, his dad owned this building when my grandma was alive. He passed it down to his son, Bradley Junior, when he and Mrs. McFarland moved south to retire. Like I said, Brad Junior is nice enough, but he wants his rent."

"Can't blame the guy for that." Riley shrugged.

It irritated Hannah. She wanted to shout, *Be on my side, damn it!* even though Riley was one hundred percent right.

"Now." Riley turned to face the front of the shop. "I think we need to do some updating."

"Updating? What do you mean?"

Riley pointed as she spoke. "I think we should paint the walls. This color is old and it's also bland. We want vibrant. The floor needs replacing. See the high traffic area? It's pretty obvious. The sign out front is flaking and peeling. And you're completely wasting this window display area by not using it." She turned to face the counter, and if Hannah's expression of shocked horror surprised her, she didn't let on. Instead, she pointed to the counter. "There's a lot of space here we can use. And this wall over here is empty. It's like a blank canvas. We can use that. I also think there are dozens of marketing opportunities you're not taking advantage of. This is a very small town, you need to use it. Use your regulars. Use your fellow small business owners like Shana. There's a ton you could be doing that you're not."

Hannah stood there, stunned into silence. All the changes, so many changes, how did Riley think they were going to do all these things, afford all these things? She simply stood there and blinked.

"I see, by the look on your face, that you're totally on board with all my suggestions." Riley grinned and waited. "Okay, look. I'll break it all down and put it in a report for you. All right? That should make it more palatable, and that's what I do for larger businesses I work with."

Hannah blinked some more, cleared her throat, looked around.

"It's a lot. I know." Riley glanced down at her feet. "I probably shouldn't have sprung it all on you like that, but I'm just trying to help."

"Yeah, you keep saying that, but it feels more like criticism, pointing out everything that's wrong with the way I run my business." She turned and went to the back where she turned on the popper, put coconut oil in and then kernels, set it to pop. Riley followed her, but neither of them said anything for a long time. Hannah worked. Riley watched.

Hannah took out her pot and set it on the stove. From the small fridge, she took out some barbecue sauce, and some hot pepper sauce, then grabbed some seasonings from the shelf.

"That pot looks older than I am," Riley said. There was a smile in her voice, but when Hannah shot her a glance, she grimaced.

"It is. It was my grandmother's." Hannah looked at it now, really looked at it, for probably the first time in years. It *was* old. Dented. The handle had a melted spot on it. Anybody looking at it now—Riley looking at it now—would, of course, see how old it was, how badly it should probably be replaced. She closed her eyes and sighed, gave herself a mental shake, then went to work on her Buffalo wing sauce.

"I'm gonna go," Riley said.

Hannah didn't look at her.

"I'll take the paperwork with me and get you set up in a program."

"Fine." She could feel Riley standing there for a moment before she finally turned and went back out to the front. Hannah could hear her gathering papers, shoving them into her bag, and then the bell tinkled and she was gone. Hannah stopped making Buffalo wing sauce and braced herself on the back counter with both hands. Her head dropped down between her shoulders, and she did her best to fend off the tears that had been hanging out just behind her eyes for the past hour.

Hannah didn't cry easily. She was not a crier. But there was one thing that could guarantee tears for her, and that was frustration. When she couldn't figure something out, when she was out of solutions, those things could bring tears.

When somebody pointed out all the things she was doing wrong regarding something incredibly important to her? Yeah, that would bring tears.

Fending them off wasn't working, and she felt her eyes well up until they overflowed.

Yeah, she was definitely going to need that drink tonight.

❖

"I went at her kinda hard," Riley said to Justin on FaceTime an hour later in her room. "There's so much she could do to put a new face on the shop, but I'm not sure she's willing."

"What's that saying about horses and water?" Justin asked.

"Yeah." She sighed and shook her head and gazed out the window. Tomorrow was the first day of September, and the weather had decided to emphasize that by cooling down considerably to a lovely seventy-five, as if in preparation. "I think I hurt her feelings."

Justin scoffed, and she glanced back at her phone, which she had propped up against a coffee mug. He was always incredibly put together, like he'd just stepped out of a commercial for a high-end men's clothing store. His dark hair was close-cropped, and never was there one out of place. His wire-rimmed glasses accented his large green eyes. His beard was so precisely trimmed, it looked like it had been drawn onto his face with a felt-tip pen. Today's tie was red and navy blue stripes, and Riley knew he smelled like Davidoff Cool Water.

"You're doing her a favor, aren't you?" he asked. "Does she know you gave up two weeks at the beach for her?"

Riley sighed and shook her head. "I don't think so. I mean, she knows I'm here to help, but she doesn't know I'm on vacation."

"Maybe you should tell her."

"Maybe." No, there was no way she'd do that to Hannah. Hearing what Riley'd had to say was hard enough; she didn't need to feel guilty on top of that. She finished up with Justin, instructing him on several client interactions and asking him to FedEx a package to her at the resort. Once they'd ended the call, she sat there, chin in her hand, and stared out the window of her room.

While she missed the city, she was finding that she wasn't as uncomfortable or stir-crazy here as she'd expected to be. Granted, it had only been a couple of days, but she felt relaxed. Easy. Maybe it was all the fresh, clean air. Maybe it was the more laid-back pace of Sunset Valley. Whatever, she felt more at peace than she thought she would, and what the hell was that about? Then she scoffed.

Yeah, ask me how I'm feeling in a few more days.

Moving to her bag, she pulled out all the papers she'd shoved in there and spread them out on the desk. Hannah may have been a whiz at coming up with amazing and unique popcorn flavors, but she sucked at bookkeeping. Wow.

She promised herself that if she at least went through the invoice pile, separated it into upcoming, due, and past due, then made some calls, she'd then head downstairs to get a late breakfast and maybe lounge by the pool. At the last minute, when she'd been packing, she'd grabbed a couple of novels and tossed them into her suitcase, just in case. Now they sat on her nightstand and stared at her, making her feel guilty.

"Okay, okay," she muttered. "I'll try."

She hunkered down and got to work.

❖

Shana was already seated at the bar when Hannah arrived at Henry's, five minutes late. As usual. She gave Shana a one-armed side hug and took the stool next to her. "Hey, bitch."

"What's up, bitch."

"Whatcha drinkin'?" She looked at the strangely green liquid in Shana's glass.

"I'm honestly not sure." Shana wrinkled her nose. "Davey said he"—she made air quotes with her fingers—"'invented it.'"

"Oh, no, not a Davey invention." Hannah laughed and took the glass, ventured a sip. It was cloyingly sweet, but also a bit on the floral side, likely from gin. She grimaced. "Okay, once in a while, Davey hits a home run. This is not one."

"This isn't even a single," Shana agreed. But she drank it anyway, because Davey was a sweetheart, and also because Shana had a thing for him.

"Hey, Hannah Banana," Davey said as he stopped in front of her. He was a walking, talking stereotype of a bartender in a small town, dressed in jeans and a white T-shirt with a red-and-blue flannel shirt hanging unbuttoned with the sleeves rolled up, his brown hair a bit too long, as was his beard. Hannah thought he'd be perfectly cast as the bartender-with-a-heart-of-gold in just about any Hollywood blockbuster. "What can I get you?"

"How about a Cosmo?"

"You got it." He started gathering ingredients.

Hannah winked at Shana. "You're welcome," she mouthed, knowing Shana liked to watch Davey use the martini shaker, and she couldn't blame her. Davey had some nice forearms. If you liked hairy and muscular.

"So?" Shana asked as she watched the display before her. "How did things go today? You didn't look terribly happy."

"Ugh." It was all she could think of to say, and it seemed perfectly appropriate. *Ugh.* It fit.

"Tell me."

Davey slid the Cosmo in front of Hannah, and she smiled with gratitude. Taking a sip seemed to fortify her, the tartness of the cranberry juice poking at her taste buds.

"It's just hard," she said.

Shana seemed to wait for more, then prodded when no more came. "Okay. What's hard?"

"All the stuff she wants to change."

"Change or fix?"

Hannah gave her a mock glare. "Hey. You're supposed to be on *my* side."

Shana leaned into her. "Babe. I am always on your side. Always."

" 'Kay."

"I also know that you tend to have…" Shana pursed her lips like she was searching for the right word. "Tunnel vision."

"I'm sorry, I have tunnel vision?" Hannah gaped at her friend. "Explain."

"Just, when it comes to the shop. You don't like change." The cold steel of Hannah's straightening spine glanced off Shana's raised palm like a toothpick, the snap of it forestalling any further protest. "That's not necessarily a bad thing," she said, expression softening like this morning's caramel, expert Hannah-tamer that she was. "You're driven, and it's awesome. I admire that about you."

It worked. It always worked. *Damn it.* "Nice recovery," she muttered begrudgingly.

"And you don't always want to hear suggestions."

"Hey." Hannah pouted.

Shana tipped her head as if to say *Really?*

Hannah sighed. "Fine. I'm driven." She widened her eyes and bobbled her head back and forth as she said it.

"You also don't enjoy help from others."

"Oh, we're not done." Another sip as she mentally braced.

But Shana surprised her by closing a warm hand over her forearm and waiting until Hannah looked her in the eye. "Babe. This woman is trying to help you, am I right? That's why she's here."

"I know." Hannah sighed. A big, deep sigh that came from way down in her soul. "You're right."

"Another thing?"

"How could there possibly be more?"

Shana grinned. "What do we know about her? Is she single? Does she play on your team? Because, honey, she is *fine*."

Hannah burst out laughing then, as her brother's voice echoed through her head. Again.

Riley plays on your team.

And then her brain filled up with visions of Riley. Hair up. Hair down. Glasses on. Glasses off. Dressed in shorts, an apron, and a hat fifteen years ago. Dressed in business clothes and heels now. And in all those scenarios, she was simply Riley. Hannah had no idea how to explain her complex feelings around Riley Shaw.

"She's very attractive," she said, nodding as she picked up her glass. "She's not really my type, though."

Shana blinked at her for a moment before saying, "So, your type is not successful and hot?"

"I—" Another deep sigh. "I just don't want to mix business and pleasure, you know?"

Shana frowned. "Yeah, I guess that makes sense."

They were quiet for a beat and sipped their drinks.

Then Shana said, "I'm not saying marry her, though. I'm just saying, maybe get you some. You know? It's been a while."

It had definitely been a while. Shana was right about that. Two years and change, to be exact-ish. But Riley? No. No way. Things around Riley were far too complicated, at least in Hannah's head. She knew that. She leaned in close to Shana and lowered her voice. "I don't see you making any moves on our friendly neighborhood bartender, ma'am."

Shana snorted a laugh. "Nice try, turning it around on me, but we're talking about *your* sex life. Or lack thereof."

"Story of my life." She signaled Davey for a refill, then blew out a breath. "I'm worried about the shop, Shay. Like, not just a little stressed. I'm really worried." Trying to swallow down the lump that had lodged in her throat proved difficult.

Shana nodded slowly as she watched Davey shake another Cosmo for Hannah. "I know you are. And that's why you need to focus on listening to Riley. This is what she does, right? She helps struggling businesses?"

"It's what she does. Yeah."

"Then let her do her job."

Hannah knew she was right. It shouldn't be something that felt hard. She wanted to point out to Shana how many things Riley had already suggested changing, just in the first day or two, but she didn't want to sound like some kind of annoying whiner.

"Okay." She nodded. "I'll try."

"That's all I'm saying." Shana lifted her glass, which Davey had refilled with a new concoction, this one a weird purple color. It made Hannah grin as she touched her glass to Shana's.

She'd try. She would listen to Riley, do what she asked.

How hard could it be?

Chapter Six

Something brighter," Riley was saying, waving an arm over her head and feeling like she was directing a flight to a runway. "Yellow? Pastel green? Something fun and happy."

Hannah stood next to her, arms folded across her chest, and stared. She didn't say anything. She didn't even look like she was thinking about it. She just seemed—felt, if Riley was being honest—annoyed. Okay, okay. That was fine. She dealt with people resistant to change all the time. The thing to do was to shift gears, focus on something else.

She turned and pointed to the floor behind them. "Okay. This. Here. The traffic path from the door to the counter is very clear, which tells me it's time to replace the flooring." At Hannah's blinking, she added, "Just here. Just in front of the counter. The back can stay." The back should actually be replaced as well, but she'd wait on that. It was clear Hannah could only handle small bites at a time. Which wasn't unusual. Small business owners were notoriously stubborn about change. "I'm thinking a tough, high-traffic laminate that looks like wood?"

Hannah stared at the floor for what felt like a ridiculously long time before giving one nod. "Yeah. Okay. I guess."

"Hannah." Riley said her name firmly, tried to ignore how much she liked it, and sighed internally, because ignoring that was impossible. She waited until Hannah lifted her head and focused those rich brown eyes on her. "I don't want you to guess. This is all up to you. If you don't want to make any changes, then don't. I'm not here to force you."

Hannah took off her hat, scratched her head, and put it back on backward. Which just made her look stupidly cute, despite the scowl on her face.

"My professional opinion: I know you're concerned about money. Changes cost money. But you also have to spend money to make money. It's an old adage, but it happens to be true. I've seen it happen time and time again. If the floor feels too costly, let's do the walls. Paint isn't terribly expensive, and you and I could paint this space in a late evening or an early morning. Easy peasy."

What? Was that an actual smile she saw making an appearance on Hannah's face?

"My grandma used to say that. Easy peasy."

"I know," Riley said, her voice soft. "I remember." She waited, and she could almost see thoughts and visions rolling around in Hannah's head.

"I don't hate the idea of yellow," she said quietly. "It kind of gives buttered popcorn."

Thank fuck.

"I thought so, too." Riley nodded. "That's why I suggested it." She crossed to the counter and opened her bag. From it, she pulled out three paint chips she'd grabbed from the hardware store the day before. She went to the wall and held them all against it.

"Wow," Hannah said. "That was quick."

"I was kinda hoping you'd go for the yellow. I wanted to be prepared." She scrunched up her nose, hoping to avoid any anger Hannah might have about being predictable.

"That one." Hannah pointed to the swatch in the center. It was a little less sunny, but a little more inviting.

"Speaking of quick." Riley took out a pen and put a small x on the chip. "I will get the paint ordered. I bet your brother can lend us some equipment." She closed her bag and turned to face Hannah, hands on her hips. "How do you feel about a painting date tonight? After closing. You and me. I'll bring dinner?"

Hannah blinked once. Twice. Swallowed audibly. Then gave one nod. "Fine." Without another word, she turned and headed into the back of the shop, and in a minute or two, Riley heard kernels being poured into the popper.

"Okay. Guess we're done," she said quietly to herself. Shouldering her bag, she pushed out onto the street and into yet another glorious, sunny day in upstate New York. A light breeze lifted her hair and rearranged it a bit before letting it settle back down against her shoulders. Checking both ways, she crossed the street to the Coffee Cup, pulling out her phone as she went.

Shana was behind the counter when she walked into the shop, the air heavy with the aroma of freshly ground beans.

"I know you," Shana said with a grin. "How's it going?"

"Not bad, not bad at all." She decided she needed a boost, so ordered herself a latte instead of her usual coffee and met Shana at the end of the counter a few moments later to collect it. She reached for the cup, but Shana held on.

"Listen." Shana cleared her throat, as if giving herself time to collect her thoughts. "Be patient with Hannah. Okay? She's a hardhead, and she can be infuriating, but she misses her grandma terribly, and she loves that shop more than anything. She'll do what's right for it. She's just gonna make you jump through hoops first." She said the last line with a wry grin that made Riley laugh.

"Yeah, I'm getting that already." She held up the cup that Shana finally let her have. "Thanks for the advice. Back to my hoops."

Once outside again, she texted Kyle: *Do u have painting stuff? Brushes, ladder, etc.?*

She wondered if he'd be too busy with whatever he was overseeing that morning, but the gray dots began bouncing almost immediately.

She agreed????

The four questions marks made her grin, and she typed back, *Told u I was good at my job.* She followed that with a winking emoji.

Clearly. Yeah, I have stuff. I'll drop it at the shop after lunch.

She pocketed her phone and sipped the latte, which was rich and delicious. And hot. Standing on the sidewalk, she stared at Poptacular, and the two things she'd noticed in the beginning stood out like they were highlighted.

The sign was faded. And chipping. And just looked old.

Then there was that unused window display area.

She nodded to herself slowly, then took her phone back out and snapped a couple of shots. Back at her car, she slid in and started the engine, headed back to the resort.

She had work to do.

❖

Riley set down the two gallons of paint with a grunt. That was it. That was everything. All the equipment they'd need to paint the front end of the store as soon as Hannah closed up shop for the night.

She'd had to run to a local sporting goods store to grab an inexpensive pair of shorts and a cheap T-shirt, since she hadn't brought anything with her that she was okay getting covered in paint. She'd also grabbed a baseball cap, and wore that, so she was ready.

Hannah was waiting on a customer and there were two women standing in line behind them, and it might have been the first time Riley had seen an actual line since the day she got here. It made her smile as she walked out to the front and took a look at the canvas she was about to work on.

"Oh, you were right," one of the women in line, a redhead, said quietly to the shorter woman next to her. "She *is* hot."

The pair were young—maybe in their early twenties—and both looked athletic. They stood with their heads close together as they spoke.

"She dated my friend's cousin a couple years ago," Shortbread said. "I guess she was really sweet and fun but could be kind of intense."

"You can kinda see that in her eyes, right?" said Red.

"Oh, definitely."

Out of the corner of her eye, Riley watched them watch Hannah, and she bit down on her lips to keep from smiling.

"I mean, it's like she tries to hide how hot she is." That was Shortbread, and Red nodded vigorously.

"Exactly. I'd date her. A little intense can be a good thing."

"Especially in bed, am I right?" said Shortbread, and they both laughed quietly as the customer in front of them left with their popcorn, and Hannah asked if she could help them.

Hot and intense, Riley thought as she ran a hand over the wall. Definitely accurate descriptors of Hannah. She wondered if Hannah had any idea that's how people—women, in particular, and women who dated women even more particularly—saw her.

Red and Shortbread laughed and joked with Hannah as they sampled a couple different flavors, even got the tiniest bit flirty, and Hannah actually flirted back. *What the hell?* That was surprising. Not only *that* she did it, but that she actually knew *how*. Riley was learning more and more about Hannah with each hour they spent together. She listened for another moment, but there was only so long she could pretend to stare at a wall, so she headed to the back of the shop near the popper and busied herself. More laughter, more banter, and finally, the three women said their goodbyes.

The little bell over the door tinkled, as Hannah followed the women and locked the door behind them. She turned the sign to Closed, and the happy demeanor seemed to have left along with the two customers and their popcorn.

"What flavor did they go with?" Riley asked as she dragged the tarp out to the front.

"Loaded baked potato."

"Good choice," Riley said with a nod. She could hear the water in the sink turn on, fill up a container, then turn off. She spread the tarp out on the floor along the base of the wall as Hannah appeared with a bucket. Kyle had already stopped in that afternoon and taken down the three measly shelves and the framed picture of Grams. She went to the back, grabbed the ladder, and brought it out front. "I heard them talking while they were in line. One of them said you dated the cousin of a friend a couple years ago."

Hannah nodded as she squeezed out a cloth and began to wipe down the wall. "She must've meant Tamara."

She waited for elaboration, but none came. "They also said you were hot."

There it was: a little twitch at the corner of Hannah's mouth.

"What happened with Tamara? Can I ask?"

"I mean, you just did." Hannah dipped the cloth, squeezed, washed. She lifted one shoulder as she spoke. "I guess we just kind of...drifted."

Riley sensed there was more, so she waited. It took a few moments, but Hannah went on.

"She didn't love my hours. Didn't quite get why I didn't have somebody else close the shop instead of doing it myself."

Riley nodded, made a little sound of understanding. She pried the top off a can of paint and stirred it.

"I mean, I got it. She was done working at five, like a normal person. You know? Who wants to wait an extra four or five hours for their person?"

"How long were you together?"

Hannah sighed as she took her cloth up the ladder so she could reach the highest parts of the wall. "Almost two years?"

"I'm sorry."

"Meh. Don't be. Clearly, we didn't have a solid enough connection, and I don't think she really had any concept of how much this shop means to me."

"Some people have no grasp of that kind of importance." She glanced up the ladder and saw Hannah nod.

"What about you?" Hannah asked after a moment.

"What about me?"

Hannah climbed down the ladder. "When was your last relationship?" When she got to the bottom, she gasped, and her eyes went wide. "I'm sorry. I'm assuming you don't already have somebody. I apologize."

She looked mortified, and Riley reached out to grasp her upper arm. "Stop. You have nothing to apologize for. No, I don't have somebody." Hannah's dark eyes on her made her feel suddenly… exposed. Laid bare. She cleared her throat and went back to the paint. "My last relationship was with Alex. We lasted about three years. She didn't like how much I travel. Said I was emotionally unavailable."

"And she broke up with you?"

"Yup."

"What'd you do after that? I bought a new couch to cheer myself up." Hannah's laugh was soft.

"Oh, you know. I traveled more for work." Riley's laugh was not soft. It was chilly.

"She couldn't make you stay in one place, huh?"

That had been the problem. She could have, but it terrified Riley. "Nope." *Because I don't stay. I run.* She poured paint into a tray, then looked to Hannah. "I haven't had a relationship since." She held up a brush in one hand and a roller in the other. "Cutting in or rolling?"

❖

First things first: Riley in shorts, a T-shirt, and a hat with her dark ponytail pulled through the back was more than Hannah had bargained for. It was unexpected, and it had her blood running very, very warm, like the oil in the popper *just before* the first kernel exploded into a little white cloud. What the hell was that about?

She took the paintbrush and began cutting in around the window, the door, and the trim. *Paint. Focus on the paint.*

Second, how did they end up having this conversation? She didn't like revisiting the Tamara situation, but she'd only hesitated a second before revealing to Riley her embarrassment over that relationship.

But Riley had shared, too.

"I didn't know you were gay until, like, yesterday." The words were out before she could even think about them, and it was a good thing she was up on the ladder facing the wall so Riley didn't see her horrified expression.

The sound of the roller stopped, and Hannah could almost feel Riley's eyes boring into her. "You didn't?"

"Nope."

"Kyle didn't tell you?"

"I mean, he told me yesterday. Yes."

Riley rolled the roller in some paint and then started on the wall. The yellow was buttery and warm. "This was a good color choice," she said as she seemed to let Hannah's words sink in. A beat or two went by, then, "I mean, he's known for years, though."

Hannah lifted a shoulder in a half shrug. "He never told me. And I never asked." She heard the roller stop again, and she twisted on the ladder to find Riley looking up at her. Just simply looking up at her. "What?"

"You never asked?"

Hannah shook her head.

"Huh." Riley went back to rolling, but Hannah stayed looking at her.

"What do you mean 'huh'?"

It was Riley's turn to shrug. "Nothing. I guess it makes sense, though. I was kind of a sore spot between you and Kyle. A.K."

"A.K.?"

Riley grinned, dipped her roller. "Yeah. After kiss. That's how I think of you and me. There was B.K. Before the kiss. That's when we were friends and got along and had fun together."

Hannah watched her paint, watched the muscles in her legs as she moved along the floor, squatting, then standing. She watched the beauty of her shoulders as Riley rolled the paint smoothly onto the wall, and suddenly, she felt that flutter low in her body, that gentle throb between her legs. A feeling that had become almost foreign, it was back in full force. Just from watching Riley paint a wall.

"Then there was after the kiss, A.K., when you hated me for taking your big brother away from you." Riley sighed. "We were never the same after that."

Wait. "For taking my big brother?"

Riley dipped again. "Yeah. You were clearly upset that he had grown up and was hanging out with me instead of you. I'm sure it's not uncommon for siblings as close as you two were back then."

Hannah nodded. *That's* what Riley thought? That Hannah was jealous of the time she got to spend with Kyle? *I mean, of course that's what she thought. Why would she think anything else?* She nodded some more and went back to her cutting in.

"But after that, you and I were never the same. Which was a bummer. I missed you." Riley's voice wasn't wistful or sad. It was matter-of-fact, and she continued to paint.

Meanwhile, up on the ladder, Hannah's brain whirred a million miles an hour with so many new thoughts. She gave herself a mental shake, though, and told herself to focus on what she was doing. Painting. That was all. Painting.

"You were right about this color," she said after a moment, making it clear the topic of conversation had officially changed. "Much as I hate to admit it."

Riley laughed, and it was a sweet sound, higher pitched than you'd expect from looking at her. "Believe it or not, I do know a thing or two about what makes a business work."

"The floor looks worse from up here," Hannah said with a sigh, indicating the traffic area with her eyes.

"Good thing your customers don't fly in on broomsticks."

"I mean, I do have one…"

They both laughed, then continued to paint as the darkness outside became full and the streetlights lit up Main. It only took about two hours to paint the entire front with two coats, and it made things look clean and fresh. The two of them stood side by side, Hannah with her hands on her hips, and they surveyed their handiwork.

"Looks good," Hannah finally admitted. "Really good."

"I'm glad you think so." Hannah appreciated that Riley did *not* say I told you so, which she'd have been well within her rights to do. Instead, she simply stood next to her and nodded.

There was no more talk of the past as they cleaned up their painting equipment and put things away.

"I don't think it's gonna need a third coat," Riley said. "Looks good, and by the time you open tomorrow, everything should be dry, nice and even."

"You paint often?" Hannah asked.

"Not so much anymore, but I like to paint. I like the way a fresh coat of paint can give a place a clean-slate look. It's been a while, though, so thanks for letting me help."

Hannah snorted a laugh. "Are you kidding? I do *not* love to paint. Thank *you* for helping." They stood for a moment, facing each other, eye contact feeling kind of intense for some reason. Finally, Riley broke away.

"Well, I'd better get back. I've got some other work stuff to take care of before I hit the sack."

Hannah nodded. "Sure. Thanks again."

Riley gathered up her stuff and was out the door. Hannah watched her go, watched her slide into her car, start the engine, check her phone, then back out into the street and, finally, pull away. And then Hannah stood there for a few moments longer before shaking herself into movement.

Half an hour later, she slid her key into the lock and pushed open the door to her tiny one-bedroom apartment. Once she set her stuff down, her stomach rumbled loudly, and she realized she'd eaten next to nothing all day. The galley kitchen was small but functional, and within the next fifteen minutes, her mouth watered as she toasted a grilled cheese sandwich. There was only one thing taking up more of her headspace than her hunger, and that was Riley Shaw.

God, she was gorgeous.

That wasn't a new assessment, of course, but Hannah hadn't seen her in years, hadn't really thought about her much except those rare occasions when her brain decided to hop into the Wayback Machine as she slept and send her a dream about eighteen-year-old Riley, Hannah's very first crush. That hadn't happened in a while, but it did still happen.

She cut her sandwich on the diagonal, pulled a bottle of beer out of her very bare fridge, and took a seat on her couch in the dark living room where she hadn't turned on any lights yet.

As she chewed, she tried to force her mind to other things.

That plant needs watering.

I should dust in here.

I owe Mom a phone call.

Riley has the sexiest shoulders I've ever seen.

"Goddamn it." A swig of beer didn't help the situation, and before she even realized it, she'd given in. Given in to the thoughts and the little soft-core porn movie her brain played in her head for her, featuring Riley Shaw, sexy painter. Eyes closed, she thought about Riley rolling the paint smoothly onto the wall. Up…down…up…down. Riley's leg muscles flexed, her shoulders were bronzed from her time in the sun, her dark ponytail almost corkscrewing from the back of the hat, her ass in those shorts—

"Oh my God, enough already!" She had to say it out loud because her head clearly wasn't obeying any thoughts about stopping this lust train it was on.

It *had* been a long time since she'd had sex. That was it. That's why she'd gotten stuck in a whirlybird of sexy thoughts. It was just that. She was just thirsty. She had a quick vision of fifteen-year-old Parker, from across the hall, telling her, "Ew, no, never say that again."

She finished her sandwich, shaking her head as she chewed the last bite. This was all she needed—to revert to crushing on somebody who was out of her league.

Depositing her dish and empty bottle back in the kitchen, she sighed and headed to the bathroom to shower off the day. Hoping to wash Riley Shaw out of her brain didn't work. At all. What did work was the handheld showerhead, which brought her to a crazy intense orgasm in a matter of seconds.

"Goddamn it," she said again.

CHAPTER SEVEN

"Okay, let's talk about some ways you can cut costs." Riley sat in a folding chair in Hannah's itty-bitty office. With both of them in there, they couldn't close the door, because Riley's chair sat in the doorway.

She spread out some of the paperwork she'd been going through over the past couple of days. As she started to talk, to point, to suggest, she could almost see Hannah disengage, as if she'd literally punched a Mute button and could no longer hear what Riley was saying.

What the hell?

This was not the same Hannah Kramer that had been here the night before, painting and being open about the past. No, they were clearly back to closed-off, not-interested-in-help Hannah Kramer, and Riley was frustrated with that. In a major way.

She glanced at her watch. Eight forty-five. She inhaled a deep breath, let it out slowly, then began gathering up all the paperwork until it was back into a nice, neat pile. Hannah watched her with obvious curiosity on her face but said nothing. Riley slid the papers back into her bag, slapped her thighs, and pushed to her feet.

As she folded her chair and leaned it against the wall of the office, she met Hannah's gaze and said simply, "Let's make some popcorn."

The way Hannah's face lit up surprised Riley, even though she'd been ready for it. Hannah popped up from her chair behind the desk and headed out into the kitchen area. "I want to try to make some nacho popcorn today. I think that'd be a fun flavor, yeah?"

Riley watched as she set some popcorn to popping, then got out the old dented pot. Riley recognized the ingredients for caramel from the last time.

"Do you make caramel every day?" she asked.

"Every morning," Hannah said, moving around the kitchen. Honestly, it was like the person in the office was a twin, one with little animation or verbal skills, and this one was the one who moved and talked and got things done. So weird. "It's my best seller, and I like to keep it fresh, you know? Caramel corn is supposed to have a bite to it, but when it gets old, it becomes chewy. Blech." She moved to the big, stainless steel counter and gazed at the shelf above it that held dozens of bottles of seasonings and spices. "I'm thinking chili powder, garlic salt, possibly cumin." She turned to face Riley and tapped a finger against her lips as she squinted in thought. "Maybe parmesan? I'm not sure. Cheddar would be better, though." She snapped her fingers and pointed at Riley. "Hot pepper sauce. Definitely." Turning back to the shelf, she kept talking, and Riley wasn't sure if it was to her or just in general. "We'll have to experiment a bit. I wonder if something like dried parsley would punch up the flavor…"

Riley liked to watch Hannah work.

It was something she realized in that moment. All other aspects aside, Hannah was creative and loved her job. Coming up with unique flavors for her popcorn was obviously the thing that got her juices flowing, and it was truly something to behold. Riley stepped back so she was out of the way, and she simply watched as Hannah flitted around the kitchen, stirring this and sprinkling that.

"If I use nutritional yeast, it'd be vegan," Hannah said, and again, Riley wasn't sure if she was talking to her or just talking. "Maybe I do a batch of each. Having vegan options to offer can't be a bad thing, right?" She didn't wait for an answer, just stirred the caramel until it was time to stick the candy thermometer in it. "Riley?"

"Hmm?"

"Can you put the popcorn into that pot and set it on the mixer?" Hannah pointed to everything she mentioned with her eyes, but Riley had just done it with Hannah the other day, and she remembered. A moment or two later, Hannah poured the caramel slowly over the popcorn as it tumbled and turned on the mixer.

Riley had things to do. Other clients to speak to on the phone. Emails to answer. A Zoom meeting that afternoon that she had yet to prepare for. But nothing was as riveting or entertaining as watching Hannah Kramer in her element. Sure, making popcorn might sound frivolous and unimportant to some people, but to Hannah, it was clearly life. It was the thing that lit her up from the inside, that made her smile, that got her moving and kept her going.

I can't let her lose this place.

The thought shot through Riley's brain with such force that it felt tangible, like it had shoved her, and she needed to move her foot to keep her balance. Suddenly, she felt torn. She would normally do what she needed to do, then pack up and head home, then on to the next location. She'd already been here longer than she'd expected. That antsy need to be on the move would set in soon. Yet she continued to watch the performance in front of her, folded her arms over her chest and leaned back against the wall as Hannah worked, almost as if she'd forgotten Riley was even there.

Out front in the shop, Hannah hit the lights and turned the sign— *that old, ugly-ass sign*—and then Poptacular was open. It was the dance Hannah did every morning, without fail, and she loved it. That much was evident.

Only a few moments later, Shana pushed through the front door, two cups in her hand. To Riley's surprise, she handed her one.

"Seems like you're gonna be here for a while, so I've decided two guinea pigs is better than one," she said with a grin. Shana handed the other cup to Hannah. "My new matcha blend."

They each sipped, and it took every fiber of Riley's being not to gag and throw the drink across the room.

"It's sweeter than last time," Hannah said with a nod, then took another sip. She glanced at Riley and sputtered a cough-laugh combination. "Somebody doesn't like it," she said.

"I mean…" Riley swallowed, looking for words as she tried to hide her grimace.

Shana waved her off. "Matcha is not everybody's cup of tea." Then, "Ha. See what I did there?"

"I think it's better," Hannah said. More nodding as she took a third sip. "Much."

"Awesome. I'll put it on the menu." Shana grabbed herself a small bag of caramel corn from behind the counter, and as she returned to them, Riley got the impression she was being sized up, evaluated. And then it was apparently Shana's turn to nod, which she did, but said nothing. She held up the bag toward Hannah in clear thanks and said, "Don't forget the Fest this weekend."

"I'll be there," Hannah said. Once Shana was gone, she turned to head to the back. "Not a fan of matcha, huh?"

"It tasted like grass in liquid form, like lawn mower juice." Riley followed her to the back and carried her cup directly to the sink to dump it. "What's the Fest?"

"It's a little street festival in the park. It's every Saturday from the beginning of September to the end of October to celebrate fall." Hannah turned so those rich brown eyes locked on Riley's. "Tourist season."

Riley's wheels started turning before she even realized it. "Like, local booths and such?"

Hannah nodded as she took the caramel corn off the mixer and dumped it onto the cooling tray. "Yeah, like local artisans, jewelry, food, music. It's fun. They only started it a few years ago, which is why you've probably not heard of it." She snapped on some gloves and began sifting the caramel corn, Riley knew this was to keep it from clumping.

"And do you have a booth there?"

Hannah scoffed. "Nah. It's too much work and I can't really haul my equipment to the park. Plus, I'd have to close the shop, which would lose me business."

Riley rolled her lips in and bit down on them until her frustration passed. She spoke calmly, which took a lot of effort. "Hannah, don't you think you'd sell a lot more there than here on Fest day? All those people milling around the park, strolling, hungry for a snack? Also"— she waved a hand up and down in front of Hannah—"local artisan. Duh."

"I mean…" Hannah lifted a shoulder.

Riley's cell pinged, reminding her of a conference call she had in half an hour. Instead of being annoyed by the interruption, she found herself relieved. She was frustrated with Hannah, with her lack of business savvy, with her resistance to any kind of change. But Riley had some ideas. She just needed to put them into play.

"I've gotta run," she said, glancing down at her phone. "But I'll text after my meeting later, okay?"

Hannah nodded but said nothing, and again, Riley found herself wishing for painting Hannah, the open, fun girl from the night before.

How could she get her back? Because, God, she wanted her back. And that scared the shit out of her.

Out front, she gathered her things together. Hannah came out with several bags of the fresh caramel corn and set them on shelves as the little bell over the door tinkled.

"Hi, honey." It was Hannah and Kyle's mother, and aside from her hair having gone a bit gray, she looked exactly like Riley remembered her—tall and lean, the same brown eyes as both of her children, a perpetual smile on her face. She was one of the nicest people Riley had ever met.

"Hi, Mrs. Kramer," Riley said with a smile.

Mrs. Kramer met her gaze, held it for a moment as she narrowed her eyes, clearly trying to place her. Riley could tell exactly when she did, those brown eyes opening wide and her eyebrows climbing up toward her hairline. "Riley Shaw? Oh my God, how are you, sweetie?"

And the next thing she knew, she was wrapped in one of Mrs. Kramer's signature hugs. Riley let herself sink into it, let her face squish into Mrs. Kramer's shoulder, inhaled her perfume, slightly floral, but in a warm and comforting way. In that moment, she missed her own mother so badly, her eyes welled up, and she had to consciously swallow them back.

"Let me look at you." Mrs. Kramer held her at arm's length, gripping both of Riley's upper arms. "My God, you're gorgeous. How long has it been? What are you doing here? How long are you staying? Do you want to come over for dinner? No, that's not an invitation, it's a request. You will come to dinner. Billy will be thrilled to see you. God, look at you."

"Mom. Stop fawning all over the poor woman," Hannah said, but her tone was light. Riley hadn't even noticed that she'd approached them and was standing close.

"I can't," Mrs. Kramer said with a laugh, sifting some of Riley's hair through her fingers. "Last time I saw you, you were off to college." Then she dropped her hand, and her eyes went soft. "I was so sorry to hear about your mother, sweetie. So sorry."

Riley nodded, felt the tears threaten yet again. She cleared her throat. "Thank you. It's been…hard."

"Of course it has." There was a beat of silence, and then Mrs. Kramer blew out a breath and said, "Okay. Change of subject." Then she laughed her sweet and gentle laugh, and all was right again. She'd always been able to do that—take you from deep, dark emotion back up to the light again.

"I'll leave you to it," Riley said, hiking her bag over her shoulder. "It was so good to see you, Mrs. Kramer."

"I was serious about dinner," Mrs. Kramer said, pointing at her.

With a nod and a smile, she glanced at Hannah and said, "I'll text you this afternoon and we'll set up another meeting. Okay?"

"I'll be here." Hannah's tone was a bit more enthusiastic than expected, and Riley decided not to question it, to simply take it while she could.

She pushed out the door.

❖

"Riley Shaw," Hannah's mother said. "I don't know that I ever expected to see her again."

"Yeah, well." Hannah went back behind the counter and counted the inventory there. She needed to make more dill pickle, more cotton candy, and the cheddar was running low. She opened the bin and tasted it. Low and stale. She sighed and pulled the bin out.

"She was always such a nice girl," her mother went on. "Polite. Gentle. Your brother was crazy about her. I always thought they'd make such a sweet couple."

"She's gay, Mom." Hannah didn't mean to blurt it out like that, but she didn't want to listen to the dreamy tones of *How Sad Kyle and Riley Aren't Married Now.* She didn't have to look at her mother to know she was blinking at her in surprise, and Hannah gave herself a point for having rendered her speechless. She turned back to face her. "What?"

Her mother shook her head. "I'm just surprised is all."

The bell tinkled, and Mr. Daniels came in, thank fucking God, to save them from any more of this ridiculous conversation.

"Morning, Mr. D.," Hannah said. "How's life?"

"Life can always be worse, Hannah, so this man will not be complaining." He leaned forward and lowered his voice. "At least not today." He straightened back up as they laughed and looked around. "You painted."

"We did." Hannah nodded and followed his gaze as it moved around the front.

"It looks terrific," he pronounced after a moment. "Not too bright, but definitely warm and inviting. Looks a bit like melted butter."

"Exactly what I was going for."

He pointed a bony finger at the wall to his left. "Your grandmother's picture. You're putting it back up, right?" His voice held a tinge of… was it worry?

"Absolutely. We only just painted last night and wanted to make sure it was thoroughly dry before we hang things back up."

The relief on his face was clear as he nodded and turned his attention to first Hannah's mother with a "How are you, Diana, nice to see you" and then to the popcorn display case. "I think I need some more of that dill pickle," he told Hannah. "What's new?"

"I'm working on a nacho flavor," Hannah said. "Just started, so I'm still experimenting."

Mr. Daniels nodded. "I'd say chili powder, cheddar, maybe some cumin." He squinted as he stroked his chin. "Some lime zest?"

Hannah grinned and pointed at him. "Lime zest is a fabulous idea." She handed him a bag of the dill pickle and he paid. "I should have some ready later today or tomorrow."

"Looking forward to it." He dropped a twenty into the tip jar as Hannah shook her head with a smile.

"Thank you, Mr. Daniels."

Hannah and her mother watched him leave. Once the door was closed and he walked out of sight, Hannah's mother said quietly, "He adored your grandmother. Such a crush."

"He still does," Hannah said, propping her elbows on the counter and her chin in her hand. "He looks at her picture every time he comes in. Did they ever date?"

Her mother shook her head. "I don't think so. Mom was just too busy with the shop. I was constantly telling her to hire help so she could take time off, have a life outside of popcorn, but she never did. I don't know if she didn't know how or didn't want to." She shrugged, her eyes still on the front door, and then two more customers came in, sending the bell to tinkling and putting an end to the conversation. "Honey, just let me have some of the cotton candy for when the twins come by later."

She gave her mom a bag, waved off her money, and gave her a kiss on the cheek.

Her hand on the door, her mother turned back and said, "Don't forget, dinner on Sunday. Oh! Bring Riley." And she was gone.

Bring Riley.

Hannah snorted. *Yeah, that's just what I need. Riley Shaw at my family's dinner table, telling them everything I'm doing wrong with my business. No, thank you.*

She shook the thought away and turned her focus to her customers.

Business ended up being fairly steady, which was a nice surprise. Kaitlyn came in at two in the afternoon, giving Hannah a break to eat something. She ordered a tuna wrap at the diner down the street, picked it up, and wandered another block to the park, where she found her favorite empty bench under a maple tree and sat down to eat.

The park was always bustling in the summer, and this bench was her favorite spot to people watch. She took a bite of her wrap and looked around. Today, the park was filled with people preparing for the Fest, the first one of the season. Tables and booths were being set up, lots of splotches of white indicating where they'd be.

Hannah loved the Fest. It had only begun about five years ago when the town council decided Sunset Valley needed a few ways to capitalize on its tourist seasons: fall and winter. Leaf peepers came in the fall, and winter was ski season. The population of the town sometimes doubled during tourist season, and for many businesses, these next six months were what got them through the rest of the year financially.

People hurried by, carrying boxes and linens and chairs. Several waved to Hannah or stopped to chat for a moment before hurrying on. She thought back to Riley asking if she'd ever had a booth at the Fest and why her answer was no. She just never had. It seemed like too much. Dragging her equipment to the park and trying to set it up. Closing the shop because there'd be nobody to run it, so she'd lose that business…

She chewed her wrap and blew out a breath through her nose. She supposed she could hire an extra person or two just for the weekends of the Fest, but what a pain in the ass. No, it just felt like too much. Her shop was close enough to the park that she got some of the traffic going to and from. Riley should be able to see that.

Riley.

Seemed like Riley was everywhere now. All of a sudden. Hannah hadn't thought about her in a very long time—though she did tend to show up in the occasional dream—and suddenly, there she was. In the shop, on her phone, smiling, suggesting, directing. It was a little crazy, if she was being honest.

"Hey, Hannah," called John Tucker, the owner of the diner a couple doors down from Poptacular. He carried a couple of boxes in a stack as he smiled at her.

She waved back. The diner had a booth, too, and John had a lot more crap to haul to the park than Poptacular would. She shook her head, not wanting to admit that maybe Riley was right, and maybe she should set up a booth and give it a try.

Too late now.

Shaking her head, she stood up and tossed her garbage into a nearby can, then headed back to the shop.

Saturday morning dawned bright and sunny, but the temperatures were already beginning to act more like fall and less like summer. A high only in the low sixties, perfect as far as Riley was concerned. She'd gotten caught up yesterday on her conference call, then did some research and made another call, and by the time she'd remembered about the package waiting for her at the front desk, it was too late for her to take it to its destination. She'd grabbed it and brought it back up to her room, where she'd ordered room service and watched a movie just to decompress.

Today, though, she had a plan.

She'd used the resort's fitness center and did a quick strength training workout. It felt good to work her muscles after more than a week of not doing so. Pumping iron always pumped her up mentally as well. She took her time with her morning, then finally showered and dressed in a pair of softly worn jeans, a short-sleeved shirt, and a full-zip hoodie left unzipped. She grabbed her bag and the FedEx package and headed into town. It was almost noon.

Kaitlyn was working today. Riley remembered that Hannah had extra help on the weekends, so there'd likely be a third person as well. Her prediction proved right when she walked into Poptacular and found somebody she'd never met at the counter, a gangly teenage boy with braces and shaggy brown hair.

"Hi, can I help you?" he asked with a grimace as his voice cracked.

"Is Hannah in?" she asked, then saw her in the back, along with Kaitlyn.

"Hannah?" the boy called over his shoulder. "Somebody's here for you."

Hannah met her eyes and Riley called out, "Can I come back?"

Hannah waved her back.

"Hi," she said when she reached her and gave Kaitlyn, who was stirring something in a small pot on the stove, a wave. It smelled amazing in the shop, as usual, and today's aromatic air held hints of hot peppers and cumin. "Still working on the nacho flavor, huh?"

Hannah nodded, sprinkling some seasonings over the popcorn tumbling around in the mixer.

Riley held out the package she'd had FedEx'd. "Brought you a present."

Hannah blinked at her. She looked at the package in Riley's hand, then back up at her, then back down to the package. "You did?"

"Mm-hmm. Here. Open it."

Hannah wiped her hands on her apron and took the package. She sliced it open and gasped when she saw the brand-new laptop. "What? What is this?"

Riley grinned, loving the surprise on Hannah's soft face. "It's a new computer for you. I had some software installed on it, too. New accounting software that'll make it super easy for you to keep track of things. And I reached out to a couple of clients in food service about how they best like to keep track of their recipes, ingredients, and such, and I put their suggestions into a document on there, too."

Hannah pulled the computer out of the box and ran her hand over the smooth silver surface of it. "I…I don't know what to say."

"We can sit down in the next day or two and go over some of it, if you want."

Hannah nodded. "Yeah, okay. I'd like that." She looked up at

Riley, and the emotion in those rich brown eyes started a tiny flutter low in Riley's body.

"As for today," Riley said, taking the laptop from Hannah's hands. "We have plans." She crossed to the tiny office and set the laptop on Hannah's desk.

"We do?"

"We do." She waved at the popcorn that was in progress. "Finish up what you're doing. Tell your employees they're on their own for a bit. I'll meet you out front." She didn't wait for a response; she didn't want to give Hannah a chance to protest or come up with a reason not to follow her. When Hannah opened her mouth, Riley held up a hand, and whatever Hannah was going to say died in her throat. "I'll meet you out front," she said again, this time with a grin. She pushed through the front door and lingered on the sidewalk and waited.

A few clouds had appeared in the formerly clear blue sky, and there was a slight breeze, but it was all so absolutely lovely. A gorgeous early fall day. While it was true that she missed Boston, the quiet here, the slower pace, and the clean, fresh air really were amazing for her head and her stress levels. She was used to firing on all cylinders all the time, and somehow, some way, Sunset Valley made her just…stop. Stand still. Breathe.

She wasn't used to that, and it frightened her in a way she couldn't explain.

Hannah came out then, looking just this side of frazzled. Also, kind of annoyed. "Okay, I have half an hour. What are we doing?"

Riley looked at her. Just looked at her, until Hannah shifted her weight, clearly wanting to squirm. She held up a finger. "Stay here." She went back into the shop.

The boy at the counter looked surprised to see her again. Kaitlyn was putting bags of rainbow-colored popcorn on the shelves.

Riley lowered her voice. "You guys got this, right?"

Kaitlyn turned to face her, while the boy looked slightly con-fused.

"Kaitlyn? You two can handle things here for a couple hours? I know Hannah doesn't like to leave you, but you got this, right?"

To her credit, Kaitlyn snorted. "I've been working here since I was fifteen. Yes. We got this." She waved Riley away with a dismissive hand, which made her laugh. "Loosen her up, would you?" And with that, Kaitlyn headed back into the kitchen.

"I'll do my best," Riley said, and headed back outside. "Okay. Ready?"

"What are we doing?" Hannah asked when Riley started to walk. It was almost a whine. Not quite, but almost, and it made Riley laugh.

"Oh my God, you're ridiculous." She spun around so she was behind Hannah and pushing her forward. "We're going to the Fest."

"What?" Hannah stopped walking and faced Riley. "Why?"

Riley looked back at her, let her own gaze roam over Hannah's gorgeous face, her smooth skin, the little divot between her eyebrows that said she was slightly irritated. When she spoke, Riley's voice was soft. "Because I want you to show it to me."

Hannah blinked at her. Simply blinked as if she didn't know what to do with that. "Oh. I mean, yeah, okay. I can do that."

"Yeah? I thought it would be fun. They didn't have it when I lived here. You can show me around, introduce me to your friends and other business owners, we can eat some good food. I think I saw a stage, too. Is there music?"

Hannah nodded. "There is. Local bands, but also bands from other towns." She glanced over her shoulder back at the shop. "But…"

Riley grabbed her hand. "They've got it."

"What?" Hannah looked back at her, and again, their eyes locked.

"Your people," Riley said softly. "Kaitlyn and Squeaky Boy. They've got it. No worries."

Hannah's grin was slow to break out across her face, but it was fun to watch as it appeared. "Michael."

"Hmm?"

"Squeaky Boy. His name is Michael."

"Oh," Riley said with a laugh. "Got it. My bad. Come on." She gave Hannah's hand a tug, and it was easier than she expected to get Hannah to follow her. She'd expected more protesting, maybe even some digging in of her heels. But that didn't happen. She threw one last glance in the direction of her shop, looked back at Riley, and gave one nod.

"Okay. Let's go."

They headed for the park.

CHAPTER EIGHT

Hannah had lived in Sunset Valley her entire life, had rarely left, even for a vacation, so that meant she knew just about everybody. And just about everybody knew her. Small town, USA, and all that.

John Tucker was running the booth for the diner, and when Hannah introduced him, Riley said, "Your tuna melt is probably the best one I've ever had. And I've had a lot of them." Seeing John's chest puff up with pride was sweet, and Hannah smiled at Riley, who seemed to have that effect on people. She knew just what to say to make them light up.

They moved on to the booth for Hopsville, the new microbrewery that had opened about six months ago. The owners were brothers, Stephen and Jacob Grant, and they'd graduated two years behind Hannah in high school. She and Riley sipped samples of their new brews in tiny plastic cups.

"Ooh," Riley said, holding up the cup with the darkest beer. "Stout?"

Just like John at the diner booth had, Jacob Grant stood up a little straighter and grinned. "Yes, our oatmeal stout."

Riley nodded and sipped again. "I can tell. It feels a bit…" She squinted as if searching for the right word. "Creamier than the wheat beer."

"It's my favorite of ours," Jacob said. He was cute in that laid-back, casual, *you'll never catch me in a suit* kind of way. Hannah had always thought so.

"I can see why," Riley agreed and finished off her sample. Then she reached out a hand and shook Jacob's. "Thanks, man."

"Come on back any time," Jacob called after them, and Hannah added him to the list in her head of folks Riley charmed in a matter of moments.

"This is awesome," Riley said quietly, leaning close to Hannah as they walked. Close enough that Hannah could smell her, breathe in that coconutty sunshine scent of her. "I mean, I love this kind of thing, and I love Quincy Market back home in Boston, but it's so big. Enormous. This is so much more…manageable. You can actually stop and talk to people. You know?" She met Hannah's gaze, her smile wide like an excited little kid's.

Hannah nodded as they walked on. Clouds had rolled in, and the breeze made it slightly cooler. Hannah wore her Poptacular T-shirt but kind of wished she had her sweatshirt with her. As if reading her mind, Riley took off her zip-up hoodie.

"Here. You've got goose bumps." She put the sweatshirt over Hannah's shoulders, and it was still warm from Riley's body when Hannah slipped her arms into the sleeves. And it smelled like her, that summer smell enveloping her in its gentle warmth. Before she could utter a thank you, Riley squealed. Literally squealed. "I love cotton candy!" And she was off toward Marika's cotton candy truck parked under a tree.

Hannah stayed back, watching Riley in her joy. It made her smile; she couldn't deny it. When she came bouncing back with fluffy pink cotton candy on a stick, Hannah grinned at her.

"Happy now?" she asked.

"Ecstatic," Riley said, her grin wide. "She's nice," she commented, looking back at the truck.

Marika waved and Hannah waved back. "That's Marika. She actually helped me get my cotton candy popcorn just right."

"Oh, that's very cool. So, I'm guessing that's her favorite popcorn flavor of yours?"

Hannah shook her head as they walked. "Nope. She gets enough sweet stuff in her daily life. She prefers savory for her popcorn. Cheddar bacon is her favorite."

Riley was looking at her now.

"And Jacob likes caramel, though his brother Stephen prefers the mac and cheese. John's a traditional butter and salt guy." She realized a couple steps along that Riley had stopped walking and was simply standing there, blinking at her. She went back. "What?"

"You seriously know what each of your customers likes?"

A shrug. "I mean, the regulars, yeah."

"Hannah, you are a much better businesswoman than you give yourself credit for. Do you realize that?"

Hannah gave an almost-bitter chuckle. "Yeah, I don't know about that. If I was, I wouldn't need you to fix things, would I?"

"Listen, everybody struggles here and there. And I'm not fixing anything. I'm just helping out. That's all." She smiled that hundred-watt smile of hers and Hannah felt something warm inside her, like there was a glow within her caused by that smile.

They wandered some more, saying hi to various folks. Not everybody was from Sunset Valley, but Hannah knew the ones who were. Every time they walked away from the booth of a local, Riley would ask about their favorite popcorn flavor. Hannah never missed a beat.

"This is the coolest party trick ever," Riley said with a delighted laugh.

"I'm glad you think so," Hannah said.

"And I'm very proud of you." They sat on a bench just out of the path of Fest attendees with their bowls of nachos from the Mexican food truck that came every week from three towns over.

"You are?" Hannah put a cheese-slathered chip into her mouth. "Why?"

"Because you haven't checked your watch once and you haven't complained at all about being away from the shop." Riley grinned and took a bite of her own chips.

Hannah blinked at her in surprise because she was right. She hadn't worried about the shop. She was simply enjoying her time with Riley, showing her around, eating all the food. As if on cue, a band that had been setting up on one of the small stages nearby started to play. Again, Riley's face lit up in delight, and she turned her body slightly so she could see better. In doing so, her hip pushed up against Hannah's and stayed there.

Hannah recognized the trio onstage, and they launched into some peppy jazz that instantly had Riley bopping her head and Hannah tapping a foot. She lost track of how long they sat there, literally joined at the hip, enjoying their nachos, listening to live music and watching as people passed them this way or that.

Hannah couldn't remember the last time she'd felt so…contented. She leaned forward so her mouth was close to Riley's ear. "Hey."

Riley tipped her head closer, and Hannah could smell the citrusy scent of her shampoo. "Hmm?"

"Wanna come to my parents' for dinner tomorrow?"

Riley turned her head and met her gaze with those blue eyes, the color of a summer sky. "I'd love that."

"Good." Hannah nodded once, then turned her attention back to the music.

Later that night, as she lay in bed, she replayed the day in her head. Over and over and over. For many reasons.

First, she tried to analyze what it was that made her feel so relaxed, so not in a hurry to get back to her shop, so not worried that she'd left Kaitlyn and Michael on their own.

Second, she tried to analyze why it was Riley that had helped her stay that calm, be that *not* worried about being away from her shop, be that happy to simply sit and enjoy the weather, the fresh air, the people, the music. How had Riley done that?

She recalled those blue eyes, that just a tiny bit husky voice, her hands as she'd draped her hoodie over Hannah's shoulders, the closeness of her face when she had…

"Jesus, Han," she whispered into the dark of her bedroom. "Get a grip."

She'd invited her to dinner! At her parents' house! Good God, Kyle was going to have a field day with that. Because of course, the fact that they were both gay meant they were destined to date. That's what he seemed to think—that two people being gay meant that of course they'd date. Why wouldn't they? She could almost hear him now.

When's the wedding?

Who's renting the U-Haul?

Are you moving to Boston or is she moving here?

This is, like, your teenage wet dream. Happy now?

Okay, maybe that last one was her and not her brother, but still. Still!

Her brain kept her up until the wee hours. She knew what would help her get to sleep: the same thing she'd done the last time her thoughts had gotten stuck in an endless loop of Riley Shaw. She could…take care of herself.

"No," she said out loud. "I can fall asleep on my own."

She lasted another twenty minutes before giving up and reaching into the drawer of her nightstand for her vibrator.

Riley's face filled her head.

Riley brought her release in under three minutes.

How would she face her tomorrow? At her parents' house? She was such an idiot.

"Goddamn it."

When the doorbell rang at Hannah's parents' house the next day, she didn't move. She busied herself stirring the pasta salad she'd helped her mother make, pretending the door wasn't her job. Which it wasn't, but Riley was her guest.

Still, she waited for a beat, and as she expected, Kyle said, "I got it," and disappeared from the kitchen. She could hear greetings and laughter and then Riley walked into the kitchen.

Hannah felt her breath catch, her stupid lungs not wanting to work, apparently, as she met Riley's smiling face. She looked—God, how did a person look so incredibly attractive in normal, regular clothes? She didn't understand it. Riley was wearing jeans and a simple black T-shirt with capped sleeves. Simple. Almost boring.

But not on her.

Jesus.

Her hair was down, and the combination of the darkness framing her face and the black of her shirt made the perfect environment for her blue eyes to stand out like sapphires among coal, bright and sparkling and undeniably beautiful. She grinned at Hannah, the white of her teeth only adding to the color contrast.

Hannah's mother walked in then, and suddenly, she was gushing about having Riley over and hugging her, and over her shoulder, those blue eyes still fixed on Hannah.

Riley smiled at her and gave her a wink.

Something in the center of Hannah melted, and she smiled back.

"This is for you," Riley said, once Hannah's mother had let her go. She handed over a bottle of wine. "It's a very buttery Chardonnay. I thought it would go well with stuff on the grill."

"Well, aren't you sweet," Hannah's mother said and held the bottle up. "Should we open it now?"

"I'd have a glass," Hannah said, and her mother handed her the bottle.

"Would you do the honors?" she asked. Then she pointed at Kyle. "Help me bring dishes out? We're going to eat outside, Riley. Is that okay with you?"

"Oh, of course, sounds great. It's gorgeous out."

And then it was Hannah and Riley alone in the kitchen with a bottle of wine.

"Hi," Riley said.

"Hi," Hannah said back, then rooted through a drawer to find the corkscrew. She went to work on the bottle, and when she glanced up, Riley was watching Hannah's hands. Something about the way she stared sent that now-familiar flutter flitting about in Hannah's body. "Can you grab glasses? They're up there." She indicated the cabinet with her eyes, and Riley snapped out of her trance and did as she asked.

When the wine was poured, Riley held up her glass. "Thanks for inviting me."

Hannah touched her glass to Riley's. "Thanks for coming."

The gentle ping faded away, and they sipped.

"Oh, that's delicious," Hannah said, sipping again.

"It's my favorite," Riley said. "I was glad to have found it."

"Did you go to Barker's? The liquor store on the corner?"

Riley nodded. "Nice older guy was working."

"That's Chris." She grinned and added, "He prefers the turtle popcorn."

Riley laughed. "I'd like to try that flavor."

"That can be arranged."

They stood there for a moment, holding each other's gaze over the rims of their glasses.

"It's crazy to be back here," Riley said after a moment. She looked around the kitchen. "It's changed a lot, but it's also stayed the same."

And then the sliding glass door opened, and Kyle leaned in. "Hey, Riley, come meet my wife and kids."

Riley's eyes were still locked with Hannah's as she said, "Coming."

Once the sliding glass door slid closed behind Riley, and Hannah was left in the kitchen alone, she felt like she could breathe again. What the hell was happening? She took another sip of the wine—which really was excellent—and watched out the window over the sink as Riley held out a hand to shake Ashley's, but Ashley stood up and threw her arms around Riley in a big hug that, judging by Riley's suddenly wide eyes, caught her off guard. Kyle was laughing and then pointing at Brody and Brianna, both playing on the swing set Hannah and Kyle played on as kids.

She was so caught up in spying on everybody out the window that she didn't notice her mother walking toward the door, and when it slid open, Hannah jumped.

"Dinner's just about ready," her mother said, body half in and half out. She held her gaze for a beat, then smiled and asked, "You coming?"

Hannah nodded—too much nodding, Jesus—and said, "Yeah. Yeah, on my way."

Her mother watched her for another moment, then headed back out, the door sliding shut.

"Jesus Christ, Hannah, get a grip," she muttered as she refilled her wine glass, then carried the bottle out into the back yard.

The backyard barbecue setup was nothing new to Hannah. In fact, it was very, very regular. But the addition of Riley seemed to give it an elevated boost, like adding a pop of spice to a dish or fireworks to a quiet evening. Riley hadn't been to the Kramer household in what? Eighteen years? Yet it was like she'd never left, like she'd been here last weekend. She slid seamlessly right back into the Kramer family, laughing with Hannah's dad, who stood by the grill wearing his Grill Sergeant apron. She joked with Kyle like they were still teenagers. Even Ashley looked somewhat enamored of Riley. How could she not? She'd heard stories of the infamous Riley Shaw since the day Kyle had brought her home and told her all about growing up in this back yard.

"Dinner is served," Hannah's dad said, setting a plate of freshly grilled burgers in the center of the table, half of them covered with cheese.

"Dad makes the best burgers," Ashley commented, snapping up Brody as he ran by. Kyle grabbed Brianna, and soon both toddlers had been wrestled into booster seats.

"I remember," Riley said with a grin. "Where should I sit?"

"Right here," Hannah said, patting the seat next to her. Riley smiled and sat.

"Hey, fill me up?" Riley asked softly, leaning close to Hannah. Her scent enveloped Hannah, who had to work hard not to inhale deeply and obviously.

Hannah reached for the wine and topped off Riley's glass. "Doing okay?"

"Doing great." Those blue eyes locked on hers for a moment until Hannah's mother spoke, breaking what felt a lot like a spell of some kind.

"So, Riley, Kyle tells me your job takes you all over the country." And they were off.

Hannah did more listening than participating. She knew a lot of what was being told to her parents—though the actual extent of just how much traveling Riley did was new information. It seemed like she was all over the place, all the time. Home a lot less than away. Ashley seemed fascinated and asked a ton of questions. And there were plenty of interruptions from the kids, who needed juice or more pasta salad or to tell Riley a story because she was, after all, the new girl. Riley never missed a beat, answering questions, smiling at the babies, and generally being the life of the party.

When dinner had been eaten and the table cleared, they all sat down in various lawn chairs or lounges with wine and brownies Hannah's mother had made. A big bowl of popcorn was passed around. Riley looked at it, then up at Hannah.

"Turtle," Hannah said. "Told you it could be arranged."

Riley's grin grew, and she dug out a handful of the chocolatey-caramel goodness.

Hannah's dad sat down in his lounge chair with a satisfied groan and swirled his peanut butter whiskey in his rocks glass. "How long will you be in town, Riley?"

Riley glanced at Hannah as she finished chewing the mouthful of popcorn, then lifted one shoulder. "I'm not sure yet. I haven't really made a decision about that."

Hannah didn't want to analyze all the feelings those words caused as they flip-flopped around inside her.

"Besides," Riley said as she turned to meet Hannah's gaze,

"Poptacular has a booth at the Fest next weekend, and I want to be around to help out."

"What?" Hannah said at the same time her mother did.

"Are you kidding?" Hannah's dad said. "We've been telling her for three years now that she needs to do that. How'd you manage to convince her?"

Riley nibbled her bottom lip as she spoke, her eyes never leaving Hannah's. "I kinda didn't. I just booked it, thought it would be easier to ask forgiveness than permission?" She phrased it as a question and wrinkled her nose in a clear sign of hopefulness.

Hannah felt all eyes on her. What was she supposed to do, say no? In front of everybody and look like the bad guy? Riley had ambushed her, and she had to admit, it was a brilliant way to get her to agree. She wasn't happy about it, but had no choice. Still staring back at Riley, she said, "I am going to work your ass into the ground."

The relief on Riley's face was clear, and she held up her wine. "I would expect nothing less."

As the family cheered and celebrated, Hannah sipped quietly. Yes, Riley had played dirty. And yes, Hannah was annoyed by it and would need to say something about that once they were in private.

Also, yes, Riley would be here for at least another week.

Hannah smiled and sipped her wine.

Riley sat in her car and sipped her coffee. Shana made a terrific dark roast, there was no denying it. She felt its strength, its caffeine ooze into her bloodstream, waking her up to the day.

It was time to face the music.

It wasn't new. She'd had plenty of small business owners—and a few big business owners—question her methods. They didn't like being blindsided. They didn't like being told what to do by some woman who didn't know the first thing about their business.

And that's where they were usually wrong. It was Riley's job to know their business, and most owners had zero idea how much research and studying she did before each visit. By the time she met face-to-face with a client, she knew almost everything there was to know about their business. How they ran it, how they treated their employees, whether they paid their bills on time, what their customers thought of them, all of it. Now, in the interest of not embarrassing or shaming a client, she'd often pretend not to know as much as she did. But it was all there, sitting in her head, crouched and waiting to pounce if she needed to use any of it.

Poptacular was no different, and she had known, beyond a shadow of a doubt, that the only way to get Hannah into the Fest was to force her there.

She'll thank me later.

Today, though? Today Hannah was going to be mad. She hadn't been able to scold her last night. She wouldn't do that in front of her family. Riley had known that as well, which was exactly why she'd delivered the news then. She knew Hannah wouldn't kill her while her parents watched.

This morning, though, there was nobody to save her. Hannah could go up one side of her and down the other, and she'd be well within her rights to do exactly that. So Riley was prepared. And she'd come bearing gifts.

She inhaled deeply and slowly, filled up her lungs, then let it out little by little until she felt centered. Grounded. Then she opened her car door, tucked the package under her arm, grabbed the additional cup of coffee she'd purchased from the Coffee Cup, and headed for the front door of Poptacular, where she could already smell freshly popped popcorn.

She rapped on the door as the ratty old Closed sign stared her in the face. Through the glass, she could see Hannah working in the back. Hannah, who looked right at her and went back to what she was doing.

"It's okay," Riley whispered. "Play your game. I can wait." She wouldn't give Hannah the satisfaction of knocking again. She knew she was there. She sipped her coffee and watched Main Street come alive as she waited. She kept her back to the door.

Nearly ten minutes later, the door unlocked behind her and Riley turned with a smile. "Morning," she said cheerfully as she stepped in past Hannah, who locked the door again behind her. She handed one cup to Hannah, who took it and let a second of gratitude cross her face before schooling her expression back to *I'm so pissed at you*. Riley almost laughed at how obvious it all was. "Brought you a present." She handed over the flat package wrapped in brown paper but decorated with a big, red bow.

Hannah narrowed her eyes, clearly suspicious, clearly ready to lay into Riley but too curious about the package. She sighed, set down her coffee on the front counter, and took the package from Riley's hand.

"Are you trying to bribe me into forgiving you for going behind my back?" She didn't look at Riley as she asked the question. "'Cause that was kinda shitty."

"Not a bribe. Just a gift."

"Mm-hmm." Hannah tore the paper off the rectangular-shaped package, and Riley heard her catch her breath. "Oh," was the only thing she said, but she stretched it out so it was more like *ooooohhhhh*.

It was the photo of Hannah's grandmother that they'd taken down when they'd painted the wall. The photo itself was gorgeous, bright colors and Grams with a huge smile. The frame had been lackluster and boring.

"I snagged it after we painted. I thought it could use some sprucing up. Grams deserved a nice setting." The frame shop had matted it, using a muted orange Riley had chosen to bring out the colors in Grams's clothes and also to complement the new yellow of the wall.

Hannah ran her hand over the glass, over her grandmother's picture, and when she looked up at Riley, her eyes shimmered with unshed tears. "It's beautiful, Riley. Thank you."

Something about the sight of Hannah about to cry squeezed emotional things inside Riley, and she had to clear her throat before she could speak. "You're very welcome," she finally managed to say.

"This doesn't mean I'm not still mad at you."

"Of course not."

They stood there smiling at each other for what felt like a long time.

"Could I at least have some caramel corn to munch while you yell at me?"

Hannah sighed a comical sigh and said, "I suppose so," like the most put-upon woman on Earth. Riley followed her into the back.

Instead of talking, they took the next forty-five minutes and made caramel corn, the day's supply. They worked well together. Riley had snagged an apron off a hook on the wall and tied it around her waist, and the two of them worked in tandem. Smoothly. Hannah made the caramel. Riley filled the mixer with popcorn and watched it tumble and coat itself in caramel. Hannah dumped it onto the cooling rack and Riley sifted through it, eliminating clumps.

"We still work well together," Riley said, tying a fastener around the last bag of caramel corn.

"I'm still mad at you." Hannah took the bag and set it on the shelf.

"I know." Riley waited. Three…two…one…

"You had no right," Hannah said, her tone clipped.

"Let me ask you something." Riley folded her arms over her chest and leaned back against the counter. "Would you ever have signed up for a booth at the Fest on your own?"

Hannah blinked at her.

"Be honest."

Hannah nibbled her bottom lip. "I mean…" She shrugged, then let out an annoyed breath. "No, probably not."

"Okay. So, how about this? We try it. We go on Saturday, we set up our booth—we don't have to bring the popper, we pop it all here, fresh that morning—we decide on your top, what? Five flavors? We don't have to bring the whole shop there. I'll be there with you, and you can get either Kaitlyn or Squeaky Boy to man things here in case somebody wants one of the other flavors we'll make sure they know about."

Hannah was clearly trying to hide a grin.

"What?"

"Michael. His name is Michael."

Riley grinned back. "Michael. Right. Him." Their gazes held for a moment. "I'll be there every step of the way, okay? We'll do it together. And if it's a giant epic fail, I'll take the blame, you can say I told you so, and we'll never speak of it again. Deal?" She held out her hand.

Hannah pursed her lips, obviously rolling it all around in her head before finally grasping Riley's hand. Hannah's was warm, her grip firm, and Riley felt a subtle current of electricity run up her arm and straight down to her groin, where it settled. "Deal."

Another beat went by as they stood there, hands linked. Then, as if they'd both been poked, they jumped into action. Hannah hurried out front to open the shop, and Riley busied herself with dishes.

Once she had the sink filled with warm, soapy water and had

begun washing, Riley heard the bell over the door tinkle and could see two customers walk in. She smiled softly, trying not to think about how absolutely comfortable she felt here. It wasn't something she needed to dwell on; she'd have to leave some time.

She watched Hannah, listened to her voice as she explained the ingredients of the new nacho popcorn, and something deep inside her went all mushy. She basked in the feeling for a few seconds before giving her head a literal shake and returning her focus to the dirty dishes.

This is a job.

She said that line to herself over and over. Yes, it was a favor to Kyle, but it was also a job. That was all. She had to remember that.

Hannah was a job. That was all.

And then her mind's eye filled with Hannah's smiling face, her soft laughter. Riley let her head drop down, chin to her chest.

"Fuck," she breathed out.

CHAPTER NINE

That looks *so* good," Riley said, her voice cheerful and her blue eyes dancing.

She wasn't wrong. Hannah could admit that, as she stood looking at the Poptacular sign. It used to be a faded yellow-ish. It used to hang on the front of her shop. Now? Now it was bright green. Not neon, exactly, but bright and cheerful, like the inside of a lime. Now it lay across two sawhorses, glimmering in the sunshine with its fresh coat of paint.

The day was bright and sunny. They'd talked on Monday about painting the sign, and Hannah had balked, as she did with everything Riley suggested, as if it was required at this point. Now it was Wednesday, and here they were. She put her hands on her hips and gazed off into the distance. They were just outside of town at the contracting lot Kyle ran. He'd taken the sign down with his tools and ladder and coworker, tossed it into his pickup, and driven it out here as Hannah and Riley followed in Riley's very nice car. He left them with the sign set up on the sawhorses and a promise he'd be back in a few hours. Riley had picked up the paint and had the stuff they'd used to paint the walls in her trunk. Together, it had taken them about two hours to do two coats.

"What do you think of this one?" Riley was leaning on her forearms, her laptop open on the trunk of her car, and she pointed at the screen.

Hannah wandered over and leaned to look over her shoulder. Riley was looking at new Open/Closed signs. Hannah didn't mean to sigh, but it happened.

"What?" Riley turned to meet her gaze. Their faces were only inches apart and Hannah could make out the black ring that circled Riley's blue eyes. "You don't like it? How about this one?" She clicked to a different one.

Hannah stood back up and waved a hand. "Sure. Whatever." She could feel Riley's gaze on her, but didn't meet it. In her peripheral, she could see Riley close her laptop and stand up.

"No worries. We can look later." She came and stood next to Hannah, and they both stared off into the distance. The contractor lot was next to a huge field where sheep roamed. Every now and then, the breeze would gift them with a whiff of manure strong enough to make their eyes water. "Do you like the color?" Riley asked the question quietly—it was amazing how silent the lot was with everybody out on a job—and Hannah could almost feel the heat of her body standing close.

She nodded. "I do."

"Good. I think it's really gonna pop when we put it back up. We want people to be able to find the place after we fill them full of popcorn on Saturday."

Riley was so cheerful, so happy all the time. Hannah turned to her. "Are you always like this?" It wasn't an accusation or even tense. It was just a question.

Riley's dark eyebrows dipped down above her nose. "Like what?"

"This…up. Cheerful. Don't you ever get down? Sad? Angry? Bummed out?"

Riley blinked at her for a moment, as if she didn't quite understand the question. When she finally answered, she seemed to choose her words carefully. "Of course, I do. I just…" She blinked again, rapidly this time, and cleared her throat. "What is there to be bummed out about?" Her grin grew and she stretched out an arm to encompass the field, the sheep, and maybe the sky as well. "Look at this! It's gorgeous!"

Her enthusiasm was contagious, Hannah couldn't deny it, and she smiled back. "It really is."

"Good. Okay. So. How do you feel about lunch?"

Hannah frowned. "I really should get back to the shop."

Riley had expected exactly that answer, Hannah could see it in the way she nodded before Hannah had finished her first word. She hated that she was so predictable. But you know what else she was?

Responsible. And it wasn't responsible of her to leave Kaitlyn to fend for herself all day while Hannah was out having a leisurely lunch with Riley. Didn't matter how damn sexy she was.

Oh, no. Nope. Not going there.

"Okay," Riley said, interrupting that train of thought, thank goodness. "Let's get you back. Kyle will bring us the sign this afternoon and put it back up."

She'd taken the wind out of Riley's sails, she could tell as they drove and Riley stayed mostly quiet. She'd chattered nonstop on the way there, but now, it was like Hannah had made her words into a self-fulfilling prophecy, and Riley was sad. Or at least bummed out. Whichever it was, it was Hannah's fault, and the silence was oppressive.

Good job, Han. Excellent work. You should be proud of yourself.

She gazed out the window as they entered town again, not wanting Riley to see her grimace. John Tucker was outside the diner, helping to unload a delivery truck of produce. She caught a glimpse of Shana heading inside the Coffee Cup. Mr. Daniels was strolling slowly down the street toward the shop, and as they passed him, Hannah was glad she'd be there to wait on him.

Riley slipped her car into a parking spot but didn't turn off the engine or make any move to get out.

"You coming in?" Hannah asked.

Riley shook her head. "Nah. I've got some work I should probably do. I'll come by later when Kyle brings the sign."

"Oh. Okay." She had zero right to be disappointed, but she was, and it was obvious, she knew. With a swallow, she pulled on the door handle and got out of the car. Leaning back down, she said, "Thanks, Riley. See you later."

Riley nodded, and Hannah had barely reached the sidewalk before she was backing out of her spot. Hannah watched as she drove on down Main, feeling like she'd let Riley down somehow.

It bothered her how much that bothered her.

With a soft groan, she headed into the shop, which had some customers in it, much to her surprise.

"There she is now," Kaitlyn said, indicating her with a wave of her arm. "Hannah, these customers are wondering if you can do custom flavors."

And her business day began. Again.

She dealt with the customers, and when Mr. Daniels came in, they oohed and ahhed together over the newly framed photo of Grams. At one point when she looked up at him, his eyes were wet, she was pretty sure. She made popcorn, researched some ideas for new flavors on her brand new fancy laptop, and before she knew it, Kyle was calling her name.

"Han. Come look."

She glanced up to see her big brother standing in the front door, gesturing for her.

Outside, he and his buddy had put the sign back, but now, instead of being its normal, subtle, quiet yellow, it was a bright, cheerful pop of color against the building.

"Wow," she said before she could stop herself. "I...wow." She held up a finger, telling him to wait, and then she turned and crossed the street. In front of the Coffee Cup, she turned to look at her shop, and damn if that sign didn't call to her from the other side of Main.

"That looks fantastic." Shana was suddenly next to her, and they stood there together, just looking.

"It really does, doesn't it?"

"No way anybody misses your shop now."

"Nope."

They stood there quietly, just looking, until Kyle lifted his hands from across the street in a gesture of *What are you doing?*

She and Shana both laughed softly. "Gotta go," she said.

"It looks great," Shana reiterated. "That Riley knows what she's doing."

She wasn't wrong.

"You've got Omaha next week," Justin said.

"Shit. That's right." Riley knew that. She didn't get where she was by not being able to keep an accurate schedule. But being back in Sunset Valley was messing with her head, slowing her down, distracting her.

Okay. No. That wasn't accurate at all. It wasn't Sunset Valley. It was Hannah Kramer.

Her cheeks puffed as she blew out a breath. "I'll be there."

"Was there a chance you wouldn't be?" Justin asked, his thick brows reaching up toward his hairline.

"No. No, of course not." She scratched at her neck and gazed out the window of her room in the resort.

"Hey, you okay, Riley?"

She returned her gaze to the screen of her laptop where her assistant's face showed an expression of concern. Justin was super handsome. Like, Disney prince handsome, complete with perfect dark hair and a slight curl that grazed his forehead. Behind the lenses of his wire-rimmed glasses, he squinted slightly at her, clearly worried. Not only was he her assistant, he was her friend, probably the closest friend she had.

"You don't seem like yourself lately," he said.

"I mean…" She shrugged and returned her gaze to the window. "It's kind of strange being here. Lots of memories. Things I'd forgotten about."

"Your mom." It wasn't a question. Justin knew her well.

"Yeah. My mom."

"It's also the longest you've stayed in one place in a long time," Justin pointed out. "Maybe you're going a little stir-crazy, you know? Maybe it's a good thing you've got Omaha next week."

Maybe that *was* it. She thought about that for the rest of the day, as she mixed work and relaxation. After all, she was supposed to be on vacation, and the weather was still beautiful. The leaves hadn't changed yet, but lots of trees had some sporadic color—a yellow leaf here, a half-orange leaf there, peppered among the green ones. She took her Kindle and headed out to sit by the pool. She didn't love super-hot weather, so the low seventies of the day was perfect for her. She spread a towel out on a lounge, turned it so the sun was shining on her, slathered herself with sunscreen, and began to read.

She'd barely gotten through a chapter before her eyes grew heavy. And then there was Hannah. Hannah, in a red bikini, her dark blond hair in a high ponytail, red-rimmed sunglasses, walking toward Riley in all her half-naked glory with a big smile on her face. Riley could only blink at her, at this vision, this sexy woman who'd lost her ever-present apron and baseball hat, and who now looked even sexier. Which Riley hadn't thought possible. When Hannah reached Riley's chair, she didn't stop. No, she lifted one leg up and over and then sat directly on Riley's hips, straddling her.

Riley sucked in a surprised breath. "Hannah? What are you doing?"

"What am I doing?" Hannah's voice was breathy, different from the way she normally sounded. Breathy and sexy and dominant. "If you have to ask, I must not be doing it right. Here, let me try again." She ground her center into Riley's hips as she leaned forward, catching herself with both hands on Riley's breasts. Riley had just enough time to gasp before Hannah's mouth was on hers. She groaned.

And that startled her awake.

She sat up quickly, the Kindle sliding off her and clattering onto the concrete. She swallowed hard and her gaze darted around the pool deck. She was grateful to be wearing her sunglasses so nobody could see what was probably a little crazy in her eyes. The only other people were an older couple on the other side of the pool, both lying flat, a woman sitting at a table under an umbrella talking quietly on her cell, and two kids in the pool who probably didn't even know she existed.

Thank God.

She blew out a relieved breath and lay back in her chair. Holy shit, that had been intense. Not normally somebody who could recall her dreams in vivid detail, she remembered every single moment of this one, and her brain was now actively replaying it for her. Over and over. That red bikini…

Hannah probably doesn't even own a bikini. She's not exactly the bikini type.

She blew out another breath as her heart rate slowly returned to normal.

She'd had a sex dream about Hannah. What the actual fuck was she supposed to do with that?

Justin's right. I've been here too long.

Okay, yeah, that's what she was supposed to think. Justin *was* right. She'd stayed in one place for a much longer time than usual, and clearly, her brain wasn't happy about that if it had resorted to sending her uncomfortable dreams.

Sexy, uncomfortable dreams…

No. No, she had to move. It's what she did when she started to feel strange: She moved. She went. She had to go.

The Fest was this Saturday, and she'd promised Hannah she'd help. She was not a person who'd go back on her word. No. She'd stay through the Fest, but then she needed to head home so she could turn around and head to Omaha. It was that simple.

Having a plan in place instantly made her feel better, helped her system relax. She lay back in her chair and watched the kids in the pool for a moment. They were taking turns diving to the bottom to grab a rubber ring, then tossing it again for the other kid. The older couple was still lying next to each other on separate lounges, but now their heads were turned to face each other. Their hands were linked, and as Riley watched, the woman laughed heartily, a musical sound that carried across the pool and made Riley smile. The man looked happily satisfied to have made the woman laugh, and Riley felt a little clench in her heart. It had been a long time since she'd had a person who looked at her the same way that man had looked at that woman.

A literal shake of her head rattled that thought loose so she could banish it, and she picked up her Kindle.

A few more things to help with. The Fest. And then she was out of there.

It was that simple.

Making popcorn kept Hannah calm.

She had no idea how or why, but it did. It had since she was a teenager. Maybe it was the routine of it. Maybe it was because it was almost mindless for her, she'd done it so many times. She could do it with her eyes closed. She knew that, and it helped immensely when she was feeling anxious about something.

Like now.

It was Friday night, and she'd closed the shop, locked the door over an hour ago. Tomorrow was the Fest, and it bothered her how nervous she was about it. She had her table and shelving all stacked up in the back, leaning against the wall and ready for Kyle to come by with his pickup super early tomorrow so she could get set up. She had the swiper thingy for her phone, in case anybody wanted to use a credit card, as well as a cash box with some money in it. She looked at the boxes taking up space around her sink. Boxes filled with bags,

bags filled with popcorn. Different flavors and colors, all made today. She'd make the caramel corn in the morning, which meant she'd have to be back here in only a few hours. She and Riley had agreed to stick to her top four best sellers, but as of about three hours ago, Hannah had upped that to her top eight flavors, and now she was making another batch of bacon and cheddar. And then she wondered if she'd made enough pumpkin spice. It was only September, but it was closing in on autumn, and that's what people wanted in autumn: all things pumpkin spice.

"Oh, God, I'm gonna drive myself mad," she muttered to the empty shop. "They're gonna find me giggling uncontrollably in a giant box of popcorn. It's only a matter of time."

The rapping on the front door startled her so badly, she jumped, letting out a cry of surprise. She glanced up toward the door, and there she stood.

Riley.

Smiling, though also looking slightly bewildered. Hannah crossed the front and unlocked the door.

"Hey," she said as Riley came in. "What are you doing here?"

Riley followed her to the back as she explained. "I was driving by and saw your lights on, thought I'd stop and see what you were doing…" Her voice trailed off as she glanced around, taking in all the bags that were boxed up. "Panic popping, I see."

"Yes. That. Exactly that." Hannah felt keyed up. Wired. She shook out her hands, feeling suddenly overly energized. Not in a good way.

"Hey." Riley grabbed her hands, held them in her own. "Hey," she said again and waited until Hannah met her gaze. "Breathe."

Hannah darted her eyes away, but Riley gave her hands a gentle squeeze.

"Breathe," Riley said again, when Hannah's gaze came back to her. She inhaled through her nose, then exhaled through her mouth, demonstrating. "Smell the flowers," she said as she inhaled again. "Blow out the candles," she said as she exhaled. At Hannah's curious look, Riley shrugged and said, "My neighbor's kid watches a lot of Ms. Rachel, and this is what she recommends when you need to calm down." Her lopsided grimace was super cute, and it made Hannah smile.

"I had no idea you were an expert in kids' shows. Or in relaxation."

"Oh, I'm not an expert in either. But I get nervous, too, and this definitely helps." Riley waited a beat, then asked, "Feel any better?"

"A bit, yeah. Thanks." She glanced around at all the boxes. "I may have overdone it."

Riley waved a dismissive hand. "Nah. We can sell all of this."

"You think?"

"Absolutely. More popcorn is just gonna make our booth look even cooler."

Hannah wrinkled her nose in uncertainty. "It won't look like I'm the crazy popcorn lady who got carried away?"

Riley tipped her head. "I mean, it might, but if it sells popcorn, that's okay, right?" She gave Hannah's hands another squeeze to show she was teasing.

Hannah sighed. "True. The town already thinks that of me, anyway. Probably."

"Probably." They stood there in silence for a moment, both grinning, Riley still holding her hands. "How about we close up shop and go grab a drink?"

Hannah looked down at herself. Her apron was dirty, but under that, her clothes were fine. And a drink sounded perfect right about now. "Let me fix my hair?"

Riley's smile grew, and she nodded and let go of Hannah's hands.

Fifteen minutes later, they were strolling down Main. While it wasn't exactly what Riley would probably think of as bustling, there were definitely people out and about, and Hannah smiled at her little town.

As if reading her mind, Riley said, "I didn't expect this much activity, to be honest." A group of twentysomethings passed them, laughing at something one of them had said.

"It's tourist season," Hannah said. "It'll be like this—and get progressively busier—until after the new year."

"I like it," Riley said, and Hannah watched her as she looked around, smiling the whole time. Hannah hadn't seen her at all the day before, and she tried hard not to latch onto the thought floating around in her head that said she'd missed her. But she had. She watched her out of the corner of her eye, took in the jeans and how they hugged her ass. Riley had a great ass. A spectacular ass, actually. Hannah hadn't seen a better one in a very long time. Her top was a simple button-down with short sleeves, and she'd definitely gotten some sun recently. Even with only the streetlights, Hannah could see a new bronzing of Riley's skin, and she recalled their teenage years, how envious she'd been of Riley's ability to tan while Hannah had two color choices for her skin: pasty white or lobster red.

"Here?" Riley's voice cut into her thoughts as they stopped walking in front of Hopsville, the microbrewery. Music wafted out from inside, not too loud but loud enough.

"Sure."

Riley held the door and in they went.

The place was hopping, and Hannah was glad for Stephen and Jacob, the brothers who owned the place. They'd created a unique establishment: part microbrewery and part hometown bar. They often had live music, but tonight, the stage in the corner was bare and the music was coming through speakers in the ceiling, a song she didn't recognize with a beat she liked.

Square tables were set up in the area, most of them occupied. Along one wall stood bistro tables, higher with long-legged stools, and the left side of the room housed a couple dartboards, two pinball machines, a pool table and, in the corner, a thing that made Riley's eyes light up.

"Oh my God, I thought I noticed this when I was in here last week." She hurried over to the puck bowling table. Nobody was playing, and Riley seemed to be in her glory. And then she was bending over, looking along the sides of the long table.

"What are you doing?" Hannah asked.

"I don't think they make these anymore. They're vintage, and when I was in here last week, I saw it out of the corner of my eye." She switched to looking at the other side. "And I wondered if—yes!" She stood up, her finger pointing.

"I have no idea what's happening right now," Hannah chuckled, stepping near Riley and following her finger. There, carved into the side of the game, scratched into the black veneer coating, were initials.

R.S.

Hannah glanced back up at her. "Is that you? You carved your initials into a game table?"

"Yes. When I was seventeen. Remember the bowling alley?"

Riley scrunched up her face and snapped her fingers. "I can't remember the name of it now…"

"Baker Lanes," Hannah supplied. "It shut down two years ago when Mr. and Mrs. Baker retired and headed south. It's a gym now."

"Baker Lanes. That's it. When I was in here last week, I caught a glimpse of this and thought *huh, that looks just like the one in the bowling alley I carved my initials into.* I meant to take a look, just for giggles, but then forgot. And I was right."

"The Bakers sold off a lot of their equipment. Steve and Jake must've snagged it."

"Well, we have to play. I mean, we have to." Riley's eyes were lit up like a little kid's, and Hannah couldn't help but grin at her.

"How could we not?" she asked.

Fifteen minutes later, they each had a Hopsville-created beer—the chocolate stout for Riley and a wheat beer for Hannah—and Riley was set to slide the metal puck down the table at the "pins" that hung from the hood. Under the pins on the table were little metal tabs. As the puck—which was basically a steel circle with a giant ball bearing in the center—slid over the tabs, the corresponding pin would fold upward, indicating that it had been "knocked down." The score was kept just like actual bowling.

After playing four frames and getting refills on their beers, two things became very clear:

One, Hannah was very good at this game.

Two, Riley was not.

"Explain this to me," Hannah said with a laugh, as Riley hunkered down over the table and made a show of squinting her eyes in concentration.

"Shh. I'm shooting."

"Sorry," Hannah whispered, and held a finger to her lips.

Riley shot.

She knocked down one pin, then stood up looking confused.

"Explain this to me," Hannah said again.

"Explain what?" Riley sipped her beer.

"Explain how somebody who is so good at just about everything in life can possibly be this bad at"—she stopped and scanned the top of the table for the actual name of the game—"puck bowling."

"I'm not that bad," Riley said with a pout. She glanced at the scores and winced.

"You are *painfully* bad." Hannah was still laughing as she set down her beer and took her turn. She got a spare.

"Damn it," Riley muttered, but it was good-natured muttering, and Hannah knew she was having a good time.

They both were.

"Thanks for talking me into coming out," she said, her voice a bit softer.

Riley stopped lining up her shot and met Hannah's gaze. "Thanks for coming out." She smiled at her and went back to her turn.

Riley really did have a gorgeous smile. Hannah had always thought so. It was the first thing that had caught her attention when they were young. Well, her eyes were first. Her eyes were always the first thing people noticed. Anybody who said otherwise was lying, because you couldn't *not* notice Riley's eyes. All that bright blue tucked into all that dark? There was no way to *not* be drawn in by them. But her smile? Wide and infectious, it could make the world melt away.

Okay, maybe ease up on the microbrews, Han...

Riley took her shot. She missed a spare and the game ended with Hannah the winner. By a lot.

They stood side by side and gazed at the score.

"Wow, you really suck," Hannah said.

Riley sighed. "I really do, don't I?"

They laughed together, and Hannah drained her glass. With a sigh, she said, "I should probably head home. Early day tomorrow."

Riley nodded and followed her toward the bar, where they set down their glasses and waved goodbye to Jacob, who was tending bar. "Good to see you, Hannah," he called after them.

"You should do a pairing with them," Riley said as they pushed out the door. "Seems like they know you. I bet they'd be into it."

"I don't hate that idea," Hannah said truthfully, her brain already deciding which popcorn flavors would go well with which beers.

"I'll take that as a win," Riley said with a soft laugh.

The night was beautiful—warm, and the breeze lifted Riley's hair from her shoulders and played with it as Hannah watched. They strolled in silence for a bit, and it didn't take long before they were back at Poptacular and standing next to Riley's car.

"That sign really does look better," Hannah commented, her eyes on the shop, the sign cheerful and easily legible, even in the dark.

"Once in a while, I know what I'm talking about," Riley said.

"Seems like it." Hannah turned back to her, and their faces were very close. She swallowed audibly, and when she spoke, her voice was husky. "Bright and early?"

"I'll be here." Riley held her gaze for another delicious moment before pulling the car door open.

"You okay to drive?"

Riley nodded. "I am. You?"

"Yeah."

"Okay. Tomorrow. We're gonna sell the crap out of your popcorn."

Hannah grinned and nodded, then strolled three cars down to her own decade-old Toyota. She started the engine and waited until Riley had pulled out and coasted up Main toward the resort before she backed out and headed in the opposite direction.

She felt good. Relaxed and loose and content.

She liked spending time with Riley. She could admit that, right? And tomorrow, they would have the whole day together. As she drove, she grinned, and one surprising fact became crystal clear.

She couldn't wait.

CHAPTER TEN

The booth looked damn incredible, if Hannah said so herself. She stood back, hands on her hips, and took it in.

Kyle had met her at the shop at five that morning—she'd gotten there at four thirty and made a fresh batch of caramel corn—loaded up his truck with everything she'd need, and they'd driven to the park together. Riley had met them there, and the three of them needed less than an hour to get everything set up. Now they had a table, shelves in a U shape, and a rainbow of popcorn flavors. Riley had printed out signs that named each flavor in bright, swirly colors, along with a larger sign that announced pricing, broken down by bag size.

Riley came to stand next to her.

"What do you think?" Hannah asked her.

"I think we're ready to sell some popcorn."

Hannah turned and met her smiling face and nodded in agreement.

Kyle stood up from behind the back shelf and slid his wrench into his tool belt. "Okay, I think that'll do it." He pointed as he spoke. "No rain in the forecast today, but the tent top will keep the sun off you and the bags so they don't get condensation inside or get sticky. I've got stakes in the ground, so nothing should tip. Everything should stay in place, even with people touching things."

Speaking of people, folks were starting to show up and stroll around the park as other booths opened for business.

"It's good to have a brother who's a contractor," Riley said with a smile, and Hannah had never been more grateful than she was right then.

"It really, really is." She pushed up on her toes and wrapped her arms around her brother's neck. "Thank you," she said quietly.

She felt his arms tighten around her. "Anytime," he said. They parted and his cheeks were tinted a light pink under his beard. "I'll be back tonight to take it down." And he was off.

"He's a good guy," Riley said, as she and Hannah watched him go.

Hannah was suddenly reminded of that day.

The moment.

The second she'd opened the door of the back room and found Riley and Kyle making out, how her whole world had felt like it had shattered. "I really thought, after I caught you two together, that you'd end up married or something." She snorted a little laugh to hide her sudden discomfort with the thought. "I mean, I was only thirteen, but that's what it felt like."

Riley's smile seemed slightly pained as she moved into the booth and began straightening bags of popcorn. "I always regretted that day," she said quietly.

That was a surprise to Hannah, and she wondered if her face showed it. "You did?"

A nod, but Riley didn't look at her. "I worried for a long time that I'd single-handedly ruined your relationship with your brother. You guys were so close, and I felt like after that day, you weren't. I was the girl who took your brother, and you guys were never the same, at least from what I saw."

Hannah stood completely still, watching Riley's hands—those beautiful hands—as she fixed things that didn't need fixing. Finally, maybe sensing the stillness, Riley turned and met her gaze.

Hannah tipped her head and said quietly, "You weren't the girl who took my brother from me, Riley. My brother was the guy who took *you* from me. Did you seriously never get that?"

Riley blinked. Once. Twice. A quick shake of her head, then, "What?"

"All my following you guys around, constantly tagging along?"

"I thought you just loved your big brother, wanted to be like Kyle."

A laugh escaped Hannah. She hadn't meant it to, but it just did, just popped from her lips. "Riley, I followed you guys everywhere because I had a massive crush on you. Yes, I loved my brother, but I wanted to be around *you*." She took a moment to enjoy the fact that she'd clearly rendered Riley speechless. "I mean, I was young, and I didn't fully understand what was going on with me, but I wasn't upset that I'd lost Kyle to you, I was upset that I'd lost you to him. *That's* why things changed between you and me after that."

"Oh, wow. I—" Those were the only words Riley was able to speak before some customers arrived at the booth, and they had to table the conversation.

Hannah had tiny, shot-sized plastic cups filled with each flavor of popcorn for sampling, so customers would know what they were getting, and the woman and her daughter who stepped up to the booth asked to try some. Hannah smiled at them, shot a look back at Riley, who seemed to literally shake herself, and they were off.

The business day began.

They worked nonstop for nearly four hours before the first stretch of time they could sort of call a break. Riley had scooted off early on to grab them both coffee from one of the breakfast trucks, but aside from that, the stream of customers had been steady.

"Oh em gee," Hannah breathed out and turned to look at Riley, whose cheeks were flushed, smile wide. "That was crazy."

"I told you," Riley said. "Did I not tell you?"

"You did. You told me." She moved back to check the shelves. "Wow, I knew the pumpkin spice would be a hit, but the dill pickle is a surprise. We're almost out." She tapped a finger against her chin, then spoke her thoughts aloud. "Kaitlyn's at the shop, and I could ask her to switch with me while I make some more. Maybe a dozen bags?"

"No." Riley's voice interrupted her thoughts.

"No?"

Riley shook her head. "No. Whatever sells out, you leave the shelf empty, so people see they missed it. Hopefully, that drives them either to the shop or back here next weekend."

"Oh, I see what you did there." Hannah grinned at her. "Next weekend, huh?"

Riley lifted one shoulder as she said, "Being successful today would illustrate the benefit of participating more often."

"And you knew I'd be successful today, did you?"

Riley tipped her head. "Ms. Kramer, you don't seem to understand that I am very, very good at my job."

Their gazes held. Deliciously. Hannah felt a gentle throb make itself known low in her body. "I'm starting to see the appeal, Ms. Shaw."

Fate seemed to understand that right then was a great time for a customer to appear, and one did. Hannah gave it one more second before she broke off the gaze and turned herself, complete with her damp underwear, and got back to the business at hand.

❖

"I am *starving*." Hannah groaned as they walked, bending her knees, her arms hanging by her sides, like a person whose energy was running out.

"I have no idea why," Riley said with a soft laugh. "You've had nothing today but coffee and popcorn." Then she gasped and pointed. "Oh my God, is that a *poutine truck*?"

Hannah grinned. "That it is, my friend. I think the chef's name is Guillermo. He drives down from Ontario and hits all the festivals during the summer and early fall. His poutine is to die for, and now that it's in my head, there's nothing I want more."

"I am totally on board with that. Poutine, here we come!"

Ten minutes later, they were strolling the Fest, poutine in hand, and Riley was gushing. She couldn't get herself to stop humming in delight. "His cheese curds are so creamy, and this gravy. My God. A thing of beauty, that's what this lovely red-and-white paper bowl is. With its little wooden spork to stab the cheesy, gravy-covered, potatoey goodness? A thing of beauty."

Hannah laughed, and Riley gave herself a point. Hannah didn't seem to laugh terribly often, so every time Riley got her to, she drew herself an imaginary point in the air. She was on eight today. A new world record, she was sure of it.

With a quick glance over her shoulder in the direction of the Poptacular booth, Hannah said, "Do you think they're okay?"

"That's the fourth time you've asked me that since we left, so I will tell you the same thing I told you three previous times, okay? Are you ready?"

Hannah rolled her eyes, but the smile was still there. "Yes. I'm ready."

"Okay. Brace yourself. Here it is: Kaitlyn and Squeaky Boy know exactly what they're doing, and it's all fine." She waited until Hannah looked at her, and then she raised her eyebrows in expectation. "Got it?"

"I got it." Hannah glanced back again, but to her credit, said nothing more.

"Let's just take some time and enjoy this lovely evening, yeah? It's warm. There's food and lights and music." She ran a hand in front of herself, from the top of her head down. "There's fabulous company." That earned her another laugh. Another point.

She expected a smart-ass comment to that, but Hannah simply held her gaze as she said, "That's all very true. Especially the company part."

The little flutter was back, and Riley swallowed. There was no place in the world she'd rather be right then. That was a new realization for her, and she put another gravy-covered fry into her mouth as they kept walking.

Hannah knew everybody. It was a small town, after all, but still. Like, *everybody*. It made Riley grin every time somebody said, "Hey, Hannah" or "Good to see you, Hannah" or "That's the popcorn lady!"

"You're famous," she said after they'd reached the end of the midway. The park had a small, manmade pond at one end with a paved path around it, and by unspoken agreement, they simply kept walking. "The whole town knows you."

Hannah lifted a shoulder, then tossed her empty bowl into a trash can as she passed it. "Small town."

"I think your shop is more well-known than you think."

Hannah sighed. "Doesn't bring in money, just being known. I need them to buy. And they just...don't. I don't know how my grandma did it."

Riley didn't want to get into work talk. In this beautiful park on a stroll away from the hum of conversation and noise and light? This wasn't the place. After a day of hard work, finally having time together just the two of them? This wasn't the time. Except she was here for Hannah, not for herself.

She was here for Hannah.

With an internal sigh, she said, "Well, it was a different time as far as business goes. You know? Less overhead, more kitsch. Less distraction. Less competition for attention."

Hannah nodded, frowning.

"But"—she had to get her smiling again. Had to. It was almost a compulsion, and she didn't want to dwell on it or what it might mean— "those aren't things that can't be combatted, you know? We just have to work at it." She turned to meet Hannah's worried gaze. "That's why you have me. That's why I'm here. To help."

"I thought you weren't staying." Hannah said it softly, just above a whisper. "I thought you were leaving tomorrow."

Kyle must've told her. "I am. But I'll be back."

Wait, what?

What the hell was she doing?

Where had those words come from?

Hannah looked at her again. "You will?"

She nodded. "I have a client in Omaha that I need to take care of, but I'll be back after that." Justin was going to kill her. But it was done. She'd said it—surprising herself as much as Hannah—and now that it was done, she felt a peace settle over her, like she'd made exactly the right decision. The look of happy relief on Hannah's face only solidified that for her.

Hannah slipped her hand under Riley's arm and leaned against her shoulder as they walked. "I'm glad." She glanced up at her with a soft smile. "Kinda getting used to you being around."

Riley squeezed her arm tightly against her body, trapping Hannah's hand, and she covered it with her other hand.

They strolled.

It was beautiful. The weather was still warm, a light breeze ruffling their hair. The lights around the pond reflected in the still water, making it sparkle. A handful of others strolled as well, but none of them were close to Riley and Hannah.

This setting? With Hannah's warm body leaning against her? Yeah, Riley could walk like this for the rest of time, she was sure.

"Wanna sit?" Hannah asked as they approached a bench. "My feet are killing me."

Riley laughed softly as they sat. "I'm always amazed by people who are on their feet all day long. Mine would be crying."

"That's because you have soft little pampered feet that live under a desk."

"True, but they also don't get to spend the day in comfy sneakers like yours. They get jammed into ridiculous heels. Not so soft and pampered then."

"But how much walking do you really do in those ridiculous heels? Do you do a zillion laps around a kitchen in them?"

They were laughing now, during the back and forth, leaning into each other as they did.

"Hey, you don't know how many laps around what kind of room I do in my ridiculous heels. Don't pretend you do, ma'am."

"I mean, I'm a pretty smart girl, and I can imagine. Lemme see... parking lot to front door. Could be lengthy but probably isn't. Sit in waiting area, so your feet get a rest there. Then waiting area to office. Again, could be lengthy, but probably not..." Hannah was tapping her forefinger against her chin as she spoke, making a show of thinking.

Riley laughed harder. "Okay, now you're just mocking me." She gave Hannah a playful shove.

"You and your ridiculous heels, yes." Hannah pushed against her and suddenly, the fact that their noses were mere millimeters apart became as obvious as if there'd been an announcement saying so, but there was no pause. No moment of thinking about it. No weighing of pros and cons. They were suddenly kissing, and Riley had no idea which of them had made the move first, but it had happened more naturally than any other kiss in her entire life.

It wasn't hot and heavy, but it wasn't tentative either. It felt almost like they were establishing the fact that yes, this had been bound to happen, and as soon as that thought flitted through Riley's mind, she knew it was one hundred percent correct. She'd known almost since she'd arrived that this was where they'd end up, that kissing Hannah was inevitable. She simply hadn't wanted to believe it.

And yet, here they were.

Hannah was a damn good kisser, and Riley wasn't sure why she found that surprising, but she did. Hannah's mouth was soft, warm, sweet, and she was definitely driving this train. One hand was on Riley's cheek, the other at the back of her neck, holding her close to Hannah's face, almost cradling her. It was both gentle and assertive, which made it both sweet and sexy to Riley. She pressed in more firmly when she felt the gentle touch of Hannah's tongue, asking to be let in. Riley obliged, and a soft moan escaped her.

When they finally parted, Riley's breath was ragged, and she slowly opened her eyes. Hannah was looking at her with a smile on her face that was made of clear joy and tinted with just a slight hint of uncertainty.

Riley swallowed and took a breath, and "Wow" was what came out of her mouth. It made Hannah's smile grow, though. "You okay?" she finally asked, once she'd caught her breath.

Hannah's grin grew. "Are you kidding me? I just made out with Riley Shaw. Teenage Hannah is doing a little victory dance in my brain right now."

Riley laughed. "Well, I'll take *that* as a compliment."

"As well you should."

"And…how's current adult Hannah doing?"

A couple holding hands walked past them, and Hannah tracked them, stayed silent until they'd headed around the curve of the pond. When she turned back to Riley, her eyes were soft, and so was her voice. She picked up Riley's hand and interlocked their fingers. "Current adult Hannah is really glad you're coming back."

CHAPTER ELEVEN

Poptacular was technically closed on Sundays, but Hannah and Kyle had hauled all the stuff back from the park that morning, minus what little was left of the popcorn, which they'd brought back to the shop the night before. They stacked the tables and shelves up in the back, Kyle left, and Hannah thought while she was there, she'd straighten things up a bit.

Yes, she was trying to keep busy. She knew that. Keeping busy kept her brain from running off to places it didn't need to go. Kept it from asking questions it shouldn't be asking.

Questions like, when had she ever been kissed like that before? Questions like, what did she do with that now? Questions like, what if Riley actually *didn't* come back?

"Just because she said she would," she whispered to herself in the empty shop, "doesn't mean she will. She hasn't been back in more than a decade, why should she come back again this time?"

And then her mind reminded her of the kissing last night. Again. Played it in her head like a movie, the two of them in a ridiculously romantic setting, sitting on a bench by a beautiful pond in the moonlight. Come on, a movie set couldn't have been heavier on the romance. It was perfect. The fact that they'd ended up kissing should have come as no surprise to anybody.

But it was Riley. Riley Shaw. The woman who made Hannah understand and accept her own sexuality, the woman she'd been fantasizing about since she was a teenager. It was *Riley*. And that made things so much more complicated.

The knocking on the front door yanked her back to the present, and there she was: Riley, standing at the door of the shop, smiling. And now that they had full-on made out, Hannah's eyes apparently had decided on their own that overtly roaming over Riley's body was not only allowed but encouraged.

She started at the bottom, at the casual sandals she wore, up to the jeans that Hannah knew would be cradling Riley's perfect ass like they were sewn to do just that, up farther to the simple white T-shirt with *Boston* arched across the front in faded red letters. Her dark hair was in a ponytail and those intense blue eyes were watching Hannah look at her. They were dark. Hooded. As they stood on opposite sides of the full-length glass, Riley uttered three words, her voice low and husky.

"Let me in."

Hannah didn't need to be told twice. She unlocked the door, let Riley in, and before she could utter a word, Riley's mouth was on hers. Hands on either side of her head, Riley kissed her hard, pushing her tongue into Hannah's mouth and pulling a moan from her.

Hannah's hands grasped at Riley, at her shirt, at her neck, as Riley walked them backward several steps until Hannah's back hit the counter and she was trapped between it and Riley.

There was nowhere she'd rather be in that moment, held captive in this delicious space, owned by Riley Shaw and her shockingly talented mouth.

Hannah had no idea how long they'd been making out before she heard a rapping, a knocking, that seemed to start from far away and grow louder, and when they finally wrenched their mouths apart and turned toward the front door, there stood Shana, two coffee cups in her hands, big brown eyes a little bit bigger than normal.

"Crap," Hannah muttered, giving Riley a gentle nudge. She went to the door and opened it, avoiding looking Shana in the eye.

"Well, it looks like a *very* good morning here at Poptacular," Shana said, her voice tinted with amusement. "I saw your lights on and wondered why you were working on a Sunday." She glanced at Riley, then back to Hannah. "I see you're not working, you're playing. Here." She handed Hannah a cup, then turned to Riley. "You can have mine if you'd like." She held up the other cup. "I don't work on Sundays but had a craving for my pumpkin spice."

Riley held up a hand. "No, thanks. I actually have a cup in my car. I stopped to grab one for my drive."

"Oh? Where are you off to?" Shana asked.

"Back to Boston. To my place. Gotta grab some stuff, then I fly west for a bit."

"I see." Shana nodded, then turned to look at Hannah. She was watching her carefully, taking her temperature, so to speak, and Hannah knew it. She could feel it. "Well, I'm sorry to see you go."

"Oh, I'll be back." Riley said it with such conviction, and when she turned to look at her, a little thrill zipped through Hannah.

"Yeah?" Shana was clearly trying to hide her skepticism.

"Yes. Definitely." There was a beat of slightly awkward silence, and then Riley clapped her hands together once. "So. I'd better get on the road." And to Hannah's surprise, she reached out and wrapped her in a hug. A tight hug.

"Come back," Hannah whispered, and then was irritated with herself for letting the words slip.

"I will," Riley whispered back. She squeezed, then let her go and added, "Check your email." Then she gave Shana a wave and was out the door.

Hannah stood there, not sure what to feel. The combination of emotions coursing through her was confusing. Sadness and elation and uncertainty and desire and fear and hope. All of it, swirling like some weird smoothie of feelings in her brain, in her heart.

There was a moment or two of quiet before Shana blew out a breath. "Wow. Okay. Well, I did not see *that* coming."

"Yeah. Well." Hannah nibbled on her bottom lip. She could still taste Riley, sweet and tangy from her coffee, plus something that was just uniquely her. She didn't want to lose it.

"You okay?"

A nod. "I am." A sigh. "Yeah. I'm good."

Shana looked unconvinced. "Do I need to worry?"

"About what?"

Shana tipped her head. "Seriously? You're gonna make me spell it out for you?" She took in a deep breath. "All right. I know who Riley is. You've told me about her. I know what she's meant to you over the years. So, my question is, do I need to worry about your heart? About your head? About you throwing yourself into work so much so that nobody ever sees you not buried in popcorn, as you tend to do when you're hurting?" She stopped and kept her eyes on Hannah, she could feel them. When she spoke again, her voice was soft and tender. "Will she come back?"

Hannah swallowed, and much to her own horror, felt her eyes well up as she remembered the times Riley had just up and left. Maybe this was different. But maybe it wasn't. When she answered, it was with a whisper. "I don't know."

❖

September was warm and dry in Omaha, Nebraska. Riley knew that. She'd been there or nearby several times, her work ethic and success spread around by word of mouth from happy clients. Unlike what she was doing for Hannah and Kyle—helping a struggling business—she also worked with businesses that were quite successful but simply wanted to streamline their company.

She'd made quite a name for herself at her organization, and she was proud of that.

It was Thursday now. Four days since she'd left Sunset Valley. Four days since she'd left Hannah. Four days since she'd kissed her face off, felt her mouth, her lips, her tongue. Riley's brain wouldn't stop showing her replays, going back to the park Saturday night, then jumping to Poptacular on Sunday morning. One, then the other. Back and forth. Over and over. It was riveting. It was sexy.

It was goddamn distracting.

She picked up her phone and typed out a text.

How's your day so far?

It was the first text she'd sent today, and she was embarrassed to admit—to herself or anybody else—just how hard it had been to wait until—she checked the time—ten fucking thirty in the morning.

"Pathetic," she muttered, scrubbing a hand over her face.

Unlike Riley herself, Hannah was playing it cool. Her texts were the tiniest bit flirty, but she seemed to have a hold of herself. She took fifteen, thirty, forty-five minutes to answer, and then the little gray dots bounced around for a million years before she finally sent a message. Like now.

Not bad. Yours?

"Ugh. Give me *something*," she muttered, and then the phone rang in her hand. A flood washed through her, a mix of excitement and relief, and she answered without even looking. "Hey. I miss seeing you. Just wanted to, I don't know, put that out there."

"Oh, uh, I miss you, too?" It was Justin.

Damn it.

Riley dropped her head to the table with a *thunk.*

"You okay, boss?" Justin sounded worried, and Riley couldn't blame him.

Maybe this was the Universe looking out for her, keeping her from saying things she shouldn't be saying. Maybe it was a good thing she got Justin and not Hannah. Maybe.

She sighed. "I'm fine. I thought you were…" She cleared her throat. "Not you."

"Sorry to disappoint you, but I am, in fact, me."

Riley gave a quiet laugh. "You never disappoint me."

"You wanna talk about it?" he asked.

"About what?"

"The person you were hoping I was?"

"I do not. But thanks. Now, how are we on those numbers I asked you for?"

After that, it was business as usual. Justin was a great guy and they got along well, talked about a lot of things. But talking to him about Hannah, about who she was and the complicated feelings she'd unexpectedly evoked, was not something Riley was ready to get into. Not yet. Maybe not ever.

They talked business and her upcoming schedule.

"So, you think you'll be finished up there tomorrow?" he asked.

"I don't see any reason why not."

"Okay, I can get you set up for Columbia, South Carolina, middle of next week. Yes?"

"No."

"No?"

"No. I'd like to go back to Sunset Valley, please. I've got some, um, unfinished business there."

There was a pause, and she could almost hear Justin's mind working, the wheels turning. "With the popcorn place?"

"Yeah."

"I mean…" He was clearly trying to find the right words to say without overstepping. She knew him well, and she could tell simply by the cadence of his voice. "That was a freebie, right? For your friend. Do you want me to just send a couple of reports with suggestions? Save you the trip?"

"No, I'd like you to book me back at the Sunset Valley Resort and Spa." She tried to keep the snark out of her voice, but wasn't sure she succeeded, and then she was annoyed at herself for taking her own confused crap out on him. "And set up a massage for me while I'm there."

"I—okay. On it."

"Thank you." She hung up before he could say anything more and before she ended up spilling things she wasn't ready to talk about.

What the hell was happening?

Since when was she not thinking about her clients? All of them. Any of them. That's what took up her life. Travel to each client, spending time with them, on to the next. Moving, moving, moving, all the time. It was what she did. It was who she was.

Wasn't it?

She had a ton of vacation time. Like, a ton of it. She rarely took time off. That's why the vacation she'd had scheduled—the one that took her to Sunset Valley in the first place—was so unusual. Because it was rare. And if her bosses wanted to give her a hard time about putting off her other clients, she'd just take more vacation. She could do that.

She sat and gazed out the window of her Omaha hotel room, stared at the blue sky, the puffy, cartoonlike clouds, for what felt like a long time and just breathed. In and out. In and out. Slowly. Deliberately.

After some time had passed and she felt more calm, less frazzled, she picked up her phone and typed out a text, then quickly sent it before she lost her nerve. *What are you doing on Tuesday night?*

The dots started almost immediately, which gave her a little thrill. Then they stopped and went away completely. Came back. Bounced. Went away. Came back. Bounced. Went away. Came back. And then words. Finally.

Was thinking of going to Hopsville Tuesday night. There's a band, and I want to talk to Stephen and Jake about this pairing idea… That was followed by the gritting teeth emoji to symbolize nerves.

"What?" she said aloud. Then typed, *Wow, look at you go!*

A couple laughing emoji came then, followed by *Got some advice from a super-hot consultant who thought it might be good for business...*

And that made her laugh out loud. It also gave her another little thrill, and she felt that flutter low in her body. *Oh, really? A super-hot consultant, you say?* She followed that up with a thinking emoji.

Super, super hot. And a great kisser.

Okay, what? Hannah had gone from playing it cool to overtly flirting in the space of about two minutes. Riley wondered, wanted to question it, but also didn't want it to stop. She typed.

I feel that being a great kisser is very important to being a good business consultant, but I could be wrong...

The dots bounced. Then, *Interesting take. How many of your clients have you actually kissed?*

Riley laughed out loud in her empty room. *Exactly one.*

More bouncing dots. *Ah, so then you're not that good a business consultant, huh?* That was followed by three winking emoji.

She laughed harder. *No, I suck.*

Hannah sent a laughing emoji, then said, *Why are you asking about Tuesday?*

This was it. Riley nibbled the inside of her cheek as she typed, *Maybe I'll go with you to Hopsville.*

No dots bounced. No words came. There was nothing for what felt like an hour but was surely only a minute or two.

Finally, Hannah's text came. *You're coming back here?*

Riley grinned as she typed. *I said I would, didn't I?*

Hannah's next text was simple, and it was followed by several smiling emoji.

You did.

Hannah's nerves were shot, and it was only Monday.

She sat at the dining room table at her parents' house, having been invited at the last minute, and deciding it was quiet enough at the shop to leave Michael alone—something she wasn't a hundred percent comfortable with, but was giving a shot: letting others take over for a bit. A plate of pork tenderloin, mashed potatoes, and green beans that looked so good they might've been a photo on a food website sat in front of her. She had a fork in her hand. She hadn't eaten a bite.

"All right. What's going on?" Her mother looked at her, one eyebrow arched in that way that had said *I can read you like a book and you're not telling me something* since Hannah was four years old.

Her father sat across from her, watching as he chewed. He was very wise, and his wisdom was clearly telling him to leave the inquiry to his wife. He cut another piece of pork, put it into his mouth, and watched her and his daughter.

Hannah knew better than to try and lie to her mother. It never worked out—her mother was too smart, knew her too well, and Hannah was a godawful liar anyway. She sighed and met her mother's eyes with her own. "Riley's coming back to town tomorrow."

Her mother's surprise was clear but also happy. "She is? Wow. That's great." She took a bite of potatoes and studied Hannah's face as she chewed. "Okay, so why is this something that has you looking all worried?"

Hannah grimaced, and words were suddenly unavailable. Her green beans became very interesting.

"Oh," her mother said, nodding with realization. "I see."

"You do?" her father asked, now looking from his wife to his daughter and back. "What do you see? Fill me in."

Hannah grinned. She couldn't help it. She met her mother's gaze, and she was grinning, too.

"Your daughter is smitten," her mother said.

"Ugh. Don't say *smitten*," Hannah said. "That's such a stupid word."

"With the Shaw girl?" her father asked.

Her mom nodded. "With the Shaw girl."

Her dad poked his fork at her. "You could do worse than the Shaw girl. She's a good kid."

"I know, Dad," Hannah said softly.

"So, what's got you so uncertain?" her mom asked.

She didn't want to get into this. Did she? Her parents would worry. They always worried. She was their little girl. They never worried about Kyle, but Hannah was a different story. She never really understood if it was being a girl or being the baby of the family or what, but they always seemed to be extra protective of her. And if she told them her concerns when it came to Riley, they'd both switch into bodyguard mode. If there was one thing she'd learned from the only boyfriend she'd had (or tried to have) in high school, it was that bodyguard mode was exhausting—not to mention it stepped all over any privacy she might think she was entitled to. No, it was better not to get into it with them just yet.

"Just some work stuff," she said, and felt immediately guilty for lying to her parents. "You know how I get when somebody tries to tell me how to run my business." She shrugged and dug into her potatoes, even though eating was the last thing on her mind.

Her mother looked at her for a long moment, and Hannah knew she was deciding whether or not to push. Apparently, she decided against it, and she asked about the latest flavors instead.

Hannah's relief was palpable as she dove into talking about her favorite thing: new popcorn flavors. "Well, the last two new ones I came up with were savory, so I think it's time to invent a new sweet." She looked from her mom to her dad. "I'm open to suggestions."

Her father shrugged. He always did. He liked leaving flavor invention up to her. Then he'd be all amazed and supportive when she brought him a sample. He was one of her favorite guinea pigs. While he liked about ninety percent of her flavors, he'd also tell her if one didn't work—like the twice-baked potato one she'd tried on him last year which, according to him, tasted like "cardboard with fake cheese sprinkled on it." Her dad did not mince words.

Her mother, on the other hand, loved to offer up suggestions. "What about some kind of coffee-type flavor?" she asked. At Hannah's dubious look, she waved a hand in the air like she was wiping it clean. "No, no, not overtly coffee, but coffee-*like*. Maybe mocha latte or something. You know? Like, it would be mostly chocolate and cream, but with just a tiny hint of coffee." She held her thumb and forefinger up a scant millimeter apart to demonstrate.

"Hmm. I don't hate that idea," Hannah said, and it was true.

"Also, I'm still waiting for peanut butter cup popcorn." Her mother punctuated that with a verbal *harumph* that made her laugh.

"I know, I know, I need to get on that one."

"It would sell like crazy. I'm telling you."

And now Hannah's brain was swirling and—as almost always happened when a new flavor idea hit—she couldn't wait to experiment.

She helped her mother clear the table and load the dishwasher. Then she kissed her parents goodbye and headed back to Poptacular, where there were two customers that Michael was handling with a smile. Kaitlyn had gone back to college, and now he was the only one left. She should hire somebody else to help him, but the thought of placing an ad, scanning through applications, and doing interviews gave her heartburn.

She gave Michael a wave and headed into the back, where she started to gather ingredients. Chocolate, which she set to melting in a double boiler, peanut butter powder, which she thought might be easier to work with than actual peanut butter itself, salt. She set them all on the counter, set some fresh popcorn to popping, and got to work.

She had to remake the coating three times, and by that third batch, it was nearing ten at night, the shop had been closed and locked, and Michael had gone home, calling back to her that it "smells like Reese's peanut butter cups in here! Yum!" making her laugh through his exit.

"That's exactly what I want," she said quietly once she was alone. And now?

She poured the third pot of chocolate–peanut butter coating over the popcorn and let it tumble in the mixer. She watched, mesmerized, something she'd enjoyed doing ever since she was a kid and working there with her grandmother. She loved watching the popcorn mix and tumble and turn over on itself, continually changing, constantly shifting. It was hypnotizing.

The best thing about it was that it kept her thoughts from zeroing in on Riley. Riley's eyes. Riley's mouth. The way Riley kissed…

She smacked a hand over her face and scrubbed it as she sighed.

"Jesus Christ, I'm in trouble."

CHAPTER TWELVE

She's gonna think I'm not coming. She's gonna think I blew her off. Those were the only thoughts running through Riley's head as she drove. She'd had a blowout on the ride, had to wait for AAA to show up because she'd never changed a tire before, which was embarrassing, now that she thought about it. Could they take her lesbian card away for that? She'd lost almost two hours with that ordeal, and Hannah was already at Hopsville, probably thinking Riley didn't really give a shit, because Riley had texted but heard nothing back.

But she *did* give a shit.

And that was the current struggle, wasn't it? It had been since she'd left last week. The whole time, all she could think about was getting back to Sunset Valley—something she'd never dealt with before. And what the hell was she supposed to do with that?

For a Tuesday evening, Hopsville was hopping—for lack of a better word. The small parking lot was full, and Riley had to park on the street. She locked her car and went in, the volume of music and conversation assaulting her like a slap.

She stood in the doorway, letting her eyes adjust to the dim lighting, scanning the crowd—and it *was* a crowd. Good for Hopsville.

It didn't take long for her gaze to zero in. Finding Hannah wasn't hard, but it was surprising, because she stood in the midst of a small group of people. Not the first place Riley would've expected to find a quiet introvert in a bar. Yet there she was, laughing at something the redheaded guy next to her said, throwing her head back to expose her neck, her throat, and Riley's brain decided now was a good time to toss her a memory…the one where she ran her tongue over that long column of soft skin while Hannah's breathing noticeably increased…

Jesus Christ.

Riley gave herself a mental shake, doing her best to pull herself together, to maintain some goddamn professionalism here—and that's when Hannah's gaze met hers.

From across a crowded room, Riley thought, and it was so silly and so clichéd, and also so true. Because it was as if everything dropped away. Other people. Sound. All of it, gone. Nothing existed but the two of them. Hannah's expression softened, her eyes crinkled slightly at the corners as she smiled. Riley grinned back, feeling something inside her settle, and she began to weave through the crowd, sidling and sidestepping until she reached Hannah.

"Hi," she said and ran a hand down Hannah's arm.

"Hey, you." Hannah held her gaze. "I was beginning to wonder if you were gonna make it."

"I know. I'm so sorry. I texted you."

Hannah pulled out her phone, then grimaced. "Damn it. I knew I should've charged it up. Dead." She held it up for Riley to see, tipping it from side to side.

"I blew a tire."

"Ugh. Dude. That sucks." The redheaded guy. Up close, he was cute. Young. Standing very close to Hannah.

Riley tipped her head. "I don't think we've met."

Hannah stepped in. "Oh, sorry about that. Ashton—Ashton, was it?"

He nodded and leaned in close so she could hear him over the crowd. "Beene. Yeah. Ashton Beene." He held out his hand to Riley as Hannah said her name in introduction. "Nice to meet you, Riley." He pointed to two other guys and one girl in the rest of the group. "This is Sully, Danny, and Jessie."

Riley shook each hand with a nod of hello, then the three of them began a conversation on their own while Ashton kept his attention on Hannah.

"They all work with Kyle," Hannah said. "Over at the construction yard."

Riley nodded her understanding as Hannah said, "Riley went to school with Kyle." Ashton had to lean down and put his ear close to Hannah's mouth. Riley was surprised by the little zap of jealousy she felt right then. "They were just a couple years ahead of me."

"Oh, right." Ashton nodded like he'd known that. "Hey, get you a drink?" He looked at Hannah's empty beer glass, then at Riley.

Hannah looked right at her while handing her glass to Ashton. "Yeah, I'd take a refill. Riley?"

"I'd love a stout," she said.

"Coming right up." Ashton disappeared through the crowd, and Riley took the opportunity to move closer to Hannah.

"He hitting on you?" The question was out before Riley could even think about whether she should ask it.

"Like a Hollywood producer on his next ingenue." Hannah grinned and seemed to study her face. "Why? Bothering you?"

Riley shook her head. "No, not at all." *Lies.*

"No? Not even a little?" Hannah arched an eyebrow, and first, it did things to her, caused something to swirl around low in her body. Then it made Riley look more closely at her. What in the—

"Are you drunk?" She lowered her voice on the last word and said it with a grin.

In response, Hannah snort-laughed and held her thumb and forefinger very close together. "I'm a teensy bit tipsy," she said in a stage whisper, then laughed again. "I didn't eat before I came, and these microbrews have *a lot* of alcohol in them!"

"No kidding." Riley couldn't help but laugh at Hannah's wide-eyed look. "Do you want me to talk to Steve and Jacob for you?" she asked. "About the pairing?"

Hannah waved her off. "Already did."

"You did?"

Hannah nodded. "We're setting it up for early October, and if it goes well, we'll do another around Halloween."

"Seriously? That's great!"

"That's why I'm having beer. I'm celebrating." She used the stage whisper again, this time on the word *beer*, and it made Riley laugh. Hannah gave her a big grin then. Almost comically big, a little bit goofy, and Riley started laughing. Okay, so tipsy Hannah was adorable. Riley could admit that.

Ashton returned, carrying three beers in his large construction worker hands, and Riley and Hannah took theirs. Ashton held his up. "Cheers." He touched his glass to both of theirs but smiled widely at Hannah as she sipped.

You poor bastard, Riley thought, hiding her grin with her glass, and while she entertained in her mind how much fun it could be for her to make it clear which team Hannah batted for, all she did was step a little closer to Hannah. Was that sudden warmth radiating from her? Certainly felt like it was.

For the next fifteen or twenty minutes, she pretended to be interested in the things Ashton was saying, nodding and smiling, but a little bored. She was usually better at this, better at taking the reins—forcefully, if need be—from men who talked only about themselves, their jobs, their lives and experiences, as if none of the women present had anything nearly as important to say. Instead, though, she just stood there like an idiot because the thing she was most aware of was Hannah. Hannah's closeness, her hand holding her beer glass. She'd removed her usual hat and pulled her ponytail up higher on her head, and the smell of her strawberry shampoo blended in surprising symmetry with the scent of freshly popped popcorn that was simply part of who Hannah was. All of it combined into a cocktail of distraction for Riley.

"Right?" Hannah said, and then Riley realized she'd been talking to her.

"I'm sorry?" she said, giving herself a quick mental shake, trying to get her head back in the game.

Hannah's smile was amused. "I was just telling Ashton here about how you're helping me improve my bottom line on the popcorn shop."

Riley nodded, probably with way too much exuberance. "Yes! Yes, absolutely. Working hard on that." Oh, God, who was she? What was the matter with her? When did she lose all power to be a normal human being having a normal conversation?

Hannah watched her, lips rolled in just slightly, as if she was trying not to openly laugh. She waited a beat, then turned back to Ashton with a nod and said with almost exaggerated enunciation, "Yes. Working hard on that."

Riley looked all around for a hole to crawl into. She prayed for an alien spaceship to come beam her up. Maybe there was a giant rock someplace she could dive under. Could the ground just swallow her up now, please? She was just thinking that when she heard Ashton's next words, spoken low and conspiratorially to Hannah.

"Hey, you wanna get outta here?" His green eyes—they really were a great color—held a sparkle, and his smile was wide. He was sure Hannah would say yes. One hundred percent. It was so obvious, and Riley stopped beating herself up so she could watch, too invested to look away.

"Actually," Hannah said without missing a beat, then ran her hand down Riley's arm and entwined their fingers. "I'm already getting out of here with her." She half shrugged with a grimace and added, "I'm sorry, though. You're super sweet."

To Ashton's credit, he smiled and nodded, then turned his attention to Riley with an apologetic half grin, half grimace. "Can't blame a guy for trying, right?"

"I cannot," Riley said with a shake of her head, the heat from Hannah's hand traveling up her arm.

Ashton slid his phone out of the back pocket of his jeans and took a look. "Crap, I'd probably better go anyway. Getting kinda late and I have an early job tomorrow."

Whether he was lying to save face, Riley wasn't sure, so she didn't point out that the late hour and his early job didn't seem to matter when he thought he'd be taking Hannah home. She let it slide, not because she didn't want to embarrass him, but because if there was one thing she was not, it was a sore winner.

She got the girl.

The least she could do was let poor Ashton leave with some of his dignity. She watched as he downed the rest of his beer, leaned into the trio of his pals and said goodbye to them, then leaned in and kissed Hannah on the cheek. He shot Riley a look that seemed to be one of respect, turned his head and craned his neck as if on a hunt for the door, then headed that way. Riley watched him go.

The two of them stood quietly for a moment.

"Well, that was fun," Riley said, and when she turned to look at Hannah, what she saw yanked the breath right out of her lungs.

Hannah's eyes were a little bit hooded. She still held Riley's hand and clearly had no intention of letting it go. She sipped her beer, her gaze never leaving Riley's. The heat and intensity of that look sent a jolt of arousal through Riley's body until it settled between her legs as a gentle but insistent throbbing.

Hannah finished up her beer and set the empty glass on the nearest table. She tugged on Riley's hand as she said, "Come with me."

Riley had only had a couple sips of her beer, but she set it down next to Hannah's glass and walked—or more accurately, was led—out the door. "Where are we going?"

Hannah didn't stop walking but did glance over her shoulder with that same intensity in her eyes as she said, "My place."

❖

Alcohol made Hannah brave.

It also made her a little bit reckless, which was why she didn't drink very often or very much. Tonight, though, was different. She was definitely tipsy, and it was definitely giving her some false bravado, some extra courage, but it wasn't clouding her judgment at all. No, she hadn't had *that* much to drink.

She knew exactly what she was doing.

And she also knew why, though that was something she didn't want to deal with right now. No, that would come later. For now, the only thing that mattered was Riley and that little spark of jealousy she'd seen when Ashton was hitting on her.

Riley didn't want somebody else flirting with Hannah. Quite the realization.

And now there was no turning back.

"What about my car?" Riley said.

"You can get it in the morning. It'll be fine." She led Riley by the hand, leading her along the darkened stretch of Main Street. It was a gorgeous fall evening, breezy and the tiniest bit cool, though not cool enough to make them cold. Hannah was pretty sure nothing could make her cold right now. It felt like her blood was hot as it rushed through her veins, spreading a fire through her body. Up ahead loomed the giant maple tree in Mrs. Kessler's yard, and Hannah didn't even stop to think twice. She tugged Riley right up to that tree, turned her so her back was against the trunk, and crushed her mouth to Riley's. The little gasp of surprise from Riley only served to ratchet her arousal up higher, which she didn't think was even possible.

They kissed deeply, Riley giving back as much as she was getting, which thrilled Hannah, and they stayed against that tree for a long while, until Mrs. Kessler's porch light came on. Hannah giggled and tugged Riley by the hand until they were headed down the street again.

They didn't say much. Each time she glanced back at Riley, there was that smile, along with a clear excitement in her eyes. Hannah was good with no words right now. She wasn't sure she could come up with anything worthwhile to say anyway, so they just kept going.

The house that held Hannah's apartment wasn't terribly far from the popcorn shop, and it was even closer to Hopsville, so the walk didn't take long. Within minutes, she was sliding the key into her front door on the second floor, Riley pressed against her back, her hands on Hannah's waist, both of them ready to fall through the doorway.

The door behind them opened.

"Hey, Han," Parker said. She held a plastic bowl labeled with the Velveeta mac and cheese logo and scraped it with her spoon.

"Oh, hey, Parker," Hannah said, brushing her hair out of her face and feeling suddenly breathless.

"What's up?"

"Oh, you know, just…going inside." She indicated Riley. "With my friend here. Riley."

Parker lifted her chin in a gesture of hello. "Hey."

"Hey," Riley said. Her hands were still on Hannah's waist, and Hannah was sure their lips were wet and kiss-swollen.

Hannah wondered if it was possible to simply spontaneously combust right where she was standing. She was hot and anxious and jittery and wanted her hands on Riley. Now. "So, yeah, I'll see you later, okay?" Without waiting for a response from Parker, she pushed the door open, and Riley followed her inside.

She barely got it closed before Riley turned the tables, and it was Hannah's turn to gasp a small *oof* as her back hit the door and Riley's mouth crashed into hers.

The same question that had been plaguing her for a week shot through her head then: How long had it been since she'd been kissed like this? How long? Months? Years? Ever? She couldn't think straight enough to come up with an accurate answer. All she knew was that Riley kissed her exactly the way she'd imagined she would in all her fantasies. Deeply. Thoroughly. Slowly for a bit, then with more insistence. Hannah felt like her legs were made of Jell-O, and any second now they'd stop holding her up.

Wrenching her mouth from Riley's, she took a moment to look in her eyes, those gorgeous blue eyes that had gone slightly dark, were now hooded and so goddamn sexy, Hannah felt a surge of arousal, dampening her underwear and causing her to grab Riley by the hand and lead her to the small bedroom.

Thank God she was a neat person, because when she'd left this morning, Hannah had no idea she'd be bringing somebody home, especially not Riley. The bed was made and there were no clothes lying around. She turned Riley so her back was to the bed, and then they were kissing again as she walked them back until Riley's legs hit the mattress and she sat. Hannah took that opportunity to straddle her lap, one knee on either side of Riley's thighs.

Oh, God, yeah, that was perfect. That position was such a fucking turn-on. She held Riley's face in both hands and kissed her senseless. She could feel Riley's hands on her, everywhere. Her back, her hips, her thighs. Finally, air became a necessity. Riley held Hannah's face until their eyes met.

"Are you sure about this?" Riley asked on a whisper.

All Hannah could do was nod, feeling as if the power of speech had left her long ago. She took a breath and found some words. "I'm sure. Are you?"

A smile grew, blossomed across Riley's beautiful face. "Absolutely."

Making love with Riley was everything Hannah had ever dreamed, ever fantasized, and more. So much more. It was filled with dichotomies: giving and taking, gentle and demanding, taking control and allowing control. They fit like the proverbial two puzzle pieces, and while Hannah had always suspected they'd be good together, she was *so* far off. They were mind-blowing together.

Riley's body was astonishingly beautiful, which shouldn't have come as a surprise but somehow did. She was long and lean, but curvy. Her breasts in Hannah's hands were like some kind of fever dream, and the feel of them cranked up Hannah's arousal to heights she didn't think were possible. And the sounds! Oh, God, the sounds Riley made when Hannah sucked in a nipple or ran her nails down Riley's bare back were a huge turn-on all by themselves. Riley was a woman who was very much in control of herself, so being able to coax sounds out of her that seemed to indicate the opposite—it was one hell of an aphrodisiac for Hannah.

The push-pull was intense and oh so sexy. One minute Hannah was on top, in control, pulling those sounds from Riley, running her hands, her tongue all over Riley's body. Suddenly, in the next minute, she'd find herself on her back, Riley above her, looking down at her with such want on her face, it made Hannah want to cry.

The hours went by like that, filled with giving and then taking, with each of them trading positions. Hannah's fingers were inside Riley, making her cry out. Then Riley's head was between Hannah's legs, making her grasp for whatever she could reach—sheets, the headboard, Riley's hair.

By the time two o'clock in the morning rolled around, they were breathless, sweaty, and spent. Riley lay on her back, Hannah on top of her, both of them breathing raggedly.

"Holy shit," Riley said on a whisper.

"Same," said Hannah, smiling against the warmth of Riley's chest.

Riley lifted her head and waited for Hannah to do the same. When their eyes met, Riley asked, "Where the hell have you been all my life?"

Hannah laughed softly. "Right here, dummy. I've been right here the whole time."

Riley dropped her head back to the pillow, shook it slowly back and forth, and repeated herself. "Holy shit."

Hannah laid her head back down with a smile on her face, and ran a finger over Riley's heated skin, tracing a path along her collarbone, around her shoulder, and back. Completely sober now, she wanted to talk, knew they should talk. But it was only a matter of seconds before Riley's breathing became deep and even, indicating she'd fallen asleep. Hannah was wrapped up in her arms, but she was able to reach down for the sheet and pull it up over them. Riley shifted slightly but didn't wake up, and Hannah settled in.

Her smile stayed on her face as she drifted off, in joyous wonder that two decades later, teenage Hannah was finally getting what she'd wanted most: to fall asleep cradled in Riley Shaw's arms.

❖

Riley had always been an early riser.

Even as a kid, she was always up and eating her cereal in front of the television before her mother even made an appearance. That had carried into adulthood, and it was rare for her to do any kind of sleeping in, even if she'd been up late the night before doing…things. Super-sexy things.

That morning was no different. The first peeks of sunshine poked through the window, and Riley floated up to the surface of sleep before opening her eyes. The first thing she noted was the weight on her body. It was everywhere. Her chest, her shoulder, her legs. And then her memory caught up, and she recalled the previous night's activities, the way Hannah had led them to where they were now, how incredible it had been. She had to admit, sleeping with Hannah Kramer hadn't been on her bingo card, yet here they were, both still naked, her body covered with a sheet and Hannah's body.

Hannah's body.

Good Lord, she was beautiful. How had Riley not expected that? She'd always thought of Hannah as very attractive, so why did her amazing body come as a surprise? Was it because she kept it mostly hidden under baggy T-shirts, an apron, and a baseball cap? She was stunning, and Riley remembered now the moment Hannah had been fully undressed in front of her last night. Her breath had caught in her throat at the sight of the shapely legs, the rounded hips, the breasts that were more than she'd expected. Jesus Christ, Riley had practically devoured her with her mouth. She'd wanted to. She'd wanted to taste every inch of her. And she had.

A new discovery: Hannah slept like the dead. Riley had to stifle her soft laughter as she moved and slid and shuffled her body out from under Hannah's and Hannah never moved or made a sound. Once upright, Riley covered her more thoroughly, found a pair of joggers and a hoodie in a drawer and a pair of sneakers that fit, brushed her teeth with her finger, pulled her hair into a messy bun, and headed out the door in search of coffee.

Downstairs in the foyer, she ran into that kid from across the hall, the girl. What was her name? She racked her brain for several seconds before it came to her. Parker. She was sitting on the porch swing, pushing it slowly with one foot and looking down at her phone.

"Hey, Parker," she said as she shut the door behind her.

"That's Hannah's hoodie." Parker didn't smile at her.

Riley looked down at the gray sweatshirt with a faded imprint of an otter. "Yeah, I just grabbed something to throw on, you know?"

"You spent the night." It was a statement, not a question.

"I did. Yes." Why was she starting to sweat?

"Mm-hmm." Parker looked her up and down as she played with the nose ring in her right nostril.

"I'm, uh, gonna go get some coffee."

"Mm-hmm." Back to her phone.

Judgment. That's what she felt. What the hell? Why was this teenager getting under her skin? She gave herself a mental shake. "Okay, see ya then." She skipped down the steps and hurried up the walk, putting as much distance between herself and Parker as she could. Man, that was weird.

Once she was out of sight of the house, she slowed her pace and chuckled internally at her own freak-out over a teenager. Whatever. She refocused her attention on the morning. Sunny and a bit chilly but refreshing. A few houses in the neighborhood already had autumn decorations out—cornstalks and pumpkins and such—and even though Riley thought mid-September was a bit early, she appreciated the exuberance for her favorite season.

She always forgot how fresh and clean the air in Sunset Valley was. Brisk and cool, lovely, invigorating. She inhaled deeply the scents of earth and falling leaves. It didn't take her long before she hit Main Street and headed toward the Coffee Cup, which was clearly bustling, given all the activity in and out the front door. Shana must do a decent business. She went inside and stood in line.

Shana was working the counter, something Riley always liked to see—the owner or CEO or boss doing the same work their employees did. Shana smiled and made small talk and seemed to know almost everybody, which made sense in a town as small as Sunset Valley. When it was her turn, Riley stepped to the counter with a smile.

"Morning, Shana."

Shana took one look at her and said, "Well, so much for not mixing business and pleasure."

Riley frowned. "I'm sorry?"

"I gave Hannah that hoodie for Christmas."

Riley cleared her throat. "Oh." She could feel the heat climbing up her neck.

"What can I get you?" She smiled, and it wasn't exactly icy, but it wasn't as warm as the smiles Riley had watched her give others. "Pumpkin spice for Hannah. And for you?"

Riley cleared her throat again and was annoyed at herself for it. "Um, just a dark roast, cream and one sugar."

Shana nodded. "Coming right up."

Riley had no reason to be embarrassed. Or to feel like squirming. She'd done nothing wrong, and Hannah was a grown-ass woman who could make her own decisions. So why then did she feel like she'd just stolen somebody's puppy?

"Here you go." Shana set two to-go cups in a paper tray, slid it in front of her, and Riley handed over her credit card. Shana rang up the purchase, handed the card back, and said, "Tell Hannah to text me."

"Will do. Thanks." Riley couldn't get out of there fast enough, and she almost ran into Kyle doing it.

"Whoa, there, Speedy McSpeederson," he said with a laugh, arms raised as he narrowly avoided getting coffee sloshed all over him. "Where are you off to in such a hurry?" His eyes narrowed slightly. "And in my sister's clothes."

Fucking small towns. Riley kept walking. "To your sister's place," she called over her shoulder as she kept moving as if she was in a speed-walking race.

Her intention had been to get some food as well, but Jesus Christ, would everybody in town recognize she was wearing Hannah's clothes? All she wanted to do was get back, and she picked up her pace, stopped to grab her car, and headed back to Hannah's.

Thankfully, Parker was no longer guarding the front door from the porch swing, and she was able to push her way into the building without any further comment on her state of dress. Once inside Hannah's apartment, she leaned her back against the door, sighed in relief, and just stood there.

It was quiet, and it smelled like Hannah.

Those were the first two things she noticed, and they somehow took away all the stress and nerves that had been building since she left. The blessed silence, apart from the clock on the wall in the kitchen, ticking softly, wrapped around her and calmed her. Hannah obviously hadn't woken up yet, so Riley carried the coffees into the bedroom, walking quietly.

Hannah was on her side, one bent arm cradling her head, the other thrown in front of her. The sheet stopped at her waist, leaving her upper body uncovered, there for Riley's eyes to feast on. She set the coffee tray on the dresser, quickly stripped out of all her clothes, and slid into bed behind Hannah, spooning up behind her. She buried her nose in Hannah's hair and inhaled deeply, smelling her strawberry shampoo, the warmth of sleep, and the lingering scent of sex still clinging to the sheets. She wrapped an arm around her, her thumb brushing over a nipple, and Hannah breathed in and turned in Riley's arms. She never opened her eyes and never said a word. She simply slid her hand around Riley's neck and pulled her in for a soul-searing kiss that ratcheted everything up again in a matter of seconds.

Had Riley ever been this turned on this quickly? By anyone in her life ever? No. The answer to that question was a resounding no, and she let herself sink into Hannah, into Hannah's soft mouth, into her warm body, let her hands roam, stroke, squeeze. She took over, sliding on top of Hannah, sucking on one nipple, then the other, until Hannah's hips were moving seemingly on their own, pushing up into her.

Riley blazed a trail with her mouth, her tongue, down Hannah's body, until she reached her legs. With a hand on each thigh, she pushed them open—not roughly, but not gently, because she had to have her, had to have Hannah. Now. Right now. She didn't bother with preamble or teasing. She didn't need to; Hannah was soaked. She dove in with lips and tongue and Hannah arched up with a cry that seemed to surprise them both. Riley grasped her hips, holding on as best as she could as Hannah undulated beneath her. She was salty and sweet and tangy and Riley couldn't get enough. When she shifted her grip and pushed her fingers inside, Hannah cried out again, grasped for the pillows around her head, and turned her face into one of them to muffle the sounds. That only made it sexier to Riley, who set up a rhythm between her fingers and her tongue until she and Hannah were moving as one.

"Oh God, oh God, oh God" were the only coherent, muffled words Hannah muttered before the explosion happened. Her hips rose up off the bed, taking Riley with them, and she held on as best she could, keeping her mouth pressed against Hannah's center, keeping her fingers buried deep inside and moving as she looked up Hannah's body and watched her climax.

It was the sexiest damn thing she'd ever seen.

Hannah came down slowly. First, her cries quieted, then her hips gradually settled back to the mattress. Her death grip on the pillow relaxed, and she threw her arm over her eyes as she blew out a big breath.

"Oh my God."

Riley laughed softly, and Hannah used the hand still in her hair to gently tug her.

"Come up here."

Taking her time, Riley slid her fingers out, which caused a little tremor in Hannah's legs she could feel. She crawled up Hannah's body, leaving soft kisses in her wake, and settled half on, half off her body. Their eyes met and their gazes held for a long moment. Riley touched her lips to Hannah's, never looking away. "Good morning," she whispered.

"Damn right it is." Hannah's dark eyes held a storm of emotion as Riley stroked a fingertip along her cheek. She could see it, no effort required. Suddenly, Hannah perked up. "Do I smell coffee?"

Riley laughed. "And moment broken."

Hannah covered her eyes with her hand, joining her in her laughter. "Sorry! I have no control over Morning Me when coffee is involved."

Still laughing, Riley slid out of bed and retrieved the coffees from the dresser. When she turned back, Hannah's expression had changed back to what could only be described as lust-filled. She pushed herself to a sitting position as she devoured Riley with her eyes.

"God, you're gorgeous," she said quietly. "Look at you."

Riley could feel herself blush—and it wasn't something she did on a regular basis—but Hannah seemed to hold some kind of power over that. She swallowed. "Thank you." She handed Hannah her cup, took her own, and settled back under the sheets, her back against the headboard.

Hannah sipped and moaned her approval.

"So," Riley began, knowing she needed to let Hannah in on the morning's activities. "I went to get coffee." She felt more than saw Hannah squint at her.

"Yes," she said, drawing the word out. "I didn't think it materialized out of thin air."

Riley took a breath. "Yeah, but I went out wearing your clothes." She pointed to the pile on the floor. "Specifically, that hoodie."

Hannah sat up straighter so she could see the shirt Riley was referring to, then sat back. "Ah." She took another sip before continuing. "So, Shana knows you slept here."

"So does your brother."

Hannah's eyebrows went up, but that was the extent of her surprise. "Oh. Well, okay then. I guess that saves us from awkward conversations." She shrugged and sipped again.

"You're okay?"

"Are you kidding me?" Hannah met her gaze. "Why wouldn't I be? The woman I've fantasized about for years spent the night with me last night. I'm great."

Riley didn't know how to respond to that, didn't even know for sure what to feel about it. But Hannah's response, her casual tone, relaxed the nerves working inside her and she let out a breath. "Okay. Okay, good."

"Are *you* okay?"

Riley took a moment to actually think about the question before she slowly smiled and gave her a nod. "I am."

"Well. Glad we got that cleared up." Another sip. "What should we do today?"

CHAPTER THIRTEEN

The next few weeks flew by in a whirlwind of marketing and popcorn and limb-melting sex.

The popcorn and beer pairing at Hopsville was such a success, the brothers asked Hannah to do one every month. Riley had helped her find a reasonably priced supplier that would do custom popcorn tins for her, so she added that to her list of sales products. She also ordered in some holiday-themed ones that were already starting to move off her shelves.

Michael—who she had to consciously *not* call Squeaky Boy to his face, thanks to Riley—had come up with a fun, playful window display that featured a red-and-white checked tablecloth over a small, round table, chairs pulled out as if ready for somebody to sit, and a bowl of popcorn on its side, with its contents spilled across the table. He changed the décor on the table to match the season or the impending holiday of the month, and as she watched him now, he was packing away the Halloween stuff, switching it out for the fake Thanksgiving dinner items Hannah had found on Etsy. The floor still needed replacing, but Bradley McFarland hadn't returned her calls about it, so she'd put that on the back burner. For now.

Her mood was light. Cheerful. Happy. Riley was coming into town tonight after traveling to Cleveland for work. Hannah hadn't seen her in over two weeks, and she was feeling serious withdrawal symptoms. She didn't particularly enjoy the fact that sex with Riley felt like some kind of drug she'd become seriously addicted to, but there it was.

She was watching the mixer spin and getting ready to add the pot of melted chocolate sauce to the fresh popcorn when she heard the bell over the door tinkle happily. A glance up told her it was Shana, who waved at her, nodded to Michael, and headed her way.

"Chilly out there," Shana said, giving her body a shivery shake. "Holy crap, it smells good back here."

"My new candy cane popcorn," Hannah said with pride as she emptied the pot and set it back down. "Gonna give that a minute to mix, then add the crushed candy canes." She nodded to the bowl of red-and-white candy pieces in the bowl on the counter. She grinned at her friend. "It'll be ready for test-tasting within the hour."

Shana threw her a salute. "Taste tester reporting for duty, ma'am."

Hannah laughed and they stood for a moment, mesmerized by the mixer, reveling in the wonderful scent of chocolate mint.

"You're happy." Shana said it out of nowhere, and when Hannah glanced at her, she was studying her. "I can tell."

"Oh, you can? How?"

"Well, first of all, I'm fluent in Hannah. So there." When Hannah grinned at her, she went on. "You smile all the time, even when nobody's talking to you. Even when you're working. Or just standing here like you are now."

Hannah continued to grin in amusement. "And I didn't do that before?"

"Nope. You concentrated before. Like this." Shana furrowed her brow and narrowed her eyes in an exaggerated look of focus.

"I never looked like that," Hannah said, gasping with humor.

"You did. Trust me. And now it's this." She fixed her face into a comical grin as she picked up the empty pot and moved it to the sink, smiling the whole time.

Hannah burst out laughing. "I object to that impression."

"Listen, it's very accurate. Ask anybody." Shana laughed with her. "Michael," she called to the front. "Who am I?" She picked the pot up again and gave a repeat performance.

"That's easy. You're Hannah." His smile was crooked and cute, and Hannah pointed at him.

"I will fire your ass so fast," she said, teasing him.

They all laughed, and as Hannah grabbed the bowl of crushed candy, she tried to remember a time when it felt this cheerful in Poptacular. A while, to say the least. She added the candy to the mixer, and it tumbled and blended with the chocolate-covered popcorn, adding festive pops of red to the brown and white color scheme. A generous sprinkle of salt went in next. She cleared her throat, knowing that Shana wasn't wrong and that there was nothing wrong with admitting it. With a tip of her head, she said to her, "I *am* happy."

Shana stepped close and put an arm around her shoulders. "I'm so glad." She made a show of looking around. "And where is the source of this happiness?"

Hannah felt her cheeks heat up at the reference to Riley. "She'll be here this evening." With a sigh, she added, "I can't wait. It's been two weeks, and I'm getting the shakes."

"So, things are going well?"

"They are." She wanted to ask about all the questions, but she knew what the answer would be. Shana was just looking out for her, as was Kyle, as were her parents, all of whom had asked similar, gently probing questions. They were looking out for her—but also likely wondering why she wasn't bringing Riley around, to dinner, to visit, to hang. She sighed quietly and kept her eyes on the tumbling popcorn as she spoke. "I'm just…kind of keeping her to myself for a while. You know?" She glanced at Shana, hoping to see understanding on her face. "I've never had this, and I don't even know what *this* is. I just want to—" She lifted her hands, palms up, and shrugged. "Bask. I want to bask in the glow of this…thing."

"'This thing'?" Shana asked with a soft chuckle. "Such romantic words."

Hannah joined her laughter. "I know. I don't know what to call it yet. Sex fest? Dating?"

"Relationship?"

At the mention of that word, Hannah gritted her teeth together and made a face. No, they didn't call it that. Not yet, at least. They hadn't really discussed it, and she couldn't put her finger on why quite yet, but it seemed like a taboo subject to Riley. "I don't…think that's it right now. Yet." She hadn't said that out loud. To anybody.

Shana seemed to take that in and digest it for a moment before she spoke. "You're okay, though? Like, tell me the truth. Are you really doing all right?"

Hannah grasped Shana's arm and squeezed it with what she hoped was a reassuring smile. "I'm great, Shay. I promise you. My business is finally on the upswing. I've got a list of new flavor ideas. And I have a beautiful woman that I like a lot who sleeps over often." She laughed to disguise how she swallowed the words *and that I'm falling hard for* before they could escape her lips and hover in the air between them. "I'm great."

"Okay." Shana nodded and seemed relieved. "Good."

Hannah let go of her arm and reached to turn off the mixer. As she pulled the big pot off and dumped the popcorn onto the drying rack, she added, "And you can tell my big brother if he has questions, he can ask me himself instead of sending you to do his dirty work." She shot Shana a grin to take out any sting her words might have.

Shana held her hands up like a robbery victim. "I don't know what you're talking about."

"Liar." Gloves on, Hannah sifted the popcorn, breaking up clumps and spreading it out. It smelled divine. She scooped up a bunch and put it into a bowl, which she held out to Shana. "What's the verdict?"

They both reached in and grabbed a handful, tasted. One thing she appreciated about Shana was her honesty. If something didn't taste right, she wouldn't lie to Hannah, she'd tell her. But today, her big brown eyes went wide, then closed as she hummed her unmistakable approval.

"Jesus God, that's delicious." Another handful. "Mmm. Fabulous. The salty sweet of it is perfect. That's gonna be a hit."

Hannah couldn't keep the smile of pride off her face. "Yeah? You think I should've used milk chocolate instead of dark? I wavered."

Shana shook her head. "No. No, the dark chocolate complements the mint better. In my opinion."

"I trust your palate," Hannah said. "And I have to agree with you."

Shana found herself a bag and scooped some into it. "I'm telling you." She pointed at the popcorn. "Stock up, baby." She spun the bag and fastened a twist tie around it, then turned and caught Hannah off guard with a hug. "I love you," she said quietly.

"Love you, too," Hannah said, her voice muffled against Shana's shoulder.

Shana let go and turned away quickly. She wasn't really a hugger, or even an emotional person, so the hug was a surprise. To both of them, apparently, as Shana hurried toward the front door and, without looking back, lifted the bag of popcorn in goodbye. "I'll be back for more of this!"

Hannah laughed and watched her friend go. Michael met her eyes and smiled, and she smiled back at him. "Hey, come here and taste this," she said to him.

"I thought you'd never ask," he said as he practically vaulted over the counter. "The smell's been making my mouth water for almost an hour."

❖

There were not a lot of places more gorgeous than Sunset Valley in the fall. Riley had always thought so, could clearly recall her mother oohing and ahhing over the colors of the leaves, but it was made even more clear to her as she drove into town that early November. The rolling hills treated her to a dazzling display of bright oranges, reds, and yellows as far as the eye could see. Once upon a time, she'd known from living there that some years were more colorful than others, and that it usually depended on whether it had been a wet or dry summer, but she couldn't remember the reasoning now. All she knew was that her drive had been spectacular.

Now, as she coasted down Main Street, she could see that though it was still technically fall, and the trees still had most of their leaves, the town was in flux, shifting from fall and Halloween decorations to Thanksgiving and holiday decorations. The pumpkins that had been scattered around town like nuts on a sundae had been replaced with cornucopias and inflatable smiling turkeys and pilgrim hats.

Rolling her neck around on her shoulders, she heard a pop and grimaced. Long time in the car. She hadn't changed or even stopped at her apartment in Boston. She'd simply grabbed her bag, headed to the parking garage, and hit the road, still in her suit.

She was fucking exhausted.

But then the bright green sign for Poptacular came into view, and all her fatigue seemed to vanish like steam off a lake in the early morning sunshine. Just dissipated. The smile came all on its own.

As soon as she pushed through the door, setting off the little bell, she was met with the most mouthwatering scent of chocolate and mint, and her stomach reminded her—somewhat aggressively, if the loud rumble was any indication—that she hadn't eaten since breakfast.

Hannah was in the back, and she turned her cap-covered head to see who'd come in. When recognition hit, her entire face lit up, Riley could see it from across the whole shop. Whatever Hannah was working on was dropped instantly as she hurried around the counter and threw herself into Riley's arms. They spun like the movie poster shot in the latest rom-com.

"Oh my God, am I happy to see you," Hannah said, then kissed her right on the lips, right there in the shop, in front of Squeaky Boy and two customers and God and anybody else who might be walking by at that moment.

Riley loved it.

She set Hannah down and touched a hand to her face. "You smell like popcorn." She grinned at her.

"What? That's crazy talk," Hannah said, then took her by the hand and led her behind the counter to the back. She handed her a bowl of popcorn that was as fresh as possible because the bowl itself was warm, and said, "Be right back."

Riley watched as Hannah headed back out front to give Squeaky Boy a hand, as the customers had questions. She could look at her a little differently now, though she supposed that was true for anybody you'd had sex with. She knew what was under those modest clothes. She knew that the baggy joggers and shapeless T-shirt and stained apron hid a figure that was not just pleasing but fucking hot, if she was being honest. She knew that tucked up under that hat was thick, silky wheat-colored hair that smelled like strawberries. Well, before that scent was chased away by popcorn. She knew what Hannah looked like when her body arched in pleasure and how her eyes hooded when she was aroused and how she gasped quietly the first time Riley's fingers touched her center.

She swallowed hard now, feeling a dampness beneath her trousers, and she smiled softly as she took a handful of popcorn and tossed it into her mouth and— *Holy shit, that's good.* Her taste buds chased away every other thought.

The customers left with three bags of three different flavors, and Hannah returned to the back, smiling. She reached out and touched Riley's face with her fingertips. "I missed you," she said quietly.

"Me too." She glanced down at the almost-empty bowl. "This is fabulous, by the way."

"A new flavor for Christmas. I was just experimenting and was going to save it until next month, but as you can smell..." Hannah waved her hand around to indicate the air.

"First thing I noticed when I came in."

"People asked about it and I started handing out samples and now there are requests." Her brown eyes went wide. "*Actual requests!*" She moved to a spot on the wall where a list of names was taped.

"Are you serious? That's incredible, baby. Wow." She ran a hand down Hannah's arm.

Hannah took a deep breath and blew it out. "So, I thought we'd go out to Chisel and Stone for dinner. Thoughts?"

Chisel and Stone was elegant and classy, and the food was amazing, and Riley wanted none of it. She sighed quietly. "I'm so tired. Can we just go back to your place and order in or something?"

Was that a zap of disappointment that shot across Hannah's face? It came and went so quickly, Riley wasn't sure. Hannah nodded and smiled. "Of course we can. Movie on the couch?"

"Ugh, that sounds divine," she said, letting her head drop back between her shoulders. When she looked back up, she reached for Hannah and pulled her into a hug. "Thanks, baby."

"Welcome." They parted and Hannah reached for her blazer, tugged on a lapel. "As sexy as you look, I can't imagine you're comfy still in your work clothes. Why don't you head back to my place, change, shower, whatever you want. Get cozy. I'll pick up Thai on my way home?"

"I could not think of a better evening." She leaned forward and caught Hannah's lips with her own, kissing her softly.

Hannah fished her keys out of her bag in the office and gave them to Riley, grasping her hand as she took them. "I'm glad you're here. I'll be home by seven."

She kissed Hannah once more, gobbled one more handful of the chocolate mint–flavored popcorn, and headed for the door, tossing a wave to Squeaky Boy on her way out.

She wanted to clean up and change, eat some Thai food, and have her way with a very naked Hannah. Not necessarily in that order.

❖

It was a testament to the power of Hannah's racing brain that she had trouble sleeping, because her body was utterly exhausted. Her muscles felt like Jell-O, her center still felt slightly swollen, and her nipples were sore. She sat up in bed, back against the headboard as Riley snored softly next to her, and took some time to study her in the moonlight that still bathed her bedroom in its glow, despite it being closer to morning than night.

Riley was beautiful. That was probably the most obvious statement a person could make about her. Right now, she slept on her stomach—something Hannah had never been comfortable doing. Her boobs got in the way, and thinking that thought made her grin. Riley had gorgeous breasts, but they were smaller than Hannah's, and she watched her sleep now, one arm tucked up under the pillow, her head turned toward Hannah. All that dark hair fanned out across the white of the sheets, and Hannah had to consciously *not* reach out to sift it through her fingers, knowing how soft it was, knowing it smelled like coconuts and the beach.

There was something akin to relief when Riley's eyes were closed. Hannah wasn't sure if it was the color, that clear azure blue, or if it was something else, but looking into those eyes made it feel like Riley could see right into her brain. Into her thoughts, into her soul. With Riley sleeping, Hannah could watch her openly without feeling exposed to her.

Riley's other hand was stretched out across Hannah's lap, and Hannah looked down at it. The throbbing in her center increased in intensity as she thought about all the things that hand had done to her in the previous hours, how it had cradled her breasts, dug into her hair, rolled her nipples, spread her thighs, slicked through her hot wetness, pushed into her body, and taken her to heights she'd never reached before. She kept her eyes on that hand because if she moved her gaze to Riley's mouth and started thinking about what *that* had done to her, she might orgasm again, right there on her own, just sitting there in her bed, just from memory.

She stifled a groan, telling herself that if she was going to lie there awake, thinking about sex wasn't really the most productive use of her time. What she *wanted* to think about was popcorn.

So she tried.

Hard.

But new flavors kept morphing back into sex. She'd think about popcorn, and she'd envision a hand grabbing a handful of it, and then the hand would turn out to be Riley's hand, then it would reach for her and—

"Goddamn it." She whispered the curse, sending it out into the quiet of the night, the silence of her room. Riley had filled her head. She was taking up much more space than Hannah had allotted her, as if she was growing, and Hannah knew why. She wasn't stupid. She absolutely one hundred percent understood why. And it terrified her.

When she blew out a frustrated breath, it sounded loud in the room, and it took a moment for her to realize that the rhythm of Riley's deep and even breathing had changed. She glanced down and she was caught. Ensnared by those eyes.

"Hi," Riley whispered.

"Hi."

"Why are you awake?" Riley's smile was soft as she pushed herself up enough to prop her head in her hand. With the other, she gave Hannah's thigh a squeeze. "You okay?"

"What are we?"

Oh, God. That question. It had been rolling around in her brain for weeks now, and she'd managed to keep it locked inside, but in these wee hours, her muscles pliable from sex and her mind wandering all over the place in the dark, it was harder. Much harder. Add in the pull of those eyes, even in the night, and she was toast. The question burst forth before she'd even known she was going to ask it, and now the words hovered in the air between them.

If Riley was surprised by the question, Hannah couldn't tell, but she did take a moment with it. She turned onto her back and pushed herself up until she mirrored Hannah's position, back to the headboard.

"What makes you ask that?"

Okay, not exactly an answer.

Hannah sighed. "I don't know. I was just thinking about it, I guess." She shrugged, internally frustrated with her own waffling.

"Are you not having a good time? With me?" Riley frowned as she reached for Hannah's hand, picked it up, and entwined their fingers together.

Hannah watched the whole thing, marveled yet again at how well their hands fit, like the proverbial puzzle pieces locking in place. "Of course I am. Hundred percent."

"Good. Me too." Riley brushed a kiss across Hannah's knuckles.

"So…what are we?"

Riley rolled her lips in for a moment, seemed to be looking for the right thing to say. "I'm not sure what that means."

"Are we dating? Are we just goofing around? Are we exclusive? Do we want something more? Do we want something less? Do we mean something? Do we mean nothing?" She snapped her mouth closed, afraid if she didn't, these inane questions would just keep coming in an endless flow of inquiry. Her swallow was audible.

"I mean, do we have to be something specific? Can't we just be… us?" Riley blinked those eyes at her, and then she leaned in for a kiss.

And damn her own inability to resist. Hannah sank into it, into Riley's lips, felt Riley's tongue press gently into her mouth, and she was lost. Riley rolled toward her, moved a hand along her arm, down her side to her hip. She pulled away from the kiss just long enough to grab Hannah's other hip with her other hand and tug her down onto her back.

No preamble this time. Riley went straight in for the kill, pressing Hannah's thighs open and lowering her mouth to what must have been a fully drenched center, and then all coherent thought was chased from her brain. There was nothing else in the world but Riley. No worries, no concerns, no questions. Only Riley's tongue stroking along her most sensitive flesh, teasingly pushing into her, then sliding around, until Hannah was gripping the sheets and Riley's hair and the pillow and anything else she thought might keep her tethered to the Earth, anything that would keep her from flying off into the oblivion of pleasure that Riley so expertly created for her. Her thighs spasmed. Her hips rolled and rocked. Riley's hands held fast to her body, one on each side, fingers gripping tightly, holding her in place as she focused her movements, zeroed in on exactly the right spot. *That* spot.

She sent Hannah over the cliff.

CHAPTER FOURTEEN

Riley had forgotten how much snow Sunset Valley could get in the winter. If she'd remembered, maybe she'd have rented an SUV instead of trusting her sporty BMW not to slip and slide her all the way into town. By the time she arrived in Hannah's driveway and shifted the car into park, her hands ached from the way she'd white-knuckled that last fifteen or twenty miles.

While it was no fun to drive in, it was gorgeous. She could admit that. She got out of the car and stretched, then simply stood there and looked. Relaxed. Breathed.

It was the end of the second week in December, and while there'd been some snow on and off through the second half of November, Hannah had said it had really begun to snow hard about a week ago. Now there had to be eight or ten inches on the ground, with more predicted over the next few days, and Riley was thankful she'd gotten here when she had.

The trees were covered, the lawns were blanketed, and everything looked fresh and clean. She lived in Boston, so she wasn't a newcomer to snow by any means. But she also traveled thirty-eight weeks of the year, and that was often to the west or the south, so being in the thick of winter wasn't common for her. Plus, snow in a busy city and snow in a small, rural town were two completely different things.

It was cold, the air almost brittle, as if she could reach out, grab a handful, and crush it in her hands. Her breaths left her in puffs of visible vapor to float away into the evening as she popped the trunk and pulled out her bag.

Hannah's apartment was in a large house on a quiet street, and she took a moment to look around at the Christmas lights and decorations that adorned almost every other house on the block. Multicolored, all white, inflatable snowmen and Santas and Blueys were everywhere, and Riley sighed. The holidays hadn't been the same for her since she'd lost her mom. Now she just put her head down in mid-November and plowed forward, not looking up until she reached January second.

She hefted her bag over her shoulder, climbed the stairs that led to the front porch, and used the key Hannah had given her to open the front door. The house held four units, two upstairs and two down. As she closed the door, a large black-and-white cat came out of nowhere, meowing loudly and rubbing against her jeans-clad legs.

"Well, hello there," she said. "I don't believe we've met." She squatted down to pet the cat. "My name's Riley. How about you?" Just then, she heard a door upstairs open.

"Beanie! Beanie-bean! Did you sneak out again?"

Riley looked up and saw Parker, Hannah's across-the-hall neighbor, standing at the top of the stairs.

"Dude, *there* you are." She took the steps down, sounding like ten people coming down at once, despite the fact that her teenage feet were engulfed in big, fluffy pink socks. She seemed to notice Riley as an afterthought. "Oh. Hey."

"Hey," Riley said, still petting the cat.

"Hannah's at work," Parker said, apropos of nothing.

"Yeah, I know." She held up her key.

"Oh." Was that disappointment? Something stronger. Disdain?

"You ready for the holidays?" she asked as she stood, feeling a weird need to find common ground with this kid.

Parker bent to scoop up her cat, then shrugged with one shoulder while not looking at Riley. "I guess." She turned and headed up the stairs. Riley followed her.

At the top, they turned in opposite directions to their doors, but Parker stopped her with her next words.

"What are you doing, anyway?"

Riley turned to meet her gaze, which was cloudy and hard to read. "I'm sorry?"

"I mean, you're like my friend Jade's boyfriend. Well, she calls him that, but none of the rest of us do."

Riley frowned and shook her head. "I'm not following."

"She's a senior, but he's in college, and he shows up when it's good for him. She waits and waits, and then he comes back for a night or a weekend. He takes up all her time when he's here, doesn't really want to hang with her friends. It's always about *his* schedule, but she loves him, so she lets that be okay. Then he goes back to college and he lives his life there, and she's left just...being this sad person waiting for him to come back. That's her whole existence: waiting for him."

Riley blinked at her for a moment, her stomach suddenly feeling a little swirly. "Why are you telling me this?"

Parker stared at her for about a second and a half before rolling her eyes so hard, Riley was surprised they didn't end up lost in her skull somewhere. With a clearly annoyed sigh, she turned her back to Riley, went inside her apartment with her cat, and slammed the door.

"What the fuck?" Riley whispered to the empty hall.

Inside the small apartment, she set her bag down and kicked off her snowy shoes. There was a note on the little table inside the door where she set her key.

Hi, babe!
I've missed you so much!
There's a plate of leftover pasta in the fridge, just put it in the microwave for a minute, stir, another 30 seconds. I left you a bag of candy cane popcorn, too.
I won't be late.
I'm so glad you're here!
H.

There was a slew of little hearts drawn all over the note, as well as a big one just before she signed her initial.

She set the note down and slid off her coat to hang it in the tiny coat closet. The living room was small and cozy, and Hannah had found a way to rearrange things to fit a five-foot Christmas tree in one corner. As she stood there, the lights clicked on, surprising her, blue and red and green and yellow flickering to life right before her eyes, clearly on a timer. Ornaments hung cheerfully from branches, and beneath it were at least a dozen wrapped gifts. On a bookshelf next to the tree, two stockings hung from the shelf about chest high. One had Hannah's name in gold glitter across the top.

The other had hers.

She reached out to them, fingered the softness of the white fuzzy tops, and something warm and happy rushed through her, though it was followed by something else, a feeling of uncertainty. Dread.

Giving her head a literal shake, she took her bag into the bedroom, set it on the floor, and looked around. Hannah's room was so very… Hannah. From the bed with the fluffy yellow comforter and about a dozen and a half pillows to the shelf in the corner that held two very obviously loved teddy bears. From the the sneakers on the floor to the photo of her, Kyle, and their parents on her dresser. From top to bottom, side to side, the room spoke of love and comfort. Tenderness.

Home.

Riley sat on the bed and let out a long, deep breath, but before she could sort through all the strange feelings she was having, the sound of the door opening, followed by stomping feet, hit her ears and then, "Babe? You here?"

She cleared her throat and blinked away the wetness in her eyes that had taken her by surprise.

"Yeah. Yeah, I'm in here."

And then there she was. Hannah didn't even stop in the doorway. She just kept coming until she'd launched herself at Riley and they were laughing and rolling on the bed.

"You're cold," Riley complained.

"That tracks, since it's December and we're in the northeast. When did you get here? The snow's really coming down." She gave Riley a quick peck on the lips, then pushed to her feet and began to undress. "I'm ready for cozy clothes and the couch with my love. You good with that? Did you eat?"

She watched as Hannah took off her bra, enjoyed the glimpse of her breasts and allowed herself a quick, tiny fantasy of licking each nipple before Hannah pulled a gray hoodie over her head.

"Ahhh," Hannah said, drawing the word out and wrapping her arms around herself. "I have been waiting for you all day." She looked at Riley and grinned. "Well, come on, silly. Get cozy. I'll put your dinner in the microwave." And then she left the room on a happy little bounce.

Riley grinned. She couldn't help it. With a slap of her thighs, she pushed to her feet. "All right," she said to the empty room. "You heard the woman. Let's get cozy."

❖

"You're coming tonight, right?" Hannah asked Riley as she sipped her morning coffee.

Riley was on the couch, her laptop open on the coffee table in front of her, sexy glasses on her face, punching keys.

"Ri."

Riley looked up at her. "Sorry. Yes. Yes, I'll be at the pairing tonight." She gave her a smile, then went back to her screen.

Hannah stifled a sigh. It had been a strange week, and she wasn't sure if she was reading into things or what, but Riley seemed...off somehow. She couldn't quite put a finger on it, and dwelling on it didn't make her feel any better. She knew she should address it, but she didn't want to do that until she had a better handle on what she was feeling.

Pushing to her feet, she said, "Okay, well, I'm off to work."

Riley nodded, her eyes not leaving her laptop.

Hannah kissed the top of her head and turned to leave when Riley's hand closed over her wrist.

"That was *not* a real kiss goodbye," Riley said, tugging her closer and reaching for her, pulling her head down until their mouths met. This kiss was *a kiss*. It started soft and tender but quickly escalated, so by the time Riley let her go, she was slightly breathless. "Better," Riley whispered. "Have a good day, honey."

Hannah pointed at her as she stood up straight. "You are bad. Very, very bad." She grabbed her coat and put it on.

"But in a good way, right?" Riley asked.

"In the best of ways," Hannah told her, and she was out the door.

The holidays were always a busy time for Poptacular, and before Hannah had realized it, most of the day had passed. She'd made several batches of fresh popcorn, starting with the usual caramel, but she'd added some holiday flavors and they were doing great, so she'd had to restock several. The candy cane was by far the most popular, but the pumpkin spice was still going strong, and she'd taken a chance on an eggnog flavor, which had been selling surprisingly well.

Joanne was working the counter. She was a regular customer, a retired schoolteacher who'd been looking for something to take up a little time in her day. When Hannah jokingly suggested that she could use a hand a few days a week, Joanne had jumped at the chance, and Hannah was thrilled to have her on board. Joanne was happy to have a part-time job, and Hannah had been able to avoid placing an ad, culling through CVs, and doing interviews. A win-win.

"Looks like your coffee delivery is on its way," Joanne called back to her.

A glance up told her Shana was heading toward the shop with a cup in each hand.

"Hoo!" Shana said as she shut the door behind her, the little bell announcing her arrival. She stomped her feet, leaving the snow on the black rubber-backed mat Hannah always brought in during the winter. The combination of wet, snowy boots and the slick linoleum floor was a recipe for disaster. The last thing she needed was somebody falling and breaking a bone in her shop. The mats were thin, long and narrow, and they led from the door to the counter to prevent such accidents. "It's getting nasty out there." Turning her attention to Joanne, she handed her one of the cups. "M'lady."

"Oh, bless you," Joanne said, taking the cup with a nod of gratitude. "What will it be today?" She knew the trade deal, that Shana got whatever popcorn she wanted.

"Are you kidding? The chocolate candy cane. Duh." Shana smiled at Hannah as she headed back. "Girl, it is awful out there, but it's supposed to let up soon. Should be okay for your pairing tonight, I think." She handed over the second cup.

Hannah took it and removed the lid so she could breathe in the scent. Vanilla and nutmeg and something else she couldn't pinpoint filled her nostrils. "That smells like Christmas," she said in delight.

"It's my Christmas Chai. Take a sip."

Hannah blew on it, then tasted. "Oh my God, it *tastes* like Christmas."

"Yes!" Shana did a little fist pump of happiness. "That's what I was going for."

"Kinda late in the season for a new holiday flavor, isn't it?" Hannah took another sip, let the tastes coat her tongue before swallowing.

"What can I say?" Shana said with a shrug. "I got bored."

"That's a valid answer," Hannah said, laughing.

"What's new with you? How's your woman?" She enunciated the last word in two very distinct syllables. Hannah must've taken too long to answer, because Shana's face went from joking to serious in half a second flat. "Oh, no. What's going on?"

Hannah glanced out to where Joanne was fiddling with the window display, and then lowered her voice. "That's just it. I don't know. She's been weird lately. A little distant. I'm not sure what to make of it."

"Have you asked her about it?"

"I'm a giant coward. So of course I have *not* asked her about it."

"Has the sex tapered off?" Shana asked, wrinkling her nose.

"Oh, God, no. That's about the only time I feel like she's with me." Hannah narrowed her eyes. "But now that I think of it…whenever I start to worry something's wrong, we end up in bed. Like she's using sex to distract me." It was the first time the thought had occurred to her, and she honestly wasn't sure what to do with it.

"I wish somebody would distract me with sex," Shana said absently.

Hannah forced a laugh. "Right? I should be careful what I wish for."

"Damn right." Shana met her eyes. "Just talk to her, babe. You know? Nothing good ever comes of letting your imagination run away with you. Or so my mother always says."

"I've met your mother. She's a wise woman."

"And she knows it." Shana gave her a playful push. "Okay, I gotta get back. Should have a delivery coming soon."

"Thanks for the Christmas in a cup," Hannah said, holding hers up.

"Thanks for the Christmas in a bag," Shana said, taking her popcorn from Joanne and holding it up in return. Then she was out the door and hurrying across the snowy street.

Hannah didn't want to dwell on the uneasy feeling in her stomach around Riley, so she was glad when the little bell tinkled, indicating customers. Snow like today's didn't stop the tourists. Most of them were there to ski at a couple of nearby slopes, so snow didn't scare them off; they relished it. A couple locals also came by: Kitty Baynard grabbed some cheddar popcorn for her son, who was due home for the holidays that night, and Mr. Daniels came to get his usual bag, and even Ashton, the cute redheaded guy that worked with her brother, stopped in on his lunch hour to grab something to munch on. The rest of the afternoon stayed fairly steady, and before she knew it, it was time for Hannah to pack up her supplies, load up her car, and head down to Hopsville for the beer and popcorn pairing. Jacob had texted her earlier that there were twenty-seven people signed up, so she was excited. She left Joanne to close up shop later and headed out.

Three hours later, she was finishing up with the very last pairing when Riley walked into Hopsville. Hannah caught her out of the corner of her eye, watched as she took a seat in the back, but didn't let it interrupt her talk as she explained that the light crispness of Hopsville's pale ale paired beautifully with her Better Cheddar popcorn. The customers were already digging in and sipping, then talking amongst themselves, nodding and smiling. Finally, she thanked them all, told them she had a few bags with her to sell or they could always stop by Poptacular, which was a short walk away. The applause was loud, and Jacob gave her a hug in the midst of it.

As things broke up and people split off, either to their own spots in the brewery or out the door to their cars, Riley wandered up.

"Hey," she said, kissing Hannah on the temple as she packed up her leftovers.

"I thought you'd be here sooner," she said, hoping she didn't sound whiny. Or ticked off. Both of which she felt at the moment.

Riley sighed. "I know. I'm sorry. I got stuck on a call."

Hannah nodded. She couldn't argue with that. Riley was working, just as she had been, though it was now nearing nine o'clock.

"Looks like it went well."

More nodding. "It did. Big crowd."

"I see that. Fantastic. What was the biggest hit?" Riley talked to her like that, showing genuine interest, for the next several moments, and Hannah started to realize her irritation was maybe unfounded. Work happened. Hell, how many times had she been late for a gathering because something had come up at work? "Hey, how are your feet? Are you tired of standing? Because it's gorgeous out right now, and

I thought we could take a walk. Maybe?" And there were those eyes. Those eyes with the blue Hannah was pretty sure she could drown in.

"That sounds great. Help me get these boxes into my car and we'll wander a bit. Yeah?"

Twenty minutes later, they were strolling down Main Street. The air was crisp and cold, but they had hats and gloves, warm coats and boots. Stars in the clear night sky shone as if somebody had flicked white paint onto a midnight blue ceiling, so many of them twinkling away. It was tourist season, and a lot of shops were still open, in addition to the restaurants and bars, and Main Street was lit up festively, bright lights in every window, Kelly Clarkson singing about things underneath the tree over the shared PA in the eaves of each shop.

"This is my favorite season," Hannah said quietly.

"Yeah?"

She nodded. "I love everything about it. The lights and the music and the snow and that feeling of warmth and love." She leaned into Riley as they walked, closing her mittened hand over Riley's gloved one. "Don't you?"

Riley breathed out, her breath leaving them on a cloud of vapor. "I do." There was a hesitancy to her tone, and Hannah waited for more. "I struggle, though."

"What do you mean?"

Riley glanced up at the sky, as if the words she was looking for were up there somewhere. "My mom loved the holidays. Like, *loved* them. She did everything. Decorated like crazy. Made a million kinds of cookies. Played Christmas music from Thanksgiving until after New Year's. Wrapped all the presents with fancy paper and ribbons. Stuffed my stocking to overflowing." Her voice caught, and Hannah glanced up at her face, her expression far away and slightly pained.

"And you miss her," she said quietly.

"Understatement of the year."

"I'm so sorry, Riley."

"Yeah. Well." Riley lifted one shoulder. "What can you do, right?"

Hannah wanted to say more, but Riley seemed to need to collect herself, so instead, she tightened her grip and leaned in as they walked. After a moment or two, she said, "Well, I know it won't be the same, but maybe we can start a couple of our own holiday traditions. You know? And my mom goes all out for dinner. We'll have a really amazing day together, me and my family, and I think you'll enjoy it. And if it gets too much, you just tell me, and we'll leave. Okay?"

"Oh." The word hung in the crisp night air, almost like it could be seen floating there. "I won't be here for Christmas. I'll be in Portland for a job."

For a moment, Hannah thought she'd misheard. "What?" She frowned, stopped walking, and looked up at Riley for clarity. Riley, who wouldn't look at her.

"Yeah, I've worked with this company before and they're having some major issues, so the CEO has asked me to meet with him on the twenty-sixth."

"I—you—you're just telling me this now?"

"I'm sorry. I thought I had. I have Columbus at the end of this week, and then I'll just go right on to Portland after that."

"No. You didn't tell me. I had no idea." What was happening? Hannah tried to wrap her brain around what she'd just been told. "Who makes somebody fly on Christmas? What kind of Scrooge is this guy? You missed Thanksgiving because of work, and now they want you to miss Christmas, too? Can't you go on the twenty-seventh instead? Make a quick trip back here first?"

"I wish I could, babe. It's already set. My flights are already booked, and I don't mess with our travel guru at work." She lowered her voice to a whisper. "I think she might be an actual witch."

Riley was trying to make light of it, but Hannah wanted to cry, and her eyes did well up. "I just…I thought we'd celebrate the holiday together. I was so looking forward to that."

Riley tightened her grip on Hannah's hand. "I know. I'm so sorry." She offered no more explanation, and Hannah didn't push, but something inside her felt like it shriveled up and fell off its vine.

That night, she lay in bed, long after Riley had fallen asleep, and stared at the ceiling, then out the window, then at the ceiling again, before finally getting up and making herself a cup of hot chocolate. She turned on the Christmas tree, quietly dragged her oversized chair to the living room window, and curled up, legs tucked underneath her. The heavy throw her grandmother had knit for her around her shoulders, she watched the snow fall.

It was beautiful. Big, fluffy white flakes floated down to the ground, blanketing the world in a fresh white cover. A new start. A clean slate. It was what she loved most about winter.

She was more disappointed than she cared to admit about Riley not being around for Christmas. She knew she didn't have a right to be—they hadn't really talked about it or about being exclusive or anything close. She'd assumed; she could admit that. Kind of thought they'd been on the same page.

She sipped her hot chocolate with a sigh and did her best to resign herself to yet another holiday alone.

CHAPTER FIFTEEN

R iley sat at a bar in Columbus International Airport, her flight delayed by more than two hours, and sipped her martini as she watched the people around her, absently wondering if the bar watered down their vodka, because she felt nothing.

Normally, she loved airports. She'd spent enough time in them over the years that she didn't have the disdain so many people did for them. She loved that people were sitting at bars and drinking at six in the morning. She loved that people were sleeping on ledges and in uncomfortable chairs. She admired the people who dressed for comfort rather than appearance—she thought this as a young woman wandered by the bar's entrance wearing what Riley was pretty sure were her pajamas and carrying a giant pillow in the shape of a penguin.

Today, though, she was antsy. She felt unsettled, a little restless and uncomfortable, like ants were crawling under her skin, and she couldn't sit still.

That's where the martini came in.

She sipped again and watched as a child of maybe five hurried by behind his parents, pulling his X-Men carry-on in his wake.

The best part of her martini was the olive, stuffed with gorgonzola, and she pulled it off the swizzle stick with her teeth, just as her phone buzzed a text.

Have a safe flight. It was followed by a heart emoji.

Hannah. It was a pretty generic text for her, and Riley was both saddened and unsurprised by that.

It was her own fault. She was a coward. She was weak. She shook her head with a long sigh and dug out her laptop.

"That sounds like the sigh of a woman with a delayed flight and a lot on her mind." The bartender was a robust middle-aged woman with her dark blond hair in a bun and eyes that looked like they'd seen a little bit of everything. She picked up Riley's empty glass and raised her eyebrows in question.

"You are not wrong, my friend," Riley said with a nod. The bartender went to work making her a new drink as a group of men in business suits came in and sat at the other end of the bar. She was glad about that, hoping they'd take up some attention. Not that Riley hadn't had many a conversation with many an airport bartender, but she didn't want that today. No, she wanted to wallow. Wallow in the murky swamp of her own making.

Abandonment issues.

That's what her last therapist said she had. And really, was that any surprise? Her father was absentee, so it was just her and her mom. When her mom died, it was just her. How could she *not* have abandonment issues? It only made sense.

Therapy sucked. She hadn't kept up with it. She didn't like looking that deeply into herself; it only served to depress her. So, after the abandonment issue conclusion, she hadn't gone back. Like she said: coward.

She picked up the phone and read Hannah's message again. So simple. So sweet. She stared at the heart emoji. Hannah was probably the sweetest, kindest, most wonderful woman she'd ever met. She was funny. She was stubborn. She was creative. She was devastatingly sexy.

And Riley had lied to her.

She called up her email on the laptop, intending to throw herself into some work before her flight, and it worked for a short time. She answered several emails she'd been putting off, went over some details and notes she'd taken while at her client's here in Columbus, and she sipped her martini. Good. This was good.

Her phone chimed again, and the text popped up on her computer screen.

Please know I'm not trying to put any pressure on you or make you feel bad, Hannah's words began. *I just want you to know I'll miss you. Tonight. Tomorrow. I wish you were here.* Next came a Christmas tree emoji, a Santa emoji, and another heart.

If Riley thought she couldn't feel more guilty or more like the cowardly piece of shit she was, she was wrong. Her eyes welled up, and she put her elbow on the bar so she could lean her head down and pinch the bridge of her nose.

Her phone buzzed again, and she almost couldn't bear to look, her guilt and shame feeling so incredibly heavy, like a suit of chain mail and lead. Taking a deep breath, she glanced at her phone.

Her flight from Columbus to Boston would be boarding in thirty minutes.

❖

"Why on earth are you open today?" Mr. Daniels shuffled into Poptacular on Christmas Eve day and posed the question to Hannah.

"Why are you looking for popcorn on Christmas Eve day?" she countered with a grin. "I'm closing in a few minutes. You just made it."

He smiled at her, his rheumy eyes sparkling. "I need something to munch on while I watch Christmas movies."

"Staying home, then?" She bagged up some caramel, made fresh that morning, along with two of the holiday flavors.

"No place to be," he said with a shrug, and Hannah felt her heart squeeze.

"You are more than welcome to come with me to my parents' house," she said. "You know that. My mom makes a stellar pumpkin pie." She'd made this offer to him for the past four years in a row, and she already knew his answer.

"You're very kind, Hannah. Thank you. I'll be fine. It's really just another day to me." He didn't seem sad about that. He didn't ever seem sad about his aloneness. It just was.

She handed over the popcorn and waved away his offer to pay. "Your money is no good today, sir," she said, smiling at him. Then she came around the counter and wrapped his tall, lanky body in a gentle hug. "Merry Christmas, Mr. Daniels." She felt him pat her gently on the back. Then she watched him go, her heart filled with the hope that he wouldn't feel lonely over the next two days.

She locked the door behind him, switched the Open sign, and got ready to head home.

Riley was on her way to Portland by now.

Hannah kept trying not to think about it as she reached her

apartment, showered, and dressed for dinner. She tried not to dwell on how the woman who'd become so important to her was going to be on the other side of the country in a three-hour time difference for Christmas, her favorite holiday of the year, that they wouldn't be together. It wasn't fair.

She should've just come out with it, with what she wanted to say, what she'd wanted to say for the past few weeks now.

Although…

Would that have helped or hurt?

Riley had acted odd for the past week, right up until she'd left last Thursday. Now here it was, Christmas Eve afternoon, and they'd only managed to text. She'd tried to FaceTime her on Sunday, but Riley hadn't answered, working with her client in Columbus over the weekend to get done in time for the holidays. It was too bad her client in Portland didn't have that kind of regard for this time of year.

With a sad shake of her head, she sighed and unfurled the silver wrapping paper with red and white reindeer and cut a piece to wrap the sweater she'd gotten for her mom. It was the last of the gifts she had to wrap, and she smiled as she added some silver ribbon, tying it off, then used scissors to curl it. Kyle would make fun of her for her meticulous wrapping, as he did every year, but then her mother would step in and compliment it, a little dance they did every year.

She checked her phone.

Nothing.

She did her best to put Riley out of her mind—easier said than done—for the rest of the day. Her mother only mentioned it once, and there must've been something on Hannah's face, because it didn't come up again.

Riley knew her number. She could call if she wanted to.

"Hey, you okay?" Kyle asked her quietly after dinner, when they were both in the kitchen. Hannah was pouring herself some eggnog, and Kyle was refilling his wife's wine glass. "You seem quiet."

His face was sincere. Hannah could always tell if he was being sweet or about to tease her, and there was nothing but concern on his face right then. She swallowed and sprinkled some fresh nutmeg onto her eggnog. "I'm fine. Just, you know, wishing Riley was here."

He nodded. "That's what I thought." He took a deep breath as he pushed a cork back into the bottle. "This time of year is hard for her.

Just keep that in mind, and maybe don't take it too personally if she's being kind of…absent."

"Okay. Thanks."

He smiled at her, and she watched him head back into the family room.

Of course! She'd been so selfish, expecting Riley to keep in constant contact. The holidays were hard when you were missing somebody. How could she not have thought of that? "God, I'm such an asshole," she muttered, pulling out her phone. She opened a text and typed quickly.

Hey, I know you're probably missing your mom right now, but just know I'm sending you a big hug, and I'm here if you need to talk. Hope everything's going well in Portland. I miss you. She hesitated on that last line, but then decided, fuck it, why not tell her the truth? She *did* miss her. There was no shame in that. She added a heart and clicked send.

Able to breathe easier, the rest of Christmas Eve went smoothly for Hannah. She felt lighter, happier. As was tradition, they each opened one gift. Christmas movies on the TV murmured in the background, and Kyle's three-year-old twins, Brody and Brianna, sat through a full forty-five minutes of *Elf* before getting bored and wandering off to the front living room that Hannah's mom had made into a playroom for them.

Hannah was always at her happiest on days or evenings like this: at her parents' house, surrounded by family, casually just being with each other. She knew in her heart that if Riley would attend a holiday here with her, just one, didn't even have to be Christmas, she'd feel the same way. Riley had no family. Hannah knew that. Her mother's parents were gone, her mother was an only child, as was Riley, her dad was MIA. And now with her mother gone, it was just Riley. Hannah tried to imagine what that must feel like, to be completely alone in the world, and her heart squeezed in her chest as she sat there in the corner of the couch, her socked feet in her mother's lap, sipping her eggnog and watching her niece and nephew run around like happy little chicks on a farm. Her family was small, but it was as close-knit as families came. She tried to imagine what it would feel like to have none of them. Not a single person in the room. Her brain simply couldn't compute such a thing, and that made her feel even more sympathy for Riley.

It was nearly eleven when she got back to her apartment, exhausted but smiling. Sometimes, she opted to spend the night at her parents' house on Christmas Eve, since she'd just be back there in the morning. But tonight she wanted some alone time, some solitary quiet time with her thoughts in her own space. And she wanted to try to call Riley.

Nearly eleven in Sunset Valley equaled only eight in Portland, so she gave it a try. She flopped down onto her battered couch and hit FaceTime, just wanting to see Riley's face.

She didn't answer.

Trying to keep her disappointment at bay, she set the phone down next to her and sat in the light of the Christmas tree. Before she could dwell too much, though, her phone rang.

Riley.

Barely able to contain her joy, she snapped up the phone and answered. "Merry Christmas, you gorgeous thing."

"Well, if that isn't the best greeting ever." There was a smile in Riley's voice. "FaceTime is being glitchy, so I thought I'd just call."

"I'm sad not to see your face but happy to hear your voice. How are you? How's Portland?"

"Meh." Riley's voice was quiet, as if she was trying not to be emotional. Of course. She was probably missing her mother something awful right then.

"Are you in a boring hotel room?"

"I'm okay," Riley said. "I had some dinner, and now I'm just chilling. Watching *A Christmas Story.* Did you know they show it for twenty-four hours straight?"

Hannah laughed. "I did know that. It's one of my favorites."

"It's definitely dated, but it's fun." She grunted like she was shifting positions. "How was your night? Tell me all about it."

For the next thirty-seven minutes, they talked and laughed, Hannah telling Riley all about the evening. From the meal to the drinks to the gifts to the two toddlers running all over the place, she filled Riley in. "You would've loved it, I think."

"I bet I would have," Riley said quietly.

Hannah sighed. "I just hate that you're alone in an impersonal hotel room on Christmas Eve. I hate it."

"That's because you're an amazing person."

"I wish you were here. How much longer do you have to be in Portland? When will you be back?" She was asking when Riley would be back in Sunset Valley, but she kept her words generic, worried she was starting to sound a little whiny.

"I'm not sure yet," Riley said. "Sometimes, this stuff is uncertain."

Hannah was suddenly super aware of her stomach, like a rock had just settled in it. "Will you be back by New Year's Eve?"

Riley's sigh was not promising. "I don't know. Maybe?"

"Not a fan of your job right now," she said, and forced a soft laugh she didn't really feel.

"I know. Me neither. I'm sorry."

"No, no." Hannah wiped a hand in front of her as if erasing her thoughts. Not that Riley could see. "Not your fault. I'm not trying to make you feel bad."

They talked for a few more minutes, until Hannah yawned for the second time. "You should get to bed, babe."

She felt her skin warm at the affectionate name. "I probably should." She sighed, long and a little sad. "I miss you."

"I miss you, too. Hey, it's after midnight. Merry Christmas, Hannah."

"Merry Christmas, Riley."

As she pressed the button to hang up, she could feel the tears coming. She did not want to cry, but her heart couldn't keep it in any longer. She'd known for a while now, though she hadn't said it out loud to anybody, and had barely acknowledged it herself.

She sat on her couch, bathed in the soft, multicolored lights from the Christmas tree, and cried silently, tears coursing down her cheeks. The fact was, she was in love with Riley Shaw, and being away from her on her favorite day of the year was killing her.

She had to tell her.

❖

Riley hated herself.

She lay in her own bed in her apartment in Boston and slowly shook her head back and forth against the pillow. Not only had she lied to Hannah about being in Portland, but she'd been too much of a chicken shit to FaceTime with her and tell her the truth. So, to keep Hannah from seeing that she was not actually in a boring, nondescript hotel room, she faked a FaceTime glitch and called instead.

How had this happened? How had she become this person?

And more importantly, how had she developed feelings for Hannah? She hadn't set out to do that. All she'd done was agree to help a friend. Kyle. *No good deed, am I right?*

And now what?

Now she could come clean or keep pretending. Neither of those things sounded like much fun to Riley. Her mind was racing, and there was no way she was going to sleep now.

"Of course not," she muttered to herself. "It's only nine o'clock in Portland." She groaned with self-irritation and reached for the TV remote. She switched the channel from *A Christmas Story* to YouTube and turned on one of those ambiance videos. This one was of a peaceful cabin living room with a crackling fire, a cozy sectional covered with blankets, and big fluffy snowflakes falling outside the enormous windows. Christmas music played softly, and Riley lay there in her bed feeling sorry for herself.

She hated Christmas.

She hated it, but she was also self-aware enough to understand she hated it because her mother had loved it, and nothing was the same without her mother. Nothing. She felt the gentle slope in front of her, the emotional one that would take her down if she let it. The one where she felt sorry for herself and angry at the world and railed against the unfairness of life.

On the TV, Idina Menzel was singing about wanting a river to skate away on, and honestly, that sounded far too perfect right now.

"Shut up, Idina," she said with irritation, and clicked the TV back to *A Christmas Story*. The little brother was in a snowsuit and couldn't put his arms down, which was pretty funny and gave her a ten-second reprieve from hating herself. But then it was back.

God, she missed her mother. She felt like she hadn't had real conversations about anything with anyone since she'd been gone. Well. Except for Hannah. She could talk to Hannah on just about any subject. Except for the subject of her and Riley's confusing feelings for her.

She lay back against her headboard and didn't even try to stop the tears when they came. "What the fuck is wrong with me?" She asked the question out loud, though only in a whisper, and suddenly felt almost desperate for some kind of answers.

She picked up her phone and typed out a text. *Am I a good person?* She sent it before she could second-guess herself, then set the phone down on her thigh. It buzzed in less than three minutes.

Are you okay? came Justin's response. *What's wrong?*

She smiled. She couldn't help it or the relief she felt that he'd responded in an instant. *Nothing. Just feeling sorry for myself.*

Where are you? he asked.

Home.

The dots bounced as Justin typed. Then, *Not in Sunset Valley? It's Christmas.* He followed that up with a thinking emoji.

She took a deep breath. Contacting Justin for reassurance was one thing, but she hadn't thought it through, because now she had to explain what an asshole she'd been. She typed. *No. I'm home. Avoiding Christmas. And my feelings.* It was brief, but honest.

Avoiding your feelings? How unlike you. Justin followed that up with a winking emoji.

"Ugh, I know." She banged her head backward against the headboard a few times before typing. *She thinks I'm in Portland.*

The dots bounced, then, *Why would she think that?*

Riley sighed. Time to face the music. *Because that's what I told her.*

The dots bounced, then stopped, then bounced some more, and she braced herself for the onslaught of whatever scolding Justin was about to give her. She pictured him in his perfectly decorated house with his gorgeous husband. She felt happy for him and worse for herself.

Ri. What are you doing? Seriously? I don't get it.

She could see his face in her mind, his thick brows meeting above his nose as he tried to work out the issue.

Another message came before she could respond. *I know the holidays are hard for you because of your mom, but how long are you gonna do this? Why won't you talk to somebody?*

He was right. She knew it. They'd talked about her returning to therapy on more than one occasion. Justin had his own therapist, and Riley considered him one of the most even-keeled people she'd ever met. "Um, gee, could that have to do with the therapy?" her inner voice tossed at her.

Again, another message came before she could respond. *Do you want to lose her? Cuz you're well on your way right now.*

"Oh, breaking out the tough love on Christmas Eve," she muttered. "Points for you, Justin." She typed, *I don't know what I want.*

Well. That was some bullshit if she'd ever seen it.

Bullshit, Justin typed back, as if reading her mind. *You know exactly what you want. You're just afraid.*

Wow. Also: ouch.

Pulling no punches on Christmas, she sent with a laughing emoji.

A moment or two went by, and she started to worry that she'd overstepped. After all, it was Christmas Eve, and she had no idea where Justin was. Home? At his family's? At a party? She was being utterly selfish expecting him to talk her off the ledge tonight. She blew out a breath and was about to set the phone aside when it buzzed with another text.

Listen. You're awesome. A queen. Truly. But the only person who can get you out of this place where you've been stuck since your mom died is you. Stop moving. Okay? Stop moving and sit still. Stop. Moving.

The lump in her throat came out of nowhere, suddenly just appeared, and she had to swallow several times to be able to breathe.

Apparently, Justin wasn't done. There was more.

Would this make your mom happy? Oh, ouch again. *Would she like knowing that your sole focus in life is work because as long as you're working, you're moving, and as long as you're moving, you don't have to sit with your feelings? I met your mom. You forget that. There's no way this is what she'd want for you.*

The lump remained, but now tears had entered the chat. Her eyes welled up, and an uncomfortable rolling began in her stomach, a stormy sea of acidic emotion.

Know what she would want? You happy. Settled down with somebody who loves you.

"Holy shit, Justin," she whispered to her empty living room as the tears left glistening tracks down her cheeks.

Another text came.

Okay, that was harsh. I apologize. But I think you're amazing, Riley, and you deserve to be happy. And I wish you'd allow yourself to be. That's all I'm trying to say.

She swallowed again, working hard on that lump. It was winning.

Listen, I gotta get back to my family, but just think about what I said, okay? You're incredible and you deserve an incredible life. Merry Christmas, boss.

She typed back. *I definitely will. Tell your mom and dad I said hi. Merry Christmas to you, too, Justin. Thanks for listening.*

Then she tossed the phone to the side and cried.

Chapter Sixteen

"Hey, Bradley, it's Hannah Kramer," Hannah said after the beep. It was the day after Christmas, and she was back in Poptacular. Not expecting a whole lot of business, but she might get some, and she didn't want to make Michael or Joanne come in on the twenty-sixth. "I just wanted to run something by you about replacing the floor in my lobby. The traffic has really worn a path in the linoleum, and it's well past being cleaned off. I was hoping we could talk about it. Give me a call when you can. Thanks and Merry Christmas."

She hung up her phone and slid it into her back pocket, then went to the back of the shop where fresh popcorn was popping.

She felt lighter today somehow. More confident. Stronger. Happier. She wasn't sure what it was, but she felt like she'd discovered some kind of newfound pleasure in her work. Not that she hadn't always loved it. She had. But this was different, like a renewed vigor.

She whistled as she made a few different flavors. And while she'd anticipated slow business that day, it had been anything but. The first customers came in around eleven, and the stream flowed steadily straight through the afternoon. As she was the only one working, the day flew by.

"We just had an early dinner at Hopsville," said one customer, who came in with a man and two kids. "They recommended we come here for dessert, and I'm so glad we did." They sampled several flavors and ended up buying four bags, and Hannah marveled once again at how some of Riley's ideas—like pairing with other local businesses—had panned out into extra business for Poptacular.

Speaking of Riley, she was scheduled to fly back from Portland tomorrow, and then she'd head toward Sunset Valley, and she was going to stay through the New Year.

"I recognize that dreamy look." Shana's voice surprised her, and when she looked up, Shana was grinning at her.

"I didn't hear you come in."

"That's because you're entertaining fantasies about your hot girlfriend," Shana teased.

"Hmm. Not sure we're supposed to be calling her that."

Shana looked skeptical. "Seriously? She spends half her time here. When she's in town, she stays with you. You guys have been sleeping together for what? Two months? Three? Yeah. You're girlfriends."

"I mean, when you put it like that…" They both laughed as Hannah snapped on gloves so she could unclump the peanut butter cup popcorn she'd just made. "Why are you working today?"

"Why are you?"

"Curse of the small business owner?"

"Exactly." Shana helped herself to the peanut butter cup popcorn as Hannah dumped it onto the sorting tray. "When does your not-girlfriend get here?"

"She's back from Portland tomorrow, so depending on what time she lands, either tomorrow night or Monday."

"And she'll stay for New Year's?"

Hannah nodded, and she couldn't keep the smile off her face. "You know what? I can't remember the last time I had somebody to kiss at midnight on New Year's Eve."

Shana wrapped an arm around her shoulders and gave her a squeeze. "I'm so happy for you, Han."

"Thanks."

They chatted a bit more, and Hannah sent Shana off with a bag of fresh peanut butter cup popcorn. Business tapered off once the evening hit, and Hannah wiped down all her equipment, then went out into the front and dusted off her grandmother's photo.

"Merry Christmas, Grams," she said quietly. Her phone buzzed in her back pocket, and her heart jumped in her chest, anticipating a text from Riley.

It wasn't Riley. It was Brad McFarland.

Hi, Hannah. Got your message. I'm afraid we need to table any updates to the shop right now. I'm actually in the midst of selling the building. I meant to tell you, and I'm so sorry, it just fell through the cracks. Being a landlord's been rough on me, and frankly, I could use the cash. The holiday slowed things down, but they should finalize by Monday. I'm so sorry, the holidays have been crazy! I know this isn't what you want to hear, but I have to think about my own situation, you know? Anyway. I'll keep you posted.

"No, no, no, no, no." She read it again. And again. And again. She scrubbed a hand over her face and read it one more time. When the bell over the door tinkled happily and she looked up, there were tears in her eyes.

Kitty Baynard walked in, wearing her usual bright smile, and headed her way. She continued to smile, but those teacher's eyes didn't miss a trick.

"Merry Christ—what's wrong?" she asked, her voice sharp and as she picked up her pace. She closed a shockingly strong hand over her forearm. "What happened?"

Hannah couldn't help herself. She spilled it all. She had to. She'd only had the news for a moment, but it was suffocating her. "Bradley McFarland sold this building." She blinked rapidly as the thoughts shot through her brain. "No new owner is going to keep my rent as is. It's been the same since Grams ran the place. Bradley was always good like that." She met Kitty's gaze. "I can't afford higher rent. I can barely pay what it is now. There's no way."

"Well, let's not get ahead of ourselves," Kitty said. "You don't know for sure, right?"

Hannah grimaced. "I'm paying the same rent my grandma paid fifteen years ago. I'm pretty sure."

"But you don't *know*." Kitty patted her arm. It was ineffectual, but sweet, and the tiniest bit comforting. "Take a breath, honey. Just breathe."

She did as she said, breathing in through her nose and out her mouth, and it did help to calm her racing heart at least a little. "I don't want to lose my shop. My grandma's shop." She swallowed hard, eyes still wet, heart heavy with reality. "I don't want to lose my grandma's shop."

Kitty did what she could to be kind and caring. Hannah knew that. In the end, she simply gave her some popcorn and sent her on her way, because the last thing she wanted to do was completely break down in front of her.

She needed to let Riley know. That's who she needed. She checked the time, subtracted three hours, and decided Riley was likely still working. She quickly typed out a text.

Sorry to bother you while you're working. Just got some terrible news.

She copied and pasted Bradley's text and sent it. It took every fiber of her being, but she managed *not* to send an additional text begging Riley to hurry and get there, that she was scared and sad and she needed her.

Please call when you can.

Phone back in her pocket, she locked the front door because she needed ten minutes to herself, then headed back to her office, where she sat down in her grandmother's chair and sobbed.

"Oh, shit." Riley whispered the words into the empty living room of her apartment. She'd just come back from a brisk walk out in the fresh December air. Her cheeks were cold and probably red, her nose was running, and her fingertips were getting numb, but it felt good to get outside. She wasn't used to sitting around.

Her phone had buzzed on her way up the stairs, and when she'd gotten inside and pulled it out to read, she'd stopped in her tracks.

Hannah's landlord had sold the building.

"There's no way a new owner will keep her rent the same," she said out loud. "No way." She'd noticed in her first perusal of Poptacular's paperwork that the rent had barely gone up over the years. Actual years. Hannah had explained that her landlord's father was a dear friend of Hannah's grandmother, had loved the shop, and did his best not to raise her rent much.

There was no way that would happen with a new owner. And Hannah was doing better, but a hike in her rent would likely eat up any extra profit she'd finally been making.

This wasn't good.

"Shit, shit, shit," she muttered as she kicked off her boots and pulled her Bruins ski cap off her head. And don't even get her started on how Hannah thought she was in Portland. "See?" she said to her reflection in the mirror over the little table next to the coat closet. "This is why you don't have anybody in your life. This shit right here. Idiot."

In her small kitchen, she clicked on her electric kettle and waited for the water to boil, her brain racing a mile a minute. Moving to the living room while waiting to make a cup of tea, she plopped onto the couch and opened her laptop where it sat on the coffee table. Why? She had no idea. It's just what she did when she was feeling stress: She worked. But it was the day after Christmas, plus it was a Saturday, and every other person—every other normal person—in the world was taking some time off. The only new email in her inbox was junk. She sat there, wiggling her fingers that had nothing to type.

Goddamn it.

Her kettle clicked off, so she went into the kitchen and made her tea, then returned to the couch and sat. She held the mug in both hands, absorbing the warmth through her skin, and glanced around her living room. Her very sparse, barely decorated living room. No Christmas tree or stockings or lights. Not a single decoration. Bare walls, as she hadn't gotten around to hanging anything. Or buying anything to hang. She had a nice TV, a sixty-inch flat screen mounted on the wall, and her couch was nice. Pricey. Pretty comfortable. And she had one framed photo of her and her mother, propped up on the table under the TV. She stared at it for a long while, until she finally blinked and realized her eyes had welled up.

"Mom," she whispered into the quiet. "Why? Why am I like this? I don't understand." She'd never felt like this before—confused, antsy, like she wanted to crawl out of her own skin. The wetness spilled over and down her cheeks as she said, "I don't know what to do. What do I do?" She leaned her head back and closed her eyes, hoping to will this feeling away.

What do you want?

Her eyes popped open, and she sat up with a gasp. "Mom?" She could swear she'd heard her mother's voice, asking that question. Which was silly. And yet…

She took a deep breath and did her best to focus.

What do I want?

Forcing herself to clear her mind and concentrate on one thing at a time was a tactic her mother had taught her a couple years before her death, and they'd used it a lot when she was in her final days. There was so much to deal with, and this method really helped Riley to separate out each individual task rather than allowing herself to be completely overwhelmed by the scope—which would've been easy to do.

She hadn't used it since. She hadn't needed to.

Taking a moment, she tried to understand why, and the answer came to her immediately: because it was a little scary. It forced her to face her truth, and that wasn't always an easy thing for Riley.

"What do I want?" she whispered aloud as she closed her eyes and let her mind roam.

It didn't take long.

"Hannah."

That was it? It was that simple? *I mean, of course it's that simple. What's not simple is the complications, the circumstances.* Another deep breath as she concentrated on the rest of it, and again, the answer came to her quickly. "I don't want to hurt Hannah. That's my biggest concern." Her mother had also taught her to say the words out loud, that actually speaking them made a difference. She said it put them out into the Universe. Riley wasn't sure if she believed that, but she did it anyway. "I don't want to hurt her," she said again, putting more emphasis on it.

Her tea grew cold as she stayed on the couch, moving through her feelings and her concerns, and it was more tiring than she expected. The strangest part was that she didn't feel alone. Somehow, some way, she felt her mother's presence. Riley wasn't a religious person. At all. But she did believe in energy, and she was certain, in that moment, she could feel her mother's.

It brought tears to her eyes.

"Thanks, Mom," she said quietly.

She picked up her phone and typed. *I'll be there tonight.* Then she headed into her bedroom and began to pack a bag.

As expected, a text came right back, and Hannah was understandably confused. *How? Aren't you in Portland? Did you get back early?* That was followed by about sixteen question marks.

Riley took another deep breath. She'd gotten herself into this fucking disaster. Now she had to get herself out of it. *I'll explain everything when I see you.* She sent that, then put her phone away. She zipped up her bag, hauled it off the bed, then caught her own reflection in the full-length mirror. The woman staring back at her looked... different somehow. Taller. Stronger. But softer in a way. She didn't quite get it, but there it was.

Back to the coat closet, and she put on her winter garb again. She could grab something from a drive-thru to eat on her way. Suddenly, all she wanted was to get to Hannah, to wrap her up and explain it all to her—the lying, the deceit. She wanted to reassure her and do everything she could to help.

Feeling both excited and anxious, she locked up and went down to her car. Trying her hardest to ignore the question bouncing around in her head didn't work, and as soon as she started the car and pulled out on the street, it blasted through her mind like it had its own bullhorn.

What if Hannah ended up hating her?

No. No, she couldn't think about that now. She called up the playlist on her phone that she'd named Mindless, and the car filled with a poppy, bouncy song about dancing. She cranked up the volume and pointed her car toward Sunset Valley.

She ended up cutting almost twenty minutes off her usual drive time because she drove like a bat out of hell, as her mother would've said. Somehow having managed not to get pulled over for speeding, she slowed her pace at Main Street. A few things were closed. After all, it was the week between Christmas and New Year's, and lots of places took time off. At the same time, this was a tourist town, so most of the restaurants, bars, and shops were still lit up, even at almost nine at night. She coasted past Hopsville, which was—true to its name—hopping. The diner was closed, but the Coffee Cup was still lit up happily. And across the street, the Open sign in the window of Poptacular was also showing. As she parked in front of it, she could see four people inside, Hannah behind the counter.

She turned off her car and waited for her headlights to extinguish, and then she sat and watched. Hannah was smiling, but Riley knew her well now. That wasn't her real smile. Her genuine smile. She was acting. She was in pain. Nobody would notice that, but Riley could tell even from the street, and the only thing she wanted to do was fix it.

What the hell had Hannah done to her?

A few more minutes went by, and just as Riley's car started to get slightly chilly, the customers waved and headed for the door.

Riley got out.

The customers were chatting and laughing as they headed down the street away from Riley, bags of popcorn in their hands. She moved to Poptacular, pulled the door open, and went inside. The second Hannah laid eyes on her, she practically flew around the counter.

She was in Riley's arms in a flash, and Riley felt her shoulders move as she quietly sobbed into her shoulder.

"What am I gonna do?" Hannah's voice was muffled. Then she lifted her head and looked Riley in the eyes. "I'm so glad to see you. You have no idea." And then she buried her face in Riley's shoulder again.

Riley held on.

"How are you even here?" Hannah asked Riley, still wrapped up in her arms. God, this was exactly what she needed. Exactly. She wanted to stay here forever. Right here, held and protected from the world by the most beautiful woman she'd ever known. Riley held her tightly, almost too tightly, and Hannah pushed that aside for the time being.

"Let's talk about that later. First, tell me everything." Riley held her at arm's length. "Let me see the text again."

"Here." Hannah handed over her phone, suddenly more exhausted than she could ever remember being. "I'm gonna close up." The lock clicked home in the front door, and switching the Open sign made a gentle flapping sound against the glass. She'd already begun her nightly cleaning ritual when the last customers had come in, so there wasn't much left to do. The warm water felt good on her hands as she wet a cloth and finished wiping her equipment down, slowly, almost lovingly, because it all felt different now. It all felt like things she might not have much longer, things that were hers that she could lose. Was it a gloom and doom attitude, as her dad would say? Absolutely. But she couldn't seem to help it.

The front lights clicked off as Riley came into the back. Hannah kept her back to her but had to sniff, which gave away the fact that she was crying. Again.

"Oh, sweetheart," Riley whispered, a hand on Hannah's back. "Don't. Nothing is for certain yet. Okay?"

She was right. Hannah couldn't explain why she felt so emotionally overwhelmed right then, but she did. Utterly exhausted. All she could do was nod.

She'd walked to the shop that morning, so grabbed a bag of the peanut butter cup popcorn, and then she let Riley drive her home. The ride was silent, but their hands were linked across the center console as Riley drove and Hannah gazed out the window at this town that was the only home she'd ever known.

What would she do if she didn't have the shop anymore? She'd have to get another job, obviously, but what skills did she have? She had skipped college to work full-time with her grandmother and learn the business. Poptacular was really all she knew.

Pretty short-sighted of her.

Her sigh was long as they pulled up to her place. Still saying nothing, Riley grabbed her bag, and they headed inside and up the stairs. Hannah set the bag of popcorn to lean against Parker's door, then unlocked her own, and they went inside.

"I need a shower," she said without looking at Riley.

The hot water was doing its best to beat her neck muscles into submission when she felt the tickle of cool air, and then Riley was behind her, wrapping her arms around her and pulling her back against her.

Hannah didn't want to speak, so they didn't. She turned in Riley's arms and gazed up at her, lost herself in the blue of those eyes. Riley's face was smooth as Hannah ran her fingertips along her cheek, then down the side of her neck and around back until she pulled Riley's head down and their lips met.

Sex in the shower was new to Hannah, and she decided then and there that she loved it. The slippery wetness of Riley's skin, the combination of the hot water and the cold tile, the creativity required being in such a small space, she loved all of it. Soon, she had Riley backed up against the wall, tongue buried in Riley's mouth, fingers buried in Riley's hot, wet center. Riley's hand was in Hannah's hair, holding fast, causing a bit of pain, but Hannah loved it, it only spurred her on, and she picked up the pace with her hand until Riley cried out her orgasm, her muscles contracting around Hannah's fingers.

This was what she'd needed: to forget for a little while. Riley seemed to understand that, because when the water ran tepid and they dried off after the shower, Riley kept touching her. Kept stroking her, kissing her, until they made it to Hannah's room, to Hannah's bed, and then it was Hannah's turn. Riley wasted no time diving down between Hannah's legs. She was already soaked; the toweling off had done nothing to change that, and at the first touch of Riley's tongue, Hannah nearly exploded. Both hands in Riley's wet hair, she held her in place, making sure her mouth stayed right where she needed it, and she came hard and fast and loud.

They went back and forth for the next two hours, kissing and stroking and tasting each other until they were both absolutely spent.

"I feel like a rag doll," Riley finally whispered as she lay on her back, spread-eagle, trying to catch her breath. "I don't think I could move my legs if there was a gun to my head."

Hannah laughed softly. "Good thing you don't have to." Her body was draped over Riley's like a human blanket, her breathing ragged, her lips kiss-swollen. The comforter was bundled near their feet, and she grabbed it, pulled it up and around them. Riley didn't move, so Hannah snuggled up against her, tucking her head under Riley's chin. Her body felt sapped, leaden, completely relaxed and sated, and now, keeping her eyes open was proving to be a chore. She felt Riley press warm lips to her forehead.

She inhaled deeply and let it out, her eyes closed. "I love you, you know," Hannah whispered as she drifted off to sleep.

When her eyes opened again, she had no idea how much time had passed. The room was still dark, but she could hear birdsong outside and determined it was probably closing in on dawn. Riley was sound asleep next to her, turned away on her side, so her back was to Hannah. Her breath was deep and even, and Hannah simply listened to it.

Propping herself up on an elbow, she wanted to hold on to this moment, this glorious peace, this escape from her reality, at least for a little while. She was pretty sure she'd told Riley she loved her before she'd drifted off, and she wondered now what the reaction had been. Intense sex had always sent her right to sleep, and theirs had been... beyond intense. For a split second, she entertained the idea of waking Riley up to ask her what she thought about the fact that she'd said she loved her, but she looked so pretty right now, so peaceful. Her dark hair fanned out over the pillow, her hand relaxed near her face. Hannah decided she didn't want to disturb what was essentially a piece of art, so instead, she snuggled in and big-spooned her, pressing up against her warm back, burying her nose in Riley's hair, pressing her pelvis into Riley's backside, and wrapping an arm around her middle. With a long exhale, she let herself relax once again.

She wanted to stay there forever.

Chapter Seventeen

The next time Hannah opened her eyes, the sun was streaming fully in through her bedroom window. She was alone in bed, and Riley's side was cold, telling her she'd been gone for a while. What the hell time was it?

She'd left her phone in her bag last night, having opted for an immediate shower and then…distraction. Her brain tossed her an image of Riley in the shower with her, back against the white tiles, eyes closed tightly, mouth open to allow her soft moans that had increased in volume…

Okay. Enough of that right now.

Once the throbbing between her legs had faded, she sighed and kicked off the covers. Dressing in a pair of joggers and a hoodie, she went in search of her phone, Riley, and coffee, not necessarily in that order.

The apartment was empty, and a tiny second of panic hit before she saw Riley's bag on the floor in the living room and breathed out a sigh of relief that surprised her. She found her own purse on the kitchen counter where she'd tossed it the night before and dug her phone out. Almost dead. The charger was right there in the kitchen, so she plugged it in just as the door opened and Riley came in, bringing the smell of the outdoors with her.

"Morning," she said with that smile that could melt her in seconds. She held a white bag in one hand and a tray with two to-go cups in the other.

"Hi," Hannah said, taking the tray from her.

"Thought I'd get us some breakfast." Riley slid out of her coat and gave a little full-body shudder. "Cold out there."

"It *is* December in upstate New York, so…" She shrugged with a soft smile.

"Can't really complain," Riley finished as she leaned in and gave her a soft kiss before opening the bag to pull out two breakfast sandwiches from the Coffee Cup. "Shana says hello." She stopped and focused on Hannah. "Seriously, is she AI? When does that woman sleep?"

"I have asked myself the same question," Hannah said with a laugh.

They moved around in the small kitchen like they'd been doing it for years, seamlessly avoiding bumping into each other as Hannah grabbed plates and Riley unwrapped the sandwiches and uncapped the coffees, tossing all the paper into the garbage.

"Couch?" Riley asked.

"Perfect."

Sitting side by side on the couch with Riley, their feet up on the coffee table, crossed at the ankle, felt indescribably perfect. Like it was not only normal but typical. Their regular routine. They ate their sandwiches in silence, aside from tandem "mmms" over how delicious they were.

"Not only does she make fabulous coffee, but this might be the best breakfast sandwich I've ever had." Riley took another huge bite.

"I'm happy to report that maybe she is *not* an artificial person, as she has a cook on her staff who makes all the baked goods and sandwiches. Bobby."

"I actually find that to be a relief."

"Right?"

"And Bobby is a god."

"He might be."

The comfort of sitting with Riley was soon overshadowed by the news from the day before, though, like a black cloud had floated into the room and stopped right above Hannah's head.

"What am I gonna do, Riley?" She hated how small her voice sounded.

Riley chewed for a moment. "Well. We don't know anything for sure yet…" She kind of let that line trail off, and Hannah gave her a look.

"Do you seriously think a new owner is going to come in and offer to charge me the same rent my grandma was paying fifteen years ago?" Riley sighed. "Probably not."

"Exactly." They sat quietly, chewing and sipping, though Hannah's sandwich was starting to feel uncomfortable in her stomach, and she set it down. Needing a change of subject, she asked, "So, what happened with Portland? Did you finish up sooner than you expected?"

Riley didn't look at her, just chewed and swallowed, then looked down at her lap. "Um."

Hannah watched her face. Waited. "Ri? What is it?"

The sigh Riley released was long. Heavy. It didn't help Hannah's roiling stomach. "I need to tell you something."

"Okay." The word stretched out like taffy.

Riley took a deep breath and said, "I didn't go to Portland."

Confusion tickled at her brain. "Oh. Okay. Did it get canceled?"

"No. No, it didn't. There was no Portland trip to cancel." Riley cleared her throat. "There was no Portland trip."

Hannah frowned. "I don't understand."

Riley said it again. "There was no trip to Portland. I made it up."

"You made it—why?" Why would Riley simply invent a work trip? What in the world?

Eye contact wasn't happening at this point. Riley was looking at her hands and shaking her head. "I don't know. I panicked."

"You panicked? About what ex—" It hit her then. Right in the face. "Oh," she said, drawing the word out as her brain kicked into high gear and finally caught up. "Oh, you didn't want to stay here for Christmas. With me."

"No," Riley said vehemently. Then she grimaced. Actually grimaced, then edited her words to, "No, not exactly."

"Not exactly? Well, that's comforting. How was it, then? Exactly?" She was getting snarky, and she knew it, but she couldn't help it. "Was the idea of spending Christmas with me so horrific that you had to, to, *make something up* to avoid it?"

Riley looked ill. "I'm…I'm not good at…" She seemed to be searching for the right words. "Staying in one place. I'm better if I keep moving."

Hannah blinked at her. "What does that even mean?"

She'd never seen Riley look like this before, cornered, panicked, almost childlike and seemingly looking for an escape. "I'm trying to explain. I—" Her swallow was audible. "I keep moving."

Hannah waited, but nothing more came. Riley looked miserable, that was true, and Hannah didn't like seeing it. But seriously? She was torn between being angry at the timing of this—while she was terrified of losing her livelihood—and being crushed at the idea that spending the holidays with her had been such an awful idea, that maybe Riley wasn't as into this thing between them as she was.

The anger was much easier to grab on to.

"Seriously, Riley? 'I keep moving'?" She didn't sneer the quote, but she didn't say it nicely. "That's your reason for not wanting to be here with me over Christmas? Jesus, I don't even know what you're talking about, but if you don't want to be here, I've got a solution for you: Don't be here." She tossed the remainder of her sandwich down on the coffee table and pushed to her feet.

"Hannah," Riley said, and Hannah tried to ignore how much she loved the sound of her name in Riley's mouth. "Wait. Please. Let's talk."

The deep breath she took did steady her the tiniest bit, but she couldn't handle this right now. "Look. I'm freaking out about the shop. Okay? It's bad. We both know that. I just…" Her eyes welled up, which only fueled her anger, but she did her best to keep it harnessed. "I don't have the bandwidth to deal with any other emotional stuff right now."

"Okay." Riley nodded. "Okay. That's fair. How about you give me some time to spend with your accounting program again, go through it, see where we can pull money to cover a likely rent increase? Would that be okay?"

She was trying, Hannah could see that, and she nodded. "Yeah. Okay. Fine." Riley's relief was clearly visible, but Hannah was still stung. "You should probably get yourself a room at the resort." Before she could see the hurt in Riley's eyes, she went into her room and shut the door behind her.

❖

"You're very lucky, Ms. Shaw. Normally, we are booked solid over the holiday, but we've had a recent cancellation, so I have one room available." The woman behind the front desk at the Sunset Valley

Resort and Spa gave her a tired smile. "It's a suite, though. I hope that's okay."

"Beggars can't be choosers, right?" She handed over her credit card, and a moment later, she was headed for the elevator.

Holy crap, she'd fucked this up. She'd fucked everything up. She sighed mightily as she tossed her bag onto the freshly made bed and moved to the window. It had started to snow again, lightly, small flakes floating down to the ground to add to the canvas of white that covered the property. Some of the trees were decorated with twinkling lights, giving the grounds a warm and festive look, but she only felt cold and alone.

"That's what I get for trying to be honest," she said quietly to the empty room. Admittedly, she hadn't given the most coherent explanation, just the one she'd remembered from her three sessions of therapy she'd tried. It hadn't been something she'd enjoyed, spilling her deepest concerns, habits, and thoughts to a complete stranger, who was being paid to listen, and after the third session, she'd given up. *No thanks, I'd rather not do this.*

She flopped backward onto the bed and stared at the ceiling, unable to get Hannah's face out of her mind. The confusion. The hurt...

Antsy was the only way to describe how she felt. Nervous and jerky, like she couldn't sit still. She got up again and stripped out of her clothes, then walked naked to the bathroom, where she turned the shower on as hot as she could tolerate and stood under the beating water until her skin was pink and the knot in the back of her neck loosened at least a little.

She wanted to go back. That seemed to be the thing to do, to try to talk it through. But Hannah had been pretty clear.

Exhausted wasn't something Riley felt often. She was a pro at staving off tiredness. The way she traveled, hopping from one time zone to another, she had to find ways to stay awake and alert, and she'd grown good at it. But this morning? God, fatigue settled over her like a weighted blanket, pushing her down, pressing on her shoulders, her neck. She dried herself off slowly. Everything she did for the next half hour, she did slowly. Moisturizing. Getting dressed. Drying her hair. She felt like she was moving in slow motion, and when she finally sat down on the end of the bed, she did feel utterly exhausted, but mentally. Emotionally. And that was extending to physically.

Feeling helpless wasn't something she handled well, so she pulled out her laptop and began on what she said she'd do: go through Poptacular's accounting again and see what kind of finagling she could do to help.

There was a Keurig on the dresser, so she made herself a very mediocre cup of coffee, slid on her glasses, and sat down to work.

The next time she looked up from her laptop, her eyes watered. With no idea how long she'd been alternately reading numbers and simply staring at the screen, she glanced at the time in the corner and did a double take. How the hell had nearly four hours gone by?

By now she was hungry, and her muscles ached from hunching over in the same position for what had turned out to be hours. She stood and stretched backward and felt several pops along her spine that always gave her pause and a little jolt of fear.

The snow had stopped and the sun had broken through the clouds, and she was nearly blinded looking out the window. The blanket of snow on the ground sparkled in the sunlight, like it had been sprinkled with tiny bits of glass, just gorgeous to look at. Riley wished she felt as happy now as she had this morning shopping for breakfast for herself and Hannah.

How quickly things change.

"No," she said out loud. "That was your fault. *You* changed things." She'd been avoiding looking at her phone because she didn't want to see proof that Hannah hadn't tried to contact her, and now she picked it up.

Nothing.

The tears that filled her eyes came as a surprise.

A new text box open on the screen, she stared for a long time before typing.

Hey, you around?

She waited for a beat, and then the dots bounced.

At HQ all day doing paperwork. You in town again? Hannah didn't mention it.

That surprised her. *Working on a Sunday?*

He typed back, *Best way to get stuff done, when nobody's here.*

She typed quickly before she lost her nerve. *Can I bring you lunch?*

Kyle's answer came quickly. *I never say no to free food.*
She grinned at the accuracy of his statement. *See you soon.* Maybe
this was out of line. Maybe she was doing an end run. She didn't care.
She needed to talk to somebody or she was going to go out of her mind,
and Hannah clearly wasn't an option right now.

Coat and purse in hand, she headed out.

Kyle's was the only truck in the lot at the construction warehouse,
and she breathed in a lungful of fresh country air before shouldering her
purse and taking the bag of food toward the office.

"There she is," Kyle said as she entered, clearly happy to see her.
He came around his desk and wrapped her in a hug, and even though
her hands were full, she sank into it, just for a moment. He moved to
the other desk in the room and grabbed the chair, rolled it over to his.
"Here. Sit."

"Thanks." She set the food on the desk and slid out of her coat.

"To what do I owe the pleasure?" Kyle asked, smiling as he sat
back down. "Hannah up to her eyeballs in popcorn? Too busy to chat?"
He grinned as he said it, and Riley marveled at how similar their eyes
were—rich brown and slightly almond-shaped. Kyle's brows were
much thicker than Hannah's, obviously, but the sandy shade of them
was exactly the same. He needed a haircut again, the ends flipping
slightly as it skimmed his shoulders.

"Something like that." She busied herself emptying the bag. "If
I remembered correctly, you're a fan of the meatloaf they make at the
diner." She handed him the polystyrene clamshell tray and he wasted
no time opening it to reveal a huge slab of meatloaf covered in gravy, a
large scoop of mashed potatoes sitting next to it.

"Oh, God, you're the best." He held the tray up and inhaled deeply.
"I'm starving. Thank you."

"Welcome." She handed him a plastic fork and knife, then pulled
out the bowl of chili she'd ordered for herself. She wasn't at all hungry,
but she couldn't bring lunch for only Kyle, then sit and watch him eat.
How creepy would that have been? "When's the last time you talked to
your sister?" she asked. Might as well dive right in.

He shrugged as he chewed. "Christmas."

"So, she hasn't told you yet."

Kyle's sandy brow furrowed. "Told me what?"

"McFarland sold the building Poptacular is in."

Kyle stopped chewing and blinked at her, as if he needed a moment to compute what she'd said. "Shit."

"Yeah."

"Hannah's gotta be panicking." He inhaled deeply, then let it out.

With a nod, she said, "She's sure the rent will go up."

"Of course it will. Bradley's been great with that, not raising the rent on her for years now. He's a good guy, knew his dad and my grandma were friends."

Riley nodded, already having all this information. She forced herself to eat a spoon of chili.

"She's gonna want you to go over numbers."

Another nod. "Did."

"And? I'm guessing no joy."

"Not much, no. She's definitely doing better, but any rise in costs is going to eat up any new profit and…" She lifted a shoulder.

"And she'll be right back where she was."

"Yeah."

"Fuck." The word came out quietly, almost under his breath. "I should call her." He pulled out his phone and she let him poke at the screen twice before she spoke.

"Wait."

He looked up, brows raised in question.

"I need to talk to you first."

"Okay." He set the phone down, put a forkful of meatloaf into his mouth, and met her eyes as he chewed. "What's up?"

Oh, she hadn't rehearsed this, hadn't played it out in her head. How was she supposed to do this? What should she tell him?

"Ri, seriously, you're freaking me out a little bit." He continued to eat as he blinked at her.

"Yeah. Okay." She cleared her throat. "So, you know how Hannah and I, um—"

"Yeah, I know how Hannah and you," he interrupted. Pointing his plastic fork at her, he said, "Honestly? Haven't seen her this happy in a long time."

Great. Perfect. Exactly what she needed to hear. *Fuck.* Riley blew out a breath and looked down at the chili in her hands. She set the bowl on the desk, the roil of her stomach making it clear she wouldn't be eating any more. "Yeah, well, she's not very happy with me right now."

Again, his sandy brows went up toward his hairline, waiting for the rest of the story.

She gave it to him.

When she finished, he sat quietly for a long moment, not looking at her, but looking down at the remainder of his lunch. He set his fork down.

"So, wait. You *pretended* to go on a business trip? To avoid spending Christmas with my sister?"

"I mean, not for that reason, but…" Shifting in her chair was probably a dead giveaway, but she couldn't help it. His stare was making her squirm.

"Did you or did you not tell her you were going to be *across the fucking country* over Christmas?"

"I did." She hated how small she sounded.

"And where were you actually over Christmas?"

Another clear of her throat. "At my apartment."

"In Boston."

"Yes."

"A four-hour drive away."

"Yes."

"Jesus, Riley. Why? That's what I don't get. Why?"

"I don't…" A shrug as she let her voice trail off. "I'm not sure…I mean I just…"

"Why?" He didn't yell the word, but it was loud and firm, and when she glanced up at him, met his gaze, his eyes flashed with what looked like a combination of anger and confusion. "Why would you do that to her?"

"Because she scares me!" The words shot from her mouth before she'd even had a chance to understand they were about to, and she blinked in surprise.

The two of them sat there for a beat, looking at each other. Blinking. Saying nothing. Then Riley pushed to her feet so quickly, her chair almost fell over.

"I have to go."

"What?" Kyle stood as well. "Now?"

"Yeah. I'm sorry." She gathered her lunch stuff, put it all in the bag, and tossed it into a nearby wastebasket. "I'm sorry." Quickly, she put on her jacket and grabbed her purse, then met Kyle's gaze once more. "I'm sorry," she whispered. She was out the door and practically running to her car in the next moment.

She held it together until she turned out of the parking lot and was speeding down the road. That's when a sob burst out of her and the tears began to flow.

The countryside flying by calmed her, so she kept going. It was one thing she'd learned about herself. As long as she was moving, she was okay.

Hannah's face popped up in her mind, as it had begun doing recently, and she felt some of her tensed muscles begin to let go, to loosen up just the slightest bit.

What the hell was she supposed to do now?

She kept driving.

Chapter Eighteen

Monday was gross.

The weather had taken a turn, snow being whipped around by the wind, the sky cloudy and dull as an old nickel. Riley lay in her hotel bed and stared out the window for so long, she had no idea what time it was. She'd woken up sometime in the predawn hours and had lain there, watching as the sky slowly began to lighten. She hadn't moved.

Her body felt heavy. Leaden.

Her head also felt heavy. And sad. Worried. Confused. Guilty.

Eventually, she forced herself out of bed and into the shower. Again, she did everything slowly. Washing her body, drying herself with a towel. Smoothing on lotion. Applying makeup. Drying her hair. Getting dressed. She did all of it at a snail's pace, and by the time she was fully dressed and ready to go, it was nearly ten o'clock.

She stood at the window and sipped her mediocre Keurig coffee as she watched the snow. She'd have to brush off her car and drive carefully. Despite the efficiency of the public works department and how well they plowed, the roads would still be treacherous. She wasn't looking forward to having to brush off her car, then navigate the streets, but she had to.

She had to.

It took a good fifteen minutes to get the car cleared and warmed up, and driving was pretty slow, but she made it to her destination before eleven. She parked out front, headed inside, and took the stairs slowly, like a dead woman walking. Half expecting Parker the teenage neighbor to be standing in the hall for no other reason than to make her feel judged, she was surprised to find it empty and quiet.

It took a moment or two for her to steady her breath and find her nerve, but she finally did, and knocked. There was movement behind the door. She could see shadows in the light beneath it, two feet standing there, and she knew she was being looked at through the peephole.

A beat went by, clearly Hannah feeling unsure about letting her in.

Riley had to make a conscious effort not to shift her weight from foot to foot as she stood there, and finally, the lock clicked and the door opened to reveal Hannah.

She looked tired. That was the first thing Riley noticed. Tired and sad, and Riley had to make another conscious effort, this time to not reach out and wrap Hannah up in her arms.

"Hey," Hannah said, then turned and walked into the living room, leaving the door open and Riley standing there.

She stepped inside, toed off her boots, and closed the door. The apartment was quiet and not exactly dark, but Hannah had no lights on other than the Christmas tree, and if there wasn't the storm cloud of bad looming there, it'd be a comforting, inviting atmosphere. A full cup of tea sat on the coffee table. Hannah, lying on her side on the couch alone under a blanket that looked handmade, didn't look at her as she walked in and sat in the chair across from the couch.

Neither of them said anything for what felt like a long time. Riley knew this was on her, it was her show. She cleared her throat.

"Your tea looks cold. Want me to warm it up?"

Hannah shook her head.

Okay. Great. Perfect. Good job, Ri.

She cleared her throat again.

"Listen, Hannah. I'm sorry. Just…let me start there." Her hands were clasped together between her knees, and now they started to wring, twisting in and around each other, as if they had minds of their own. "What I did was stupid, and I know I hurt you."

Hannah's eyes were open, so she was listening, but her gaze stayed on the tree, the colors glistening in reflection.

"I've been trying to understand the why of it. Like, why I would've…done what I did."

"Lied to me." Hannah's voice was small, and she almost missed it.

"What?"

That's when Hannah's gaze turned to her, bore into her. "*Lied* to me. *That's* what you did."

A lump suddenly appeared in her throat, big and made of stress and worry. She swallowed it down. "Yeah." She nodded. "Yeah. That."

Hannah was back staring at the tree, and this was brutal. Brutal. Why couldn't she speak? Why couldn't she organize her thoughts? Everything was a jumble, like her skull was full of spaghetti, every thought interweaving with another and another and another until it was just one mess of tangled words. Tears sprang into her eyes.

"I miss you." Those words came out in barely more than a whisper. "I miss you, and I'm so sorry I hurt you."

"Thank you." Hannah's words were quiet, and she didn't look at Riley.

Thank you? That's it? What more does she want?

Those thoughts whirled through her head, but not in a snarky way. In a simple, factual question. She'd come to apologize. She'd done that. Now what?

"I..." She sighed and turned to look at the tree as well, at a complete loss as to what to say next. She knew she needed to talk, that she was the only one who could fix this, but she had zero idea how, so instead, she sat there, staring at a Christmas tree and feeling like a child.

After what felt like a year and a half, Hannah pushed herself up to a sitting position and blew out a long, slow breath. "Look. You apologized. I assume that's what you came here for. I accept your apology. You can go now." She tipped her head to one side and glared at Riley. And yeah, it was most definitely a glare.

"I know I hurt you—" she began, but Hannah cut her off.

"Yeah, you said that. And yes, you hurt me. But I don't think you get how much. How deeply." Hannah seemed to be waiting for her to say something, anything, but Riley's voice was stuck. "Not only did you pretend to be on a business trip, but you pretended to be on a business trip so you *didn't have to spend Christmas with me.*" Again, she paused. Again, Riley couldn't find words. "That told me pretty much all I needed to know about where I rank on your list of priorities." She shook her head, clearly disgusted, and muttered, "I knew falling for you was a mistake." She lay back down and pulled the blanket over her shoulder. "You can go now."

She'd been dismissed, and it was painful and embarrassing. She should say more. She should say something. Anything. "Hannah—"

"Just go. Please." And this time, Hannah's voice was soft. She met Riley's eyes and whispered, "Please."

Pain.

It was all she could see. Hannah's pain. And she had her own, yes, but Hannah's was big, huge, it took up the whole room, and Riley had caused it and now Hannah was begging her to leave. She wanted to drop to her knees and do some begging of her own, some pleading. She wanted to apologize over and over and over. But none of that happened.

"Okay," she said instead, very softly.

She crossed the room quickly, stepped into her boots without bothering to lace them up, put one arm in her coat, and left. She hurried down the stairs, tears now rolling freely down her cheeks. As she pushed through the front door, there slouched Parker, the teenaged neighbor, and she looked up from her phone as Riley pushed past her.

"Oof, looks like you blew it," she observed.

"Shut up," Riley threw over her shoulder as she hurried to her car.

The weather hadn't improved, but traffic around Sunset Valley was minimal. She could've been more careful driving back to the resort, but her mind wasn't exactly on the road, and she fishtailed twice as she turned corners.

Back in her room, she was ready to pack everything up and flee—and she knew that's what it would be: fleeing—but the snow had picked up, as had the wind. As she stood there at the big window, staring out at the whipping whiteness, she knew trying to drive back to Boston would be beyond ill-advised.

Work.

That's what she'd do.

It's what she always did when she needed to focus her brain on something else.

Yes, it was the week between Christmas and New Year's. That didn't mean there weren't things she could do. There were tons.

She changed into cozier clothes—yoga pants and her favorite sweatshirt. She put her hair up. Then she opened her laptop up on the desk in her room and got things together—paper, pens, her phone—until she'd made herself a little workstation. Then she sat down and did her best to focus.

It was the only way to keep her mind off Hannah, off her steely eyes and her hard voice and the clear pain that was written all over her.

She inhaled slowly and deeply, did her best to center herself. Then she clicked open her inbox.

Yeah. This would work.

Surely.

❖

"Why don't you come to Henry's tomorrow night?" Shana's eyes were soft, her voice gentle, but there was also the tiniest shred of pity in her tone.

"You're very sweet, but I don't want to cramp your style when you suck face with Davey at midnight." Hannah said it teasingly, with a grin, but inside, her stomach roiled. No, she didn't want to be around anybody who'd be kissing when the ball dropped, and especially not in a bar full of people. Because she'd be kissing nobody. Again. She turned on the popper.

"Babe. Come on. You can't stay home and wallow."

"Sure I can. I'm actually pretty good at it. You'd be impressed." She could feel Shana's eyes on her, and she purposely busied herself making caramel. "This is my third batch today," she said, pointing at the pot. "Apparently, people are in a caramel-y kind of mood. They should get it while they can, right?"

Shana gave her a sad smile. "I hate the way you've just given up." She said it softly, and while it wasn't accusatory, there was a firmness to her tone now.

Hannah turned on her and narrowed her eyes for half a beat before closing them, giving her forehead a scratch, and saying nothing.

A moment of silence went by before Shana sighed quietly.

"All right, well, I've gotta get back. Those beans aren't gonna roast themselves." Shana's smile was one of apology. Hannah knew her well enough to see that. "I'll catch you later, okay?"

"Yeah."

She heard Shana say goodbye to Joanne, and as she left, a couple customers came in. Hannah found it both amusing and infuriating that business had picked up when she knew as soon as the sale of the building was finalized and the new owners took over, she'd have to close. Shana wasn't wrong in assuming she'd given up, but what was the alternative? She'd briefly entertained looking for a new location, but just a quick search had assured her the rent she was currently paying was ridiculously low.

She made the caramel sauce, then moved the popcorn to the mixer and poured it on. The smell filled the entire shop, and it was one she'd never tire of. Her eyes welled up.

"Damn it," she muttered with a sniffle.

"Hey, Hannah?" Joanne was in the doorway, her voice low.

Hannah sniffed once more, cleared her throat, and said, "Yeah?"

"There's a guy here to see you. Says he's a lawyer?"

She pursed her lips and blew out a breath as she glanced toward the front of the shop and saw a gentleman in a suit scrolling on his phone. "Yeah, okay. Can you keep an eye on this for me for a sec?"

"Of course."

She wiped her hands on her apron as she headed out front. "Hi there. Can I help you?"

The man turned to meet her gaze. A neatly trimmed brown beard accented his face. He was small-framed but handsome, clad in a navy blue suit and a peacoat. He reached out a hand. "Hannah Kramer?"

She nodded as she took it and shook. His grip was firm, but not obnoxiously so.

"Kieran Herkimer, attorney." He indicated the end of the counter by the wall, away from the cash register. "Can we?"

"Sure." Was it happening already? Bradley had said the sale would be finalized this week, but she hadn't expected a lawyer to visit so quickly. The roiling in her stomach kicked up a few dozen notches.

They moved to the end of the counter where he set his briefcase and clicked it open. "I have a new lease for you to sign." He pulled out some papers as Hannah frowned.

"I'm sorry?"

"The new owner sent me over to have you sign a new lease." It was the same sentence but still made no sense. "It'll start the first of the year. So, Friday." He gave her a smile, and she noticed the deep blue of his eyes. "Sorry about the speed. My client wanted to get it all set up before the first." With a grimace, he added, "I usually take this week off, but he insisted." He pointed out different spots on the lease between them as he spoke. "Okay, so here's the date this goes into effect. Here's your monthly rate. And he had me add in that it's not to change until he passes away."

"I—wait. What? I don't understand." Hannah was following his finger, and when they got to the monthly rate, her brain screeched to a halt. "This…this is less than I'm paying now." She looked up at Kieran and repeated herself. "I don't understand."

Dimples appeared on each cheek when he smiled. "Yeah, he said you'd be confused."

"Who said?"

"My client. Robert Daniels."

"What?" She knew her eyes went wide because she could feel it, literally feel the air on her eyeballs, so intense was her surprise. "Mr. Daniels bought this building?"

"He did. Apparently, your shop"—his gaze went to the framed photo on the wall—"and your grandmother were very important to him."

Hannah stood there and blinked. It was all she could do. Stand there. Blink.

"So." He went back to pointing at the papers. "This is your monthly rent. And then this clause here says that when Mr. Daniels passes away, the building becomes yours."

"*What?*"

This time, Kieran Herkimer laughed out loud. It was a surprisingly deep and throaty sound. "Yeah, he said you'd be surprised by that, too."

"Surprised? I—I'm—I don't understand any of this." It was as if her brain had simply stopped working. She put her hands to her temples. Thoughts wouldn't go in. Nothing would compute.

Kieran smiled at her, and he seemed to give himself a moment to slow down. "Sorry. I'm rushing through all of this, and I shouldn't do that." He took a breath. "Okay. In a nutshell: Mr. Robert Daniels put in an offer on this building a few weeks ago."

"I knew Bradley was selling, but I didn't know it was to him," Hannah said.

"Yes. In fact, Mr. Daniels has been trying to buy it for several years now."

Okay, that was a surprise. "He never said anything."

Kieran shrugged. "If I've learned anything about Mr. Daniels, it's that he keeps his cards close to the vest." He smiled at her. "He explicitly told me the first order of business once closing happened was to assure you that you wouldn't have a rise in rental costs."

Hannah did some more blinking and was now understanding that it was her go-to when she didn't grasp something.

Kieran reached out and set a warm hand on her forearm. "Ms. Kramer, all he wants is for you to remain in this building. He knows how important this shop was to your grandmother. He knows how important it is to you. And he knows how important it is to the community." With a gentle smile and a pat on her arm, he added, "He doesn't want you going anywhere."

She needed a beat to take in his words, everything that was happening. In the end, she asked for copies so she could run them by her own lawyer—and Kyle—and Kieran was happy to oblige.

She watched him leave the shop, then stared after him for a long while. Even when the bell tinkled and a customer walked in, she still stared. Joanne came out from the back and sold three bags of the turtle flavor to the customer, and once they'd left, she hesitantly touched Hannah's shoulder.

"Han? You okay?"

Hannah blinked rapidly, as if coming out of a trance. She looked down at the papers in her hand, then back up at Joanne, and she had absolutely zero control over the smile that burst across her face.

"I'm great, Jo. I am *fabulous*." She hurried around the corner, calling over her shoulder, "Can you hold down the fort for a bit? I need to see my brother and…" She left the sentence incomplete because she'd almost said Riley's name. But Riley was long gone.

"Of course," Joanne said as Hannah flew past her in a whirlwind of winter coat and rustling paper.

She started her car and let it run while she brushed it free of snow. The weather had been nasty for two solid days now, but she had snow tires and years of experience driving in it, so she wasn't worried. Her excitement had dimmed ever so slightly at the thought of Riley, who was likely back in Boston by now, and who she'd probably never see again, and the way her heart squeezed in her chest at that thought was no joke. She had to stop what she was doing for a moment and close her eyes to let it pass, pressing her gloved fingers against her chest and rubbing. All she wanted to do right now—the very first thing she wanted to do—was rush to Riley and share the news. She'd be so happy for Hannah.

The lump in her throat was stubborn, and she spent the entire ride to Kyle's office trying to swallow it down.

CHAPTER NINETEEN

The snow was still falling, but there'd been enough time for the plows to work their magic, and according to Riley's weather app, things were going to clear up as she drove.

She purposely didn't drive down Main Street on her way out of Sunset Valley; she didn't think she could bear to see Poptacular one more time. Her stomach had been churning unpleasantly since Monday, since Hannah's dismissal of her, and she'd barely eaten.

"I can live on coffee," she muttered. "People do it all the time, right?" She looked down at the paper to-go cup of coffee she'd snagged from the lobby of the hotel and grimaced. It was...not good. But stopping at the Coffee Cup wasn't an option either. She didn't want to run into Shana.

Besides the churning of her stomach and the inability to sleep, her heart also ached. Not figuratively, but literally. She pushed her fingers against her breastbone and rubbed, and her mind filled with images of Hannah. Hannah smiling, Hannah laughing, Hannah orgasming.

"Jesus Christ," she muttered and used the buttons on her steering wheel to turn up the music. Maybe she could blast the memories out of her head.

She wished her mom was here. God, how she wished that. She missed her all the time, but now? It was a hundredfold. Her mom would know how to make her feel better. Great with advice, Riley had never hesitated to go to her with a problem. And if her mom didn't have a solution, she always had words of wisdom that made her feel at least a tiny bit better.

She was on her own this time.

"What is wrong with me?" She shouted it out into the empty interior of the car as she hit the highway heading back toward Boston. "What is wrong with me?" Tears sprang into her eyes and a small sob rumbled up from her throat.

The way she felt about Hannah…she hadn't felt that in such a long time. If ever. She'd been in love before, once, but not like this.

"Wait." Was she in love with Hannah? She blew out a breath of mental exhaustion, because of course she fucking was. That wasn't hard to realize.

"But I fucked it up, so…" She shrugged, having a conversation about her love life with exactly nobody. "And I apologized, but…I guess I didn't do it right. If I had, she wouldn't have kicked me out. You know?"

Hitting her turn signal, she passed a semi. Normally, she loved driving, loved moving. Being in the car or on an airplane or even a train—those were her happy places. Always moving.

So, why did she feel restless right now? Antsy. Unsettled. A glance at her dash told her she'd been driving for about an hour. More than enough time to settle in for the ride, to relax into her seat, sing along to her playlist, think about what she wanted to pick up for dinner on her way to her apartment while she also thought about the next work trip.

But none of that was happening.

None of it.

Shifting in her seat, squirming uncomfortably, her brain shuffling too many thoughts—it was all making for a weird ride home, and she was getting irritated.

"Moving, moving, moving," she sang quietly, the silly song she hummed to herself when she was happily on her way to the next business trip.

She was not happy.

"What the *fuck*?" she asked. Loudly.

And then it hit her.

Like a bat to the head.

Like the proverbial ton of bricks falling on her.

She didn't want to be moving.

She wanted to be staying still.

For the first time she could remember since her mother died, Riley Shaw wanted to stay still.

It was such an enormous realization that she had to pull over. Hit her turn signal, slow down, and move to the shoulder where she put her car in park and sat. Stared in disbelief as her brain chugged through thoughts like a freight train.

When her mom was alive, Riley still traveled, but not as much, and she didn't live for it. She went where work sent her, but not like she did now. Back then, trips were once every two or three months. And after her mom had passed, Riley had stepped those up, taken on as many business trips as possible.

It didn't take a therapist to make her see things clearly. With her mom gone, Riley simply kept moving. Because if she stayed still…

Tears showed up out of nowhere, and she allowed them. Not something she did very often. This time? She let them come.

And come they did.

Out of nowhere, a sob racked her body and burst forth. She gripped the steering wheel with both hands and let it pour out of her.

Time passed. She had no idea how much of it. Her car rocked slightly each time a semi flew by, and finally—finally—her tears subsided. She took a deep breath, and out of nowhere, she knew exactly what she wanted.

There was tissue in her car somewhere, and she dug around—glove box, pockets, purse—until she found one. She blew her nose, flipped the visor down and gave a small cry of despair at the sight of her mascara all streaked under her eyes, so she took some time and cleaned it up. Once she looked presentable again, she carefully signaled her return to traffic and pulled out. At the very next exit, which just happened to be within five miles, she got off the highway, turned to the on ramp, and got right back on, heading in the opposite direction.

Because she knew exactly what she wanted now.

And she needed to tell Hannah.

❖

"Holy shit, Han, that's fantastic!" Kyle picked his little sister up in a hug and spun her once around before setting her back down.

"I know, right?" she said. "I still can't quite believe it."

"And you had no idea?"

"None. He never said a word, and he comes into the shop at least once or twice a week."

Kyle sat down at his desk. "Maybe he was waiting for the sale to go through before he said anything?"

Hannah glanced out the window at the construction guys moving around the yard. "Not as many guys as there usually are," she commented.

"Lotta guys took the week," Kyle said.

She inhaled deeply and let it out, then turned to her brother. "I feel so much lighter, Kyle. The relief—" She held up her hands, palms up, and closed her fingers into fists, "it's like something I can touch. Grab onto and hold."

Kyle's grin was wide, genuine. "I'm so glad. It's quite the Christmas gift."

"It really is."

They were quiet for a moment before Kyle asked softly, "Anything from Riley?"

Hannah frowned. "No." She shook her head. "I was pretty hard on her."

He scoffed and shuffled some papers around on his desk. "Yeah, well, she had it coming, didn't she?"

"Yeah." She drew the word out. Kyle was right, but that didn't make her feel any less bad about it. "All right, I'll get out of your hair. I just wanted to tell you the news in person. Poptacular is gonna be okay."

"Really happy for you, Han." He reached out a fist for her to bump, and she did. "You gonna be at Mom and Dad's tomorrow night?"

She sighed as she headed for the door. "I don't know. Maybe?"

"All right, well, we'll be there, and I know the twins would love to see you."

They said their goodbyes and Hannah headed back to the shop. She really did feel lighter, like a weight she'd been carrying around for years had, at long last, been lifted from her shoulders. And it kind of had, hadn't it? That comparison wasn't far off from her reality.

The snow had started up again, but this time, it wasn't being whipped around by a vicious wind. Rather, it fell slowly and softly in big, fluffy flakes, the kind Hannah loved. The kind that made Main Street in Sunset Valley look like the set of a Hallmark Christmas movie. She felt a tiny bit better as she drove toward the shop and parked her car but still wished for one more thing to make her day complete, and that wasn't going to happen. She sat in the car for a moment and let herself feel those feelings—the sadness, the loss, the missing Riley so much it made her chest ache.

After a few minutes, she took in a deep breath, let it out, and got out of her car.

Main Street still looked merry and bright. Light-up wreaths had been fastened to each lamppost, and in the dusk, they shone festively, their multicolored twinkle lights making her smile. Shop windows were decorated, and tourists and locals alike were wandering up and down the street, in and out of storefronts.

God, she loved her little town.

All right. Enough romanticizing.

She headed for the front door of Poptacular.

Which was surprisingly busy. With a wave to Joanne, she hurried to the back and shucked off her coat, switched it out for her apron and her ski cap for the baseball hat, and went out front to help with customers. Eight sales later, she and Joanne high-fived each other.

"When was the last time we had a rush like that?" she asked Joanne.

"Business has been good. Picked up quite a bit, I've noticed." Joanne turned to straighten the two shelves they'd nearly emptied.

"I'd better make some more of the chocolate candy cane popcorn," she said, went to the back, and started a fresh batch popping. Business had definitely increased. It was noticeable, and she owed that to Riley. The partnership with Hopsville had been a huge boon for both businesses. Doing more advertising had helped. Riley wasn't wrong when she'd said you have to spend money to make money. And now that she didn't have to worry about her rent going up—now that it was actually going *down*—maybe she could do a little more of that.

The sound of the popping corn made her extra happy this time, and she turned to watch it, the growing white kernels popping out, the pot tipping to drop them down. It was rhythmic and almost hypnotic.

When she glanced up to check on Joanne, her heart jumped in her chest.

Riley was walking in the front door.

Their eyes met across the room, the cliché not lost on Hannah, even as she stood there, rooted by shock. And just like that, everything in her relaxed, settled, unclenched. She smiled at Riley, and the relief she could see, even from that distance, made her heart jump again.

Riley gave Joanne a smile and a nod, and she indicated the back as she headed in Hannah's direction.

Joanne turned to meet Hannah's gaze, her smile just as big as Hannah's, she suspected.

"Hi," Riley said as she came into the kitchen and stopped a few feet from Hannah.

"Hi." Hannah swallowed hard. A beat went by when neither of them spoke, so she finally asked, "I thought you'd be back in Boston by now. What are you doing here?"

Riley pointed at her with a nod. "That is an excellent question. And I have an answer." She started to wander around the kitchen, not really in a circle, but not actually pacing. It was as if she needed movement to keep her thoughts clear. She touched random things as she passed them—a big spoon here, a sponge there. "I *was* headed home, back to Boston. To my," she sighed and made a fluttering motion with her hand, "rather empty, rather unremarkable apartment. And I started thinking about the things I'd done and the things you said."

Hannah was riveted, not only by Riley's looks—something she now understood would always snag her attention—but by her words and the way she was speaking them. The opposite of Riley's wandering, Hannah didn't move. She stayed glued to her spot, following Riley with her eyes.

Riley wet her lips, stopped moving, and looked at Hannah. "When my mom died, I was lost. I felt like I'd been cast out into space with no tether to anything, just floating aimlessly, no destination, no ties, just me, lonely and alone."

The lump in Hannah's throat appeared out of nowhere at those words, at the mere thought of Riley being so sad.

"But I found a way to make that work for me. The floating. The travel, if you will. I discovered that if I just kept moving, I didn't have to dwell. I didn't have to think about the fact that my mom's gone because I'd be too busy. Moving."

Hannah nodded. "Makes sense."

"It does, right?" Riley looked down at the edge of the stainless steel counter, set her hand on it, rubbed at it with her thumb. "So, I did that. For the past three years, I've kept moving, never staying in one place for very long. From client to client, airport to airport, state to state. Hell, I don't even stay in my apartment for very long at a stretch. That's why it's bare." She glanced up at Hannah. "I don't even have anything on the walls. The *white* walls." She shook her head, as if she'd only just realized how silly that was.

Hannah had questions, but she also had the feeling Riley was on a bit of a roll, so she stayed quiet, watched, and listened.

"Then I came here. I told myself I was doing Kyle a favor and that you were just another client." She looked at Hannah then. "And you were just as stubborn as many of my others, so it was easy to slide you into that category. At first." Riley cleared her throat. "And then..." She waved a hand in Hannah's direction, up and down. "It was you. It was *you*. And you were so resistant and hardheaded and protective of your business and *fucking sexy*. Jesus." She shook her head then, but with a soft smile. "And I was lost again, but in a different way."

Hannah swallowed hard and wondered if Riley heard it.

"I keep moving. I keep moving, that's what I do." Riley met Hannah's gaze and held it. Fiercely. "And you have messed me all up. You've made me want to do something I haven't wanted to do in three years."

It took some effort to find her voice, but Hannah did it. "What do you want to do?" she asked softly.

Riley closed the distance between them until they were facing each other, only inches between them. She took Hannah's hands in her own, held them tightly. "I want to stay still." A small sob escaped her then. "I want to stay still. With you. Can I do that?"

And then Hannah was crying, too. It was sudden, and she didn't even realize it until the tears were flowing. "Oh, baby, yes. Yes, of course you can." She opened her arms and reached up to wrap them around Riley's neck, hug her tight. "Of course you can. It's all I want, you know. It's all I want. Just you. Just you." Their mouths crushed together, Riley's head bumping Hannah's hat up and off as they kissed, and then Riley buried her face in Hannah's shoulder.

Hannah held her tightly, arm around her shoulders, fingers in Riley's dark hair. She felt Riley's arms around her, locked tight, and she'd never felt so safe or so desired or so at home ever in her life.

She held on.

❖

They didn't even talk as they busted through the door of Hannah's apartment. The second it closed behind them, Riley was on Hannah, pulling at her coat, her hat, stripping her of any clothing she could, right there in the entryway.

"Hang on there, Casanova," Hannah said with a laugh, and her dark eyes held a sparkle of happiness.

"Can't," Riley muttered through her kisses, even as she toed off her boots and let her coat slide off her arms. Then Hannah's face was in her hands again, and they were kissing some more, Riley backstepping her into the living room. "God, I've missed you," she said when they came up for air.

She took a moment to look around. The Christmas tree was lit up, the only light in the room, creating the most gorgeous, sensuous atmosphere. Reaching toward the couch, she pulled the fluffy blanket off the back of it and spread it out next to the tree. When she looked back at Hannah, she was smiling.

"Oh, that's what we're doing?" she asked, that sparkle still there, still visible even in the dim lighting.

"That's what we're doing." Riley took her hand and pulled her close. More kissing ensued. Deeper, more thorough kissing, and the next time they broke apart, they were breathless. Riley's fingers found the hem of Hannah's shirt and tugged it up and over her head, and for the love of God, had there ever been anybody more beautiful than Hannah, standing there in her bra, her torso bathed in the soft, multicolored lights of the Christmas tree.

She was speechless.

"Riley," Hannah whispered after a long moment.

Riley looked up, met her gaze.

"Kiss me."

She didn't have to be told twice. "Come here."

The blanket was sherpa on one side, and it was soft and fluffy against their skin as they undressed each other. Soon, both of them were naked.

"Can I make a confession?" Hannah asked, eyes crinkled at the corners as she grinned. "I've always wanted to make love under the Christmas tree."

"Yeah?"

"Yeah."

"Well, I'm here to make your wishes come true." Riley lowered her head and caught Hannah's mouth in a searing kiss before moving to her chin, then trailing a path down her throat to her breastbone. She stopped at each nipple, giving attention to one, then the other, until Hannah was shifting and writhing beneath her.

Ragged breaths.

Little gasps.

Fingers clenching her hair.

All things Riley associated with Hannah and sex. She'd paid close attention each time they were together, as if studying for the most important test of her life. She knew if she touched Hannah *there*, she'd get a little cry. And if she sucked on her *there*, a gasp. And when she stroked her tongue *right there*—

"Oh, God," Hannah moaned, and arched her head back into the blanket. Both of her hands were in Riley's hair now, tugging deliciously as she begged. "Riley. Please. Please?"

"Look at me." Riley's voice was low, its huskiness surprising even her. She was poised between Hannah's thighs, her mouth mere inches from where Hannah needed it the most. She knew that, but she waited until Hannah lifted her head. Her eyes were hooded, her cheeks flushed as she met Riley's gaze. She was the most beautiful thing Riley had ever seen. She smiled at her. "I love you," she whispered, and as Hannah's eyes went slightly wide in what might have been surprise, but could also have been relief, Riley lowered her head and went to work, giving her no more time to think about it.

Hannah tasted like love and warmth and home, and Riley took her time, savoring the tang of her, savoring the feel of the soft wet flesh against her tongue. She held on to Hannah's hips, her fingers digging in as she worked to stay with her, even as Hannah rocked and undulated beneath her hands and her mouth. She let go with one hand, but only so she could slip inside, and the slick hotness of Hannah's body holding her fingers in almost made Riley come herself. But she waited, kept moving her tongue but kept her fingers still until she was sure Hannah was close to the edge. She could tell by the soft, high-pitched sounds she made, by the way her fingers tightened in Riley's hair, and only then did she gradually pull her fingers out, then push them back in.

She set up a slow pace, matching the movements of her tongue and the rhythm of her fingers, and only sped up a little at a time. Hannah arched and rocked and clenched her fists, and the sounds she made— the little gasps and groans and words of pleasure—only served to make Riley wetter, until finally, with one last stroke, Hannah fell over the edge.

Her entire body arched up off the blanket, and Riley had to hold on, go up on her knees to stay with her. Easily the most glorious sight she'd ever seen, Riley took it in, even as she kept her tongue pressed to Hannah's center. Her skin looked warm, almost as if it was glowing green, red, and blue from the inside. Her fingers in Riley's hair were almost painful now, but Riley didn't care. In fact, she relished it, the same as she relished the pulsing throbs she could feel under her tongue and the way she relished the way Hannah's inner walls tried to hold her fingers in place.

When Hannah finally came down, when her hips finally settled back down onto the blanket and her arms fell to the floor like falling tree branches, releasing Riley's hair, only then did Riley give one last swipe with her tongue and look up at her.

There were tears in Hannah's eyes.

A moment of concern hit Riley. "Baby, are you okay? Did I hurt you?"

A tender smile broke out across Hannah's face as she shook her head. "No," she whispered. "Exactly the opposite." She reached for Riley's shoulder. "Come up here."

Again, Riley didn't need to be asked twice. Keeping her fingers tucked snugly inside Hannah, she made her way up until her face was just above Hannah's.

Hannah shifted her own position and lifted one leg until her thigh hit Riley's very wet center. Riley caught her breath.

"Oh my God," Hannah whispered. "Do I do that to you?" She pressed her thigh up again, with the same reaction.

Riley nodded, unable to find her voice.

The third time Hannah pressed her thigh up, Riley moved with her, and in the next seconds, she was riding Hannah's leg, sliding along it, her own copious wetness making the glide easy. Bracing herself up with one hand next to Hannah's head, she moved both her body against Hannah's thigh and her fingers in and out of Hannah's center, until the rhythm matched. Hannah dug her fingers into Riley's backside and helped her move, and in a matter of a few short minutes, both women cried out their orgasms under the light of the Christmas tree.

Some time later—Riley had no idea how much later because she had zero concept of time at that point—they lay under the tree, Riley on her back, Hannah draped over her and tracing little shapes on her bare skin.

"I've never done that before," Hannah said quietly.

"What? Make love under the tree? Yeah, you said."

"No. I've never come at the exact same time as my partner." She didn't look at Riley when she said it, almost as if embarrassed by it.

Riley hugged her close. "Me neither." She took a deep breath and let it out slowly. "I gotta say, though, it was pretty awesome."

Hannah lifted her head then and met her gaze. "Right?" she asked, eyes wide. "Amazing." They laughed together, and then Hannah's face suddenly became serious. "So…" She wet her lips.

"So…?"

Hannah cleared her throat. It was obvious she had something important to say, and Riley didn't want to rush her, so she waited her out, running her fingertips up and down her back. "Maybe it was just the heat of the moment—and if it was, that's totally okay—but you said you love me."

Riley nodded. "I did. I do."

Brown eyes went wide. "Really?"

Her surprise was cute, Riley had to admit it. "Really."

Hannah dropped her head down to Riley's shoulder, seemingly in relief. "Oh, thank God." Then she lifted it again. "I love you, too."

Riley had zero control over the smile the broke out across her face. She could literally feel it blossom, and she tightened her arm around Hannah. "Yeah?"

Hannah sighed and lay back down, her head pillowed on Riley's chest. "I fell in love with you when I was eleven, and I don't think that's ever gone away. I just learned how to tuck it into a box."

"Compartmentalizing."

"Oh, I am *so* good at that. You have no idea."

They both laughed softly, then went quiet. Riley wondered if Hannah was basking the way she was when Hannah suddenly popped up so quickly, it startled her.

"Oh my God, what?" Riley said, sitting up with worry.

"I completely forgot to tell you! I can't believe it." Hannah stood up, completely naked, and started to pace the floor of the small living room. The glow of the Christmas lights bathed her skin in warmth, and Riley suddenly found herself smiling, sitting back on her hands and enjoying the view.

"Tell me," Riley said. "But tell me slowly."

Hannah stopped pacing at her words and caught the lascivious expression on her face, then laughed. "You stop that."

"What, ogling your naked body? Never."

Hannah shook her head with a smile and what might have been a blush, rather than a glow of the red lights. "Fine. Ogle away. But listen to this: You know Mr. Daniels? My regular?"

Riley squinted as she thought. "The tall, lanky old guy?"

With a nod, Hannah told her about the visit from the lawyer, the papers he'd left, the reduction in the rent, and how the building would be willed to her eventually.

"You're kidding."

Hannah sat back down and traced her fingertips over Riley's thigh. "Nope. I left the paperwork at the office because I was a little distracted by this hot brunette that came in and kissed my face off, but tomorrow, I'm gonna take it over to my dad. He has a lawyer friend, so I'm gonna ask if he can take a look."

"Baby. This is incredible." Riley reached for her, wrapped her in a hug. "My God, this solves so much!"

"I know, right?"

"Allow me to be super corny and clichéd for a moment, but it's a Christmas miracle!"

Hannah laughed and Riley joined her. They put their foreheads together, kissed softly. "You know what's the real Christmas miracle?"

Hannah asked quietly. "You coming back to me. That is my Christmas miracle." With gentle fingers, she brushed some of Riley's hair out of her eyes and tucked it behind her ear. "I love you."

Riley felt like her heart was almost too big for her chest, so swollen with love was it. She caught Hannah's wrist in her hand, brought it to her mouth, and kissed the knuckles one at a time. When she met Hannah's gaze, she knew her own eyes were wet. One blink, and the tears spilled over, tracking down her cheek as she whispered, "I love you back."

EPILOGUE

Two years later

Poptacular had changed quite a bit in the past few months, and Hannah stood near the front door, ready to turn off the lights for the night, and simply looked around, pride swelling her chest.

The counter had been moved to the right-hand side of the space and a window had been installed so customers could stand and watch the popcorn being popped, coated, mixed. The floor was new, shiny and inviting, so much so that part of her still hated walking on it, and she cringed internally whenever it rained and a customer came in, treading mud and water all over it. Riley loved to tease her about that. On the left, the wall was all shelves, displaying bags of popcorn plus popcorn-themed knickknacks—an antique butter melter, a ceramic classic red-and-white striped bag overflowing with ceramic popcorn, things she'd picked up or Riley had in her work travels. It had become a sort of running joke for her to see what kind of popcorn paraphernalia she could discover when she was away from home.

Home.

A word that had taken on new meaning to Hannah in the past twenty-four months. She and Riley now shared a small house just a block over from her parents. Small, but perfect. She'd always spent so much time at Poptacular—and still did—but now she couldn't wait to get home at the end of the day.

On the wall of shelves, two portraits hung: the one of Grams that would always be there, and next to it, one of Mr. Daniels. He'd passed away last summer, and as promised, had willed the building to Hannah under the promise that she "continue making popcorn dreams for the town of Sunset Valley." Her heart always felt both heavy and light when she turned her attention to the portraits. She missed them both terribly. She also owed both of them her immense gratitude. She hoped they knew that, wherever they were.

The buzzing of her phone yanked her back to the present. A text from Shana.

Bitch, where are you?

A glance at the time told her it was after ten, and she'd promised to meet Shana at Hopsville at ten. She typed.

Sorry! Got hung up. Be there in ten!

She clicked off the lights and locked up.

The winter had been a fairly easy one so far. Main Street was still glittering with holiday lights and decorations and it was a balmy thirty-seven degrees, so she decided to walk. It hadn't snowed in several days, and the sidewalks were clear. She inhaled deeply, taking in that fresh, clean air. It made her feel lighter, something she'd felt noticeably for several months now.

Hopsville was throwing its second annual New Year's Eve party because last year's had been such a success. Steve and Jacob had brewed a holiday amber ale that people loved. Even Hannah, who wasn't a huge beer drinker, told Steve it tasted like Christmas in a glass. They had raffles and live music, and the TVs mounted in the corners would show the ball dropping at midnight.

She spotted Shana and Davey near the bar, Shana waving a hand to get her attention.

"There you are," she said, wrapping Hannah in a hug. "I was getting worried."

"You know me, always with the popcorn." Hannah laughed. While she'd gotten *a bit* better with her hours at the shop, she could still get lost in experimenting with a new flavor and lose track of time.

"Always with the popcorn!" Shana laughed and leaned into Davey, who had his arm around her waist. She handed a full glass of beer to Hannah. "Holiday amber, just for you." Her own glass held up, she touched it to Hannah's. "Happy New Year, baby."

"Not yet," Hannah said, then sipped. Damn, it really was like Christmas in a glass. Beer, yes, but also hints of nutmeg, cinnamon, cloves… She raised her gaze and met Steve's behind the bar. He smiled as she held up her glass and mouthed "Yum!"

For the next hour, she sipped beer, chatted with Shana and Davey, saw Kyle and Ashley when they came in, and threw herself at her brother to hug him.

"Had a couple beers, have you?" he teased, hugging her back.

"Two. I've had two."

Ashley grinned at her. "Popcorn doesn't absorb much."

Hannah pointed at her. "You are correct." Then she gasped as she glanced at the door. "Oh, my God, Mom and Dad are here?" Her parents pushed through the crowd to them, and Hannah hugged her mom. "What are you guys doing here? I expected you'd be in bed by now."

Her father pulled her into a hug as her mother said, "We decided not to be boring this year." She looked around. "Wow, this place is hopping!"

"What can I get you?" Hannah asked.

For the next hour, the seven of them laughed and drank and talked about anything and everything. Hannah kept glancing at her phone because everybody she loved most in the world was there with her except for Riley…who was supposed to have arrived almost thirty minutes ago.

"She'll be here," Shana whispered in her ear when she looked at the door for the twenty-seventh time.

Hannah laughed and did her best to relax her shoulders. This was a new thing: When Riley was due to show up, Hannah's entire body would feel just a little bit tense until she actually arrived. Then everything would ease, like she was letting go of a breath she'd been holding for too long.

At eleven forty-five, she pulled out her phone to send a text, and the door opened.

Hannah's world settled.

Riley's gorgeous blue eyes met hers across the crowd, and Hannah could see her face relax, too. A gentle smile settled on her face as she made her way through the crowd, her dark hair sprinkled with light snow.

"Is it coming down?" Hannah's father asked as Riley reached them and wrapped Hannah in a hug.

"Just a little." Riley shook out her hair, then met Hannah's gaze. "Sorry I'm late." She kissed her softly on the mouth.

Hannah indicated one of the TVs. "You made it just in time." She handed over her freshly poured beer and Riley took a large gulp. Hannah leaned into her, slid her arm inside Riley's coat and around her back. She took a deep breath and let it out slowly, a cleansing breath that said everything was right in her world. The feeling was still something she hadn't quite gotten used to. Like having somebody to kiss at midnight on New Year's Eve.

The ball began to drop, and the entire bar counted down from ten. Hannah glanced up at Riley, squeezed her close, then clapped her hands together in delight as they watched the ball come down.

"Three! Two! One! Happy New Year!"

She turned to kiss Riley, but she was gone. What the—? It took her a beat to realize that she wasn't actually gone.

She was down on one knee.

Holding a ring.

The entire bar had gone quiet.

Riley spoke.

"Hannah, these last two years have been the most magical of my life. I can't believe I left Sunset Valley so many years ago only to find out that what I've wanted most was right here all along. I can't imagine my life without you. You've made me happier than I ever thought I could be, and I want to start this new year spending the rest of my days making sure you feel the same way. Will you marry me?"

Disbelief wasn't a strong enough word to describe Hannah's demeanor just then. Shocked, thrilled, two more words that worked, but only a bit. And when she thought of Riley? Looked down at her now, as she held an open ring box up to her, an expression of hope on her face?

Love.

That was the word that sprang into her head when she thought about Riley. Instantly. Without thought or deliberation.

She looked down at her now, this woman who had truly been her very first love and was now asking to be her forever love. Riley's eyes were sparkling with unshed tears, and Hannah reached out to lay a hand against her cheek.

You could hear a pin drop in the bar.

"What, like I'd say no?" she said with a smile. "Yes. Absolutely, one hundred percent yes."

The bar erupted, positively erupted in applause and cheers and shouts. It was deafening. Riley stood, her face lit up with happiness in a way that only compared to when they'd signed the paperwork for their house. Taking Hannah's hand, she slid the ring on her finger, a gorgeous silver band that sparkled with diamonds in the recessed lighting of Hopsville. Then she pulled her into a hug.

"I love you," Riley said in her ear.

"I love you, too." Hannah pulled back enough to kiss her on the mouth. "I love you so much."

Kyle held up his beer and said loudly, "To my newly engaged sister and my soon-to-be sister-in-law!"

Another cheer burst forth from the crowd, and Hannah couldn't stop the tears of happiness that rolled down her face. This was it. Everything she never thought she'd have, right here in this microbrewery. Her heart was bursting.

And then out of nowhere, bags were being tossed around from behind the bar. She turned to meet Steve's eyes, and she and Riley both laughed as he shouted out to his patrons.

"Who wants popcorn?"

About the Author

Two-time Lambda Literary Award–winning author Georgia Beers has written more than forty novels of sapphic romance. She resides in upstate New York, where she was born and raised. She strongly believes in the beauty of an excellent glass of wine, a good scary movie, and the unconditional love of a dog. Fall is her very favorite season.

She is currently hard at work on her next book. You can visit her and find out more at www.georgiabeers.com or search her on Patreon.

Books Available From Bold Strokes Books

Beautiful Things by Emma L McGeown. A warmhearted romance of missed chances, undeniable chemistry, and a stubborn love that maybe, just maybe, can find its way back. (978-1-63679-934-6)

The Great Popcorn Romance by Georgia Beers. Opposites attract, and Riley Shaw stands no chance of resisting Hannah Kramer's magnetic pull. But opposites know just how to drive each other crazy… (978-1-63679-910-0)

Love Takes a Village by Karis Walsh. As Lena Preiss struggles to manage a busy restaurant in the Bavarian Christmas village of Leavenworth, Washington, chocolatier Devin Meyer brings an unexpected richness into her life, along with her delicious desserts. (978-1-63679-902-5)

Secrets of the Heart by Jenny Frame. When a beautiful stranger starts asking questions about Nikki Sharkey, head of an infamous crime syndicate, Nikki will stop at nothing to protect her daughter Isla. (978-1-63679-653-6)

Talon and the Songbird by Julia Underwood. In a world where survival depends on strategic alliances, Makayla and Talon must navigate not only complex politics but also the dangerous territory of their hearts. (978-1-63679-970-4)

Three Blissful Days by Dena Blake. Kendall Jackson attempts to make her ex regret dumping her by announcing she's dating beautiful park ranger Ivy Patterson. But there's nothing fake about how attracted Ivy is to Kendall. (978-1-63679-707-6)

Chasing Her Scent by MJ Williamz. When Sheridan Rousseau walks into Lisette Mouton's charming little bookstore in Quebec City, she unknowingly holds the key to a mysterious box hidden in a secret room. (978-1-63679-900-1)

Heart's Run by D. Jackson Leigh. Hoping to recover an escaped racing mare, stock transporter Tobie Mason locks horns with local wild horse advocate Maggie Wilkes. (978-1-63679-825-7)

Scandalous by Kris Bryant. When a Hollywood actress trades places with her twin sister, everyone's in an uproar about getting duped, but

Lindsay's more concerned about finding out which twin she made out with. (978-1-63679-874-5)

The Art of Love by Ali Vali. When Mimi and Bianca both set their sights on Jolly, sparks fly, loyalties are tested, and hearts collide as they navigate the unpredictable nature of their hearts. (978-1-63679-719-9)

The Secrets of Rhydian Hill by Ronica Black. A doctor in need of a new start. A woman running from a killer. A love story that could end in tragedy. (978-1-63679-880-6)

Feeling Lucky by Krystina Rivers. What happens when, despite suddenly having enough money to buy almost anything, Lucy and Tanner start to discover that maybe all they need is each other? (978-1-63679-876-9)

Iceberg by Gun Brooke. When Lady Arabella hires Zandra, she never expects to find love, especially not as a disaster looms on the horizon. (978-1-63679-908-7)

It Happened One Semester by Aurora Rey. After a Pride night hookup, can eager new Assistant Professor Hudson Greene and Dean of Advising Callie Shaw overcome the odds and ace falling in love? (978-1-63679-814-1)

It's Kind of a Bad Idea by Sarah G. Levine. What happens when an emotionally unavailable serial dater meets the one woman she can't help but fall for—who happens to be the one woman who told her not to? (978-1-63679-920-9)

Thankful for You by Tagan Shepard. Everyone deserves to find their person. Maybe Karen has finally found hers? (978-1-63679-884-4)

What Happens On Location by Nan Campbell. How can Helen produce a successful movie when its director is the woman responsible for the demise of her marriage? (978-1-63679-904-9)

When Love Comes Around by Radclyffe and Ronica Black. Can Maya Sanchez and Nolan Wright trust each other enough to build something real, or will the past tear them apart? (978-1-63679-930-8)